THE
THREE-NINE LINE

OTHER TITLES BY DAVID FREED

Flat Spin

Fangs Out

Voodoo Ridge

A CORDELL LOGAN MYSTERY

THE THREE-NINE LINE

DAVID FREED

THE PERMANENT PRESS
Sag Harbor, NY 11963

For information, address:
  The Permanent Press
  4170 Noyac Road
  Sag Harbor, NY 11963
  www.thepermanentpress.com

Library of Congress Cataloging-in-Publication Data

  Freed, David—
    The three nine line / by David Freed.
      pages ; cm
    ISBN 978-1-57962-399-9
      1. Logan, Cordell (Fictitious character) I. Title.

  PS3606.R4375T48 2015
  813'.6—dc23   2015013683

Printed in the United States of America

For Lisa

Acknowledgments

This book would not have come to pass without the support of many kind and generous people on two continents. My thanks in particular to retired Air Force Brigadier General Dan Cherry for introducing me to former North Vietnamese fighter pilot Nguyen Hong My, whose MiG-21 Cherry shot down after a prolonged dogfight in 1972 over North Vietnam. Though badly injured, Hong My would survive their air battle and years later become good buddies with Cherry. Believing that any friend of Dan's is a friend of his, Hong My happily piloted me all over Hanoi on the back of his motorbike, taking me to wonderful restaurants, beer halls and museums that I might've missed otherwise. It was with Hong My that I toured the infamous "Hanoi Hilton," where United States prisoners of war were housed. He also introduced me to other North Vietnamese combat veterans whose vivid recollections of war proved invaluable in my work both as a novelist and journalist. I cannot express enough my appreciation for Hong My's help. I'm also greatly indebted to his nephew, aspiring aeronautical engineer Duc Nguyen, for serving as my interpreter and stand-in chauffeur—and for making me laugh aloud at his frequent, unintentionally humorous puzzlements over modern American culture.

I would be remiss in not thanking my longtime friend and former reporting colleague from the *Los Angeles Times*, Scott Duke Harris, and Scott's wife, K. Oanh Ha, Hanoi bureau chief of Bloomberg News Service, for their generous hospitality during my stay in Vietnam.

To air traffic controller Jeff Barnhart, my gratitude for helping keep me safe in the air and, in this case, in print.

Ditto that last sentiment to copy editor Barb Anderson for her sharp pencil and sage, questioning mind. Thanks also to graphics designer Lon Kirschner for his always excellent book covers; to my agent extraordinaire, Jill Marr of Dijkstra Literary, for her unwavering support; and to copublishers Marty and Judy Shepard of The Permanent Press for continuing to afford Cordell Logan and me a home. We are both ever in your debt.

To my brilliant, beautiful partner, Dr. Elizabeth Bates Freed, who truly embodies the notion that behind every good man stands a better woman, I am blessed by your tender and steadfast presence in my life. Earthbound or aloft, there is no one I'd rather have in my right seat.

"Vengeance and retribution require a long time; it is the rule."

—CHARLES DICKENS, *A Tale of Two Cities*

The Three-Nine Line

Two widowed sisters out for their predawn stroll were the first to spot it, floating near the red wooden bridge that led to the island with its ancient temple. They thought it was the rarely seen giant turtle, the one whose sacred ancestors have lived in the lake for a thousand years. But when they made their way excitedly onto the bridge and peered over the hand railing into the dark water, what they saw was not some mythic, oversized reptile. It was a man, arms hovering buoyantly at his sides, his black sport coat humped over his back like a tortoise shell, dead.

One of the old women stayed behind while the other hobbled as best she could along the lakeshore to the police substation on Le Thai To Street, a quarter mile away. The two officers on duty were sipping tea from cloisonné cups and smoking Marlboro Lights, engrossed in a television soap opera about sixteenth century Chinese warlords. The woman told them what she'd found and implored them to come quickly. The cops said they'd be along as soon as their show was over. That was before she let it be known that her son was a ranking Party member and that he knew others, higher still. The taller of the officers grudgingly grabbed a flashlight, the other a pack of cigarettes. They drove her back in their patrol car, a Toyota Tercel with candy bar lights and a manual transmission.

The man was dead all right. The cops agreed on that much, gazing out at the body as it lapped against the bridge supports. Probably some tourist who'd drunk too much beer in the Old Quarter and accidentally fallen in, the way tourists will do sometimes. Why, the shorter cop grumbled under his breath, did the old women have to find him when they did? An hour later and they would've both been off duty, probably getting drunk themselves. Now here they were, their immediate futures bleak with piles of paperwork and hours of unpaid overtime. But that wasn't the worst part. The worst would be having to kiss up to those ambitious overachievers from the Department of Public Security who'd be assigned to the case, the ones who actually *investigated* crimes and didn't commit them or cover them up, like the rest of the Hanoi police force. The two cops crossed the bridge onto the island. They cursed the tourist for having been stupid enough to drown on their shift. They cursed the two old biddies for having found him. Of all the lousy luck.

A wooden skiff with a square bow was roped to a stand of cattails below the temple. One of the cops climbed in. The other undid the rope, pushed off, and hauled himself aboard. There were two oars. The body wasn't far, twenty meters, if that, but the morning was already sultry, the air heavy, and by the time they reached the man, the shirts of their forest-green police uniforms were soaked through. Sweating and swearing, they looped the rope under the floater's armpits, then towed him back to land.

It took both cops to drag the body out of the water. The man's left foot was clad in a black lace-up oxford made from synthetic leather. The other foot was shoeless. His slacks were gray polyester, his sport coat a blend of polyester and wool. When they rolled him over, they saw that he was wearing a white, short-sleeved dress shirt and a red necktie, loosely knotted and adorned with a single yellow star. He looked to be in his sixties. Stocky build. A full head of bristled, close-cropped hair gone gray. An Asian face, round as a moon pie. Pinned to his lapels were a dozen military decorations. Sunk hilt-deep into his sternum was a hunting knife.

"He didn't drown," the shorter cop said, lighting a cigarette.

His partner looked over at him for a moment as if it were the dumbest, most obvious thing anyone in law enforcement had ever said, then turned and shined his flashlight beam full on the corpse's face: Skin drained of color. Jaw slack. Lifeless, half-hooded eyes. Lips curled in a half smile, like he was in on some inside joke.

"I know this guy," the cop with the flashlight said. "I read about him in the paper. They called him 'Mr. Wonderful.'"

His partner exhaled smoke through his nose like a dragon. "Who called him that?"

"The Americans did. Their pilots. The ones we shot down during the war."

"Why would they call him Mr. Wonderful?"

The taller cop clicked off his flashlight and sighed, envisioning all of the work that lay ahead.

"Because he wasn't."

ONE

The whales were a thousand feet below us—a pair of California grays to be exact, a mother and her calf. They surfaced slowly, gracefully, the most synchronized of synchronized swimmers you've ever seen. Exhaled breath misted in their wakes like gossamer. An ethereal, beautiful sight.

"*Thar* she blows, matey," the famous, fifty-something movie star occupying the right seat of my airplane said for the third time in the cheesiest Captain Ahab accent I'd ever heard. From the backseat, his two blonde girlfriends, both knockouts half his age, giggled like part of their job description was to humor him. "*Thar* she blows."

If the guy said it one more time, I was going to have to rip out his chin implant. Okay, that's not true. For one thing, I'm an aspiring Buddhist and Buddhists believe in nonviolence. For another, the famous movie star was paying me a fat five hundred bucks to show him and his gal pals a good time, flying them out over the Rancho Bonita coast for an hour in my aging Cessna 172, the *Ruptured Duck*, so they could all get their nature freak on.

"Arrgh, *thar* she blows."

I ground my teeth and counted silently to five.

We were orbiting above the ocean in a tight, thirty-degree bank. The famous movie star was wearing sunglasses with gold frames and a shiny, black leather flight jacket with the collar up, an aging James Dean. "Lower," he said, bringing the boom mike on his headset closer to his mouth. "We need to get down there so my goddesses can get a better look. They dig getting in close, if you get my drift."

He jabbed me playfully in the shoulder like we were buddies, in on some manly man joke.

"If we go any lower," I explained as evenly as I could, "our
whale friends down there'll start getting nervous. As animal
lovers, I'm sure we can all appreciate how we wouldn't want
to upset them. Also, when we're this far offshore, it's really a
good idea to maintain as much altitude as we can so that if we
have engine issues, we can glide in and not have to worry about
swimming to shore."

"The engine sounds fine to me," the famous movie star said.
"Look, if this is about the money, I got plenty." He pulled out a
fat flash roll from his jeans and held it up so his playthings in
the backseat could see it, peeled off five $100 bills, and tossed
the cash on my lap. "C'mon, Sky King. Do it. Lower."

Once upon a time, for that kind of money, I would've turned
off my transponder and gone wave skimming. But for once, I
could truthfully say, I didn't need the money. I could also say
that hard work and determination had ultimately played only
minor roles in my having achieved financial independence.
What mattered, as it turned out, was an obstinate cat, YouTube,
and sheer, blind luck.

I'm a proud graduate of the United States Air Force Academy and a former fighter pilot. For several years after that, I'd
kicked doors and pulled triggers in the employ of Uncle Sugar,
dispatching bad guys in corners of the globe that most Americans have never heard of. One might think, with such a résumé,
that running a civilian flight school and aerial charter service
in a well-heeled, seaside resort like Rancho Bonita would've
been a walk in the park by comparison. I would've assumed so,
too, which is why I'd hung in there for as long as I had, rarely
making ends meet while living in a converted garage apartment
with Kiddiot, the world's stupidest orange tabby cat, before fate
intervened. I'd pondered bankruptcy on more occasions than
I'm willing to confess. Then, during a commercial break while
watching *Monday Night Football* together, as we always did,
my octogenarian landlady, Mrs. Schmulowitz, proposed that I

should advertise my service. She even fronted me the funds for a thirty-second spot that would air twice weekly on local public access television.

"What could it hurt?" Mrs. Schmulowitz said. "My third husband, Morris, may he rest in peace, he advertised like it was going out of style. TV, newspapers, radio, bus benches, the whole *shmegegge*. Which is how he became the Bedspread King of Bensonhurst."

Morris had hit it big after featuring animals in his commercials "borrowed" from the Brooklyn Zoo where his brother, conveniently enough, was the assistant primate handler. Posing on camera with chimps, Mrs. Schmulowitz said, made her third hubby "look almost human by comparison." She was convinced that I could achieve comparable results by appearing on TV with my overweight, untrainable cat.

The script for the commercial that Mrs. Schmulowitz insisted on writing and producing herself called for me to cuddle Kiddiot in my arms as I sat in the *Ruptured Duck's* cockpit and extolled the many virtues of learning to fly. But no sooner had Mrs. Schmulowitz yelled, "Action," when Kiddiot, who's never been keen on being held by anyone, especially me, went postal trying to escape and proceeded to fillet my face and arms with his claws. The tape curiously made its way onto YouTube and quickly went viral. Virtually overnight, I had more paying customers than I knew what to do with, including the famous movie star, who lived on a lush, gated estate among the hedgerows of The Knolls, Rancho Bonita's toniest neighborhood, and whose girlfriends had apparently come across the video online.

"Let's go," he said, "lower."

I took the Benjamins he'd dropped on my lap and handed them back to him. "I just told you. It'll scare the whales."

"Okay, make it a thousand." He glanced at his girlfriends to make sure they were duly impressed, then back at me. "We can play this game all day, amigo. Don't you know who I am?"

"Yeah, I know who you are," I said, scanning my airspeed and attitude indicators. "You're the guy who made one halfway-decent action flick twenty years ago, and the same guy who's been phoning it in ever since, especially that last commando flick you did with Stallone. That one scene where you lost your arm, where you were still blasting away with the M-60, trying to rally the troops over how much their country needed them? Oh, man. All I could think about was how fortunate you were that there aren't any laws for overacting because, dude, you'd be in prison for sure."

He slowly peeled off his expensive shades, the kind I'll never be able to afford, and gave me one of those Hollywood tough guy looks.

"What did you just say to me?"

"I said we need to save the whales and your one-hour flight's over. Time to head back to the barn."

I cranked the yoke hard over, standing the *Duck* on his right wingtip, the way I used to back in the day, when I flew A-10 Thunderbolts for the air force. The maneuver slammed the famous movie star into the passenger door hard enough that he yelped. I thought he might've injured his shoulder. Turns out it was among the finest acting he'd ever done.

~~~

Lunch was a bag of Doritos and two stale Oreo cookies I found buried under some maintenance records on the metal government surplus desk inside my "office," which was really a windowless storage closet I rented from airplane mechanic Larry Kropf in his World War II-era hangar at the Rancho Bonita airport. I was booked solid that day: After dropping off the famous movie star and his girlfriends, I gave one-hour lessons to four new student pilots and sat in on a conference call with the directors of a nonprofit feline rescue agency up in San Jose. They wanted to know, in light of my sudden YouTube fame thanks to Kiddiot, whether I'd be interested in serving as their volunteer spokesman. I declined.

I topped off both of the *Duck's* wing tanks at the self-service fuel pump on the west end of the airfield and taxied back to the hangar as the sun was calling it a day. Over the ocean, puffs of altocumulus blazed crimson, dabbed on a cerulean sky. The kind of calendar-quality sunset that if you didn't know any better looked Photoshopped, the kind my late ex-wife would've quietly savored.

Larry walked over, sipping a Diet Coke as I chocked and tied down the plane on the flight line.

"How was your day?" he asked.

"Crazy busy, in a good way."

"Looked like it. Must feel pretty good, making some decent bank for a change, eh, Logan?"

"No complaints."

Larry looked to be in a rare, no-complaints mood himself. He'd recently undergone gastric bypass surgery, which had shaved eighty pounds off his 320-pound frame. He was still a big man by any measure, though, rocking an unkempt beard and black-frame, Buddy Holly-style glasses with lenses thick enough they could've fried ants. He was wearing his usual navy blue work pants, belted tightly to compensate for his recent weight loss, a vintage San Francisco 49ers ball cap, and a stretched-out T-shirt smeared with hydraulic fluid that read, "4 out of 3 people struggle with math."

"So," Larry said, "you doing okay otherwise?"

I knew what he was asking about: Savannah, my ex. More than six years after divorcing, we'd reconciled and agreed to start over. That I'd gotten her pregnant played no small role in our decision to reunite. Then she died. Half a year had passed since then, and I still couldn't bring myself to talk openly about what had happened.

"I'm hanging in there, Larry."

"Listen, if you ever just feel like talking . . ."

"I'll call Dr. Phil."

"I'm serious, Logan."

"Me, too."

He grunted and changed the subject, pointing with his chin behind me. "Helluva show."

I turned. The sun was sliding into the ocean, rimming the watery horizon with rays of light angled upward from the other side of the planet like gifts from Olympus. Or maybe gifts from Savannah. I snugged down the tie-down rope under the *Duck's* left wing and tried not to miss her so much, which pretty much was impossible.

"The wife's making lasagna tonight," Larry said. "Lemme tell ya, you haven't had lasagna until you've had hers. Sometimes I think she's trying to kill me with all that cholesterol so she can get the insurance money and marry some rich doctor, but am I complaining? You gotta die of something, right?"

I smiled.

He paused. Then he said, "She's making plenty. Why don't you come over?"

"Did you just invite me to dinner, Larry?"

"Me? Hell, no. The wife. She's inviting you over. She's got a friend coming over. Another nurse at the hospital. She wants to fix you two up." His eyebrows danced lasciviously. They looked like two fuzzy caterpillars.

"I appreciate the offer, but I'm really not looking for anything like that right now, Larry."

"Copy that. But before you say no, I've seen this gal, okay? Easily an eight, eight-plus—definitely a nine, depending on how many beers you've had. Kinda reminds me of Cindy Crawford, only Cindy's mole is smaller—not that this chick's mole is gonna destroy Tokyo or anything. Just fair warning, it's definitely there. Just so you don't get shocked or nothin' when you see her, okay?"

"*Destroy Tokyo?*"

"Okay, forget I said anything about the mole. I'm probably making more of it than it deserves." Larry lowered his voice: "Listen, between you and me and the wall, I'd do her in a heartbeat if I didn't think the wife would find out and blowtorch my crotch."

I didn't mean to sound ungrateful. And it's not like I was particularly happy spending my nights alone with my cat. It's just that I wasn't ready to have dinner with any woman other than the one I'd lost.

"Please thank your wife for me," I said, "but I have plans tonight."

"Plans? What plans? Go home to that cat of yours? That cat's a menace. He has it in for you. Come on, Logan, come to supper. It'll do you some good."

"I'll take a rain check. How's that sound?"

"Sounds like I'm gonna be in big trouble. I promised the wife you'd come." Larry puffed out his cheeks and exhaled. "Oh, well, you can drag a horse to water, right? Can't say I didn't try. Catch you *mañana*, Logan."

"*Mañana*, buddy."

I watched him walk back to his hangar, wondering if maybe I'd erred in not taking him up on his offer. The fact was, though, I *was* busy that night—only not in a way I could've ever anticipated.

~~~

"N-32 . . . N-32."

The old man leaned over the bingo machine and extracted another randomly selected ball with a number on it. He was all dentures, hearing aids, and glasses, a living cadaver in red golf pants and a yellow golf shirt. He probably wasn't a day over ninety. On second glance, maybe he was.

"All I need is one more number, just *one* more," Mrs. Schmulowitz said with her pink bingo dauber at the ready, surveying the five cards spread out on the table in front of her as we sat in the ballroom of the Rancho Bonita Elks Lodge. "C'mon, O-66, O-66, baby, O-66 . . ."

"O-65 . . . O-65."

"Oy, so close!" She shook a fist and hollered at the geezer running the machine. "Hey, Mr. Bingo, let's have some *good* numbers for a change."

None of the players looked up from their cards. They were all apparently used to such outbursts from my Brooklyn-born landlady, a retired junior high gym teacher who took her bingo as seriously as she did televised football games. I'd agreed to drive her to her weekly sessions at the Elks in lieu of anything else to do in my free time. Looking around the crowded ballroom, I realized I was easily the youngest person there by thirty years.

"I-17 . . . I-17."

I glanced down at the lone card I was playing, saw I-17, and said, "Bingo."

"We have a bingo. The youngster sitting with the ever lovely Mrs. Schmulowitz."

Groans of disappointment drifted up from the crowd. Mrs. Schmulowitz gave me a congratulatory pat on the knee—"Way to go, *bubeleh*"—while the cadaver in the golf shirt shuffled over, reviewed my card, confirmed aloud that I had, in fact, a valid bingo, and handed me a twenty-five dollar gift certificate to Arby's.

An old woman sitting across the table from us in a wheelchair sucked in her sallow cheeks and smirked. "*Arby's*? That's not even roast beef. It's roasted llama. Or kangaroo. Good lord, even my dog wouldn't touch that stuff."

"Come off it, Edith," Mrs. Schmulowitz said. "I've *seen* you at Arby's. You're just jealous you didn't win."

"Am not."

"Are, too."

"Why don't you just go to hell, Mrs. Schmulowitz?"

Fortunately at that moment, my phone rang.

"This is Logan."

The unmistakably gravelly voice on the other end of the line said, "How's your scrotum?"

Relieved that I wasn't about to intervene in a catfight between two octogenarians, I stood and quickly headed for the door. The caller was my old buddy, Buzz. We'd served together in Alpha, a since-disbanded Tier One counterterrorist group whose mandate had been to revoke the get-out-of-jail-free cards of jihadists and miscellaneous other miscreants. In theory, we were supposed to take them into custody after hunting them down. In truth, they usually never made it that far. Buzz, a former Delta Force operator, had later gone to work for the Pentagon's Defense Intelligence Agency. He was now in charge of a small, newly formed covert organization, the name of which and mission specifics he'd repeatedly refused to share with me unless I agreed to come work for him. After pondering his offer for a week, I declined. My thoughts had remained scattered after losing Savannah, my mind too distracted to return to the razor-edged world of black ops. Now six months later, he was calling again. Only this time, he said, he wasn't offering. He was demanding.

"This is not a drill, Logan. I need you to un-ass yourself from whatever mindless civilian activity you're presently engaged in and report for duty A-SAP."

Two old men were milling about outside the entrance to the Elks Lodge, puffing fat cigars. I walked past them and into the parking lot, far enough away that they couldn't hear me.

"I'm listening, Buzz."

"I've got a C-37 inbound to the Rancho Bonita airport as we speak. He's due in to Signature Flight Support at 0630 Zulu. You *will* be onboard that aircraft, copy?"

Zero-six-thirty Zulu. That was a half hour before midnight, local time. I checked my watch: the jet would be landing in less than ninety minutes.

"What's the op?"

"I'll give you the full dump when you get here. We can talk money then, too."

"Where's 'here'?"

"You don't need to know that right now, Logan. All you need to know is that your country needs you."

I laughed.

"What's so funny?"

"You couldn't come up with something less cliché than, 'Your country needs you?' "

"Bite me. It's the truth. I won't take no for an answer, Logan. I can't. Not this time."

I rubbed the back of my neck. Buzz was a force of nature whose judgment I'd come to trust implicitly. When he wanted something done that he deemed important, it invariably got done.

"I'll have to reschedule a few things," I said.

"Fine, do whatever you have to, but do it quick. I'll be waiting for you when you get here. You'll be gone for about a week. And don't worry about bringing a weapon. You won't need one." A pause, then he added, "Hopefully."

Buzz snorted like a pig—his version of a laugh—before the line went dead.

I slipped the phone back in my jeans and realized that my hand was shaking ever so slightly with adrenaline in much the same way it did when I was with Alpha, those anxious butterflies that always disappeared the moment you felt that first bullet whiz past and muscle memory took over. I dug the feeling. It reminded me that my time on this planet was not without purpose, that my life still had meaning beyond merely taking famous movie stars and their girlfriends whale watching.

Two

Mrs. Schmulowitz offered to feed Kiddiot, as she invariably did when I left town. I gave her a list of my student pilots' names and their numbers as I drove her home and asked her to call them in the morning to postpone their flying lessons until I returned. She didn't ask where I was going. I was grateful for her discretion; I couldn't have answered her questions anyway.

"I'm gonna try a little scientific experiment on that cat of yours while you're gone," Mrs. Schmulowitz said as I steadied her by her elbow, helping her from my truck and onto her front porch. "He won't eat any cat food you serve him, am I right?"

"True."

"So, my theory is he won't eat cat food because he *knows* it's cat food. The problem is, he doesn't think he's a cat. He thinks he's Donald Trump, this cat! So what I do is, I go to Whole Foods, okay? I get a quarter pound of tuna salad. It'll cost me twenty bucks, but what do I care? I'm loaded. My second husband, he saw to that, may he rest in peace. Then I come home. I make sure the cat's not watching. I take the tuna salad. I put it in another bowl and I put the bowl in the fridge. Then I take the Tender Vittles that he won't eat. I put the Tender Vittles in the Whole Foods container that had the tuna salad in it. I wait until he sees me, wave it under his nose, give him a little smell, right? Then I make a big deal of spooning the Tender Vittles out of the Whole Foods container into his bowl. He thinks he's getting tuna salad from Whole Foods. It's gonna work, I guarantee it."

I wished her luck and went to pack. Per Buzz's directive, I left behind my reliable, two-inch, .357 Colt Python that had been my backup weapon with Alpha, a revolver I carried as a civilian whenever the need arose.

Kiddiot came to see me off as I threw my duffel bag into the back of my truck. Anyway, that's what I assumed he was doing as he hopped out of the cat door of our converted garage apartment and sauntered toward me—only to keep going, tail straight up, squeezing through Mrs. Schmulowitz's backyard gate and disappearing down the alley.

That's gratitude for you.

It was nearing midnight by the time I got to the airport. An unmarked Gulfstream V executive jet, known in air force parlance as a C-37, was parked on the ramp in front of Signature Flight Support, one of two luxury, fixed-base operations that cater to the many showbiz luminaries and corporate bigwigs who call Rancho Bonita home. I pressed the intercom button next to the glass front door.

"May I help you?" The voice on the speaker box was female and surprisingly pleasant, given the lateness of the hour.

"Cordell Logan."

The electric lock on the door clicked open. I passed through a hangar occupied by a single-engine Pilatus and entered a well-appointed reception lounge that fronted the flight line. Two men wearing the ubiquitous black slacks and white short-sleeved dress shirts of corporate pilots put down their Styrofoam coffee cups and stood as I walked in.

"Mr. Logan?"

"That would be me."

I handed my driver's license to the one with the four captain's bars on his shoulder epaulets. The receptionist sitting behind the counter, a young blonde in a dark blue skirt and blazer, gave me a toothy smile while he studied it.

"We're good to go," he said after a long moment, then handed me back the license.

The blonde buzzed us through the door leading to the flight line. The pilots and I walked out to the jet. I asked them our destination but they ignored me, closing the cockpit door behind them. Waiting at the top of the stairs with his burly, tattooed arms folded was a bearded, dark-haired young man in a tight-fitting black T-shirt, tan pleated Dockers, and tan, lace-up combat boots. Holstered under his left shoulder was a .50-caliber Desert Eagle pistol.

"Welcome aboard, Mr. Logan. My name's Best. I'll be your flight attendant this evening."

"Normally I flirt with the flight attendants, but in your case, I think I'll make an exception."

He grinned. "I need you to raise your arms for me, please."

"I'm not packing, if that's what you're wondering."

"It's S-O-P, sir. I apologize for the inconvenience."

I complied. He frisked me down quickly but efficiently, then searched through my duffel bag. When he was finished, he pulled the jet's cabin door closed.

"You want something to drink before we launch?"

"I'd like some fresh-squeezed guava juice, please."

"It's a government flight. How 'bout some fresh-squeezed bottled water?"

"Got any coffee?"

"How do you take it?"

"Black."

He disappeared into the aft galley. The jet's passenger cabin was as swank as any Fortune 500 boardroom: creamy leather recliners and sofa, soft lighting, plush carpet, and fold-out, burl-wood tables for dining and writing. I plopped down into a recliner and peered out the window. We were rolling toward Runway two-six. I could see the *Ruptured Duck* where I'd tied him down in front of Larry's hangar. My plane might've been nearly as ancient as I was, what with his sun-faded yellow and orange paint job, his outdated avionics and ragged upholstery that looked like a jilted lover had taken a razor to it, but he was still a good and reliable bird.

I'll be back soon, old friend. We'll go flying then.

Best brought me my coffee and took a seat across the aisle from me. Inked on his left forearm, amid a miasma of other military tattoos, was a fragmentation grenade.

"Army?"

"Seventy-Fifth Ranger Regiment," he said. "How'd you guess?"

"Marine tats usually aren't nearly that classy."

We bumped fists. The jet turned smartly onto the runway, engines spooling up, and swiftly thundered into a moonless sky, pushing me in my seatback. Within a minute, we were banking left and heading out to sea, followed soon after by another climbing left turn to the east.

"I need you to write down what size clothes you wear," Best said, handing me a retractable pen and slip of paper across the aisle. "Chest, neck, sleeve length, inseam, the whole nine yards."

"What for?"

"To buy you a new wardrobe."

"Say again?"

"I don't ask, Mr. Logan. I just do what the boss tells me."

You learn not to ask too many questions of those higher up the food chain when you've been in the military. That's just the way it is. I jotted down my measurements.

"Would you like me to make up the bed for you?"

"The *bed*?"

Best nodded toward the leather sofa. "It folds out. You can catch a few z's en route. From what I hear, you're gonna have a long day."

I watched him turn the sofa into a bed, replete with a down comforter and two foam pillows. I handed him my empty coffee cup and climbed in between satin sheets. Man, talk about living large. I was racked out in my own private jet, winging to some top-secret location to discuss a highly classified intelligence operation. Was I feeling self-important? You bet your bottom I was—and also feeling a little guilty. True Buddhists believe that a man can only achieve genuine compassion and enlightenment after learning how to check his ego at the door. I realized as I lay

there between those satin sheets at 35,000 feet that I still had a
fair bit to go in that department.

~~~

There are three rules to making consistently smooth land-
ings. Unfortunately, nobody knows what they are—including,
apparently, the two pilots at the controls of the Gulfstream in
which I was sleeping. The first bounce jarred me awake. The
second nearly separated me from my molars. We finally settled
onto the runway and the guys up front stood on the brakes.
Eventually we slowed and turned off the runway, but not before
Best shot me a grin that said he thought the landing sucked big
time, too.

"Any landing in which you can reuse the airplane is a good
one," I said, yawning.

"Welcome to Cleveland," he said.

I glanced outside. The sun hadn't been up very long. You
couldn't see much. "Are we stopping for fuel?"

"No, sir. This is it."

"Cleveland? That's our top-secret destination? Seriously?"

"Yes, sir."

I put on my hiking shoes while we taxied toward the executive terminal at Cleveland's Hopkins International Airport. There
was a black Chevy suburban with Ohio plates and tinted windows standing by on the tarmac, engine running. Best lowered
the jet's cabin door and stood aside. The pilots kept the cockpit
door closed, probably too embarrassed to show their faces. I
would've done the same, given the quality of the touchdown.

"You can leave your bag in the plane, Mr. Logan," Best said.
"We'll see you on the flip side."

"Fair enough."

I stepped onto the tarmac empty-handed. The air was cool
but not cold. The Suburban's front passenger door was locked. I
rapped on the impenetrably dark window and waited, but got no
response. I tried the right rear passenger door. It was unlocked.
I got in. A tinted partition blocked my view of the driver.

"How're you doing? Listen, you mind stopping off at Arby's on the way? There was no food on my flight and I've got a twenty-five-dollar gift certificate burning a hole in my pocket. Which is to say, I'm buying."

No answer.

I pulled the door shut and off we went.

I'd like to share with you my specific destination that early spring morning in the city of Cleveland, but that would be violating operational security, which the federal government tends to frown on. Suffice it to say, it was a commercial building of some height somewhere in the greater downtown area, where one of the office suites listed on the directory in the lobby said one thing, and where the actual business conducted in that suite was something altogether different.

The Suburban driver—I never did catch his face behind that tinted glass—dropped me off in the underground garage, then motored on. Buzz was waiting for me as promised. His hair was styled in that high-and-tight boot-camp style he favored. His unibrow was untrimmed, as it always was, and he wore a perpetual frown I suspect he'd been born with. Except for the black pirate patch over his right eye (courtesy of some shrapnel he'd caught on an op once outside of Tripoli when we were both with Alpha), he reminded me a little of Bert from *Sesame Street*.

"Logan, you're as goddamned ugly as ever."

"Talk about the pot calling the kettle black."

We shook hands and slapped each other on the back.

"How was the trip?"

"No complaints. Except your guy wouldn't stop at Arby's on the way in."

"*Arby's?*" Buzz squinted at me with his one good eye. "The only time I eat at Arby's is when I'm in the mood for kangaroo."

He wasn't a big man, but he was undeniably larger than life. Bombastic. Outspoken. A lover of opera. A hater of all enemies, foreign and domestic. Recipient of the Distinguished Service Cross, the Silver Star, numerous Bronze Stars and three Purple Hearts. He was as loyal a friend and as tough a warfighter as you'd find anywhere, one you wouldn't want to meet in a fire-fight, let alone that proverbial dark alley. He was ordinarily given to loose-fitting camp shirts and baggy paratrooper pants, which was why I was more than a little surprised to see him decked out in a well-tailored, conservative gray business suit and glossy black wingtips.

"Never figured you for a Brooks Brothers man, Buzz."

"I'm management now, if you can believe that bullshit. Gotta look the part, right?"

"I suppose so." I followed him to the elevator. "Cleveland? What's up with that?"

Buzz punched the up button. "Low rent and plausible deniability."

"Deniability of what?"

The elevator doors slid open. A FedEx deliveryman got out pushing an empty handcart and headed for his van. Buzz nodded to him politely and waited until he and I were safely alone inside the lift.

"Are you asking me from a hypothetical perspective?"

"I could be," I said.

"Good, because *hypothetically*, let's just say that it's a lot easier for the White House to deny running its own direct-action operation in Cleveland than it would be, say, Inside the Beltway where nobody can keep a secret."

"You're working for the White House?"

"Who said anything about the White House? I was talking hypothetically."

"Roger that."

He jabbed a button with the second knuckle of his right middle finger, the tip of which was missing. The doors slid shut. The elevator began moving. Buzz watched the floor numbers light up. "We need to get you read in and get this candle lit. We don't have much time."

I knew enough not to ask any more questions until we got upstairs.

~~~

The sign on the office door said, "General Motors Employee Relations, Midwestern Operations." Actually, it didn't say that. It said, "United Airlines Support Services." Okay, it didn't say that, either. The name of the corporation on the door can't be revealed for security reasons. Let's just say it's one you'd instantly recognize. And let's also say that what goes on inside the place has nothing to do with that corporation.

Buzz tapped a code into a digital keypad and the door clicked open. The first thing I noticed as we walked in were the two plain-faced women sitting behind a reception counter. Short hair. Tight, angular jaws. Humorless eyes that missed nothing. Both were ex-military police officers. That was my guess. I'd dated one or two MPs back in the day. A lot of fun on Saturday nights, once you got past all that girls-will-be-boys macho.

Filling the wall behind the receptionists was a large mural that advertised the operation's aforesaid corporate cover name and provided a visual representation of the work ostensibly done there—images of workers on automobile assembly lines, or of a United 747 in flight. Or neither of those. You get the picture.

One of the receptionists requested my photo ID while Buzz stood by and looked on. She scanned my driver's license into an electronic card reader like those the TSA relies on at the airport to make sure you're not cozy with the Taliban. Then she typed something on her computer and handed me a laminated pass, orange with a big blue "V" on it, which I clipped to my shirt.

Buzz tapped code into another digital keypad.

"After you," he said, holding the solid core wooden door open for me.

Glancing over my shoulder as I walked into his inner sanctum, I noticed the collapsible stock of a Heckler & Koch MP5 submachine gun within easy reach underneath the receptionists' desk.

General Motors, indeed.

THREE

In movies and on television shows featuring classified intelligence agencies, the nerve center is almost always some glassed-in, ultramodern beehive of activity where quirky but brilliant analysts can instantly access even the most obscure facts using state-of-the-art technology. Buzz's Cleveland-based operation was more true-to-real-life. In other words, it was nothing like that. Twenty or so casually dressed, mostly young people sat in cubicles, peering intently at flat panel computer screens while talking in hushed tones on telephone headsets. The atmosphere was about as Jason Bourne-like as a telemarketing bullpen, only without all the noise.

"Don't let looks deceive you," he said, pausing to proudly survey his domain. "These kiddies know what they're doing."

"What *are* they doing, Buzz?"

"Whatever the president tells us to."

"Hypothetically speaking, you mean."

"Touché."

His new command, Buzz explained, was code-named Acme, which sounded suspiciously similar to Alpha, our former employer. Both agencies were off the books, meaning neither officially existed. But unlike Alpha, which was deemed a hunter-killer operation, Acme's mandate was more hunter than killer.

"Our mission is generating actionable intelligence," Buzz said. "We leave the throat-cutting to others. In theory, at least."

"That's so antithetical to a knuckle-dragger like you."

"I'll take that as a compliment. Hey, it was a three-grade pay jump from my DIA billet. So I ain't exactly complaining, except now I spend half my time here in Ohio, wearing a suit and being slowly killed by PowerPoint presentations. The old lady doesn't seem to mind too much, though. Gets me out of the house. She can't stand living with me anyway. Says I would've been better off living in a cave, chasing mastodons."

"That certainly would be my take."

He saluted me with a single upraised finger.

"How many guys like me do you have working for you, Buzz? Any other alums from Alpha?"

"Better off you didn't know that, Logan. Compartmentalization. All that."

"Roger."

I followed him through the warren of work cubicles. The view out the window was of Lake Erie and FirstEnergy Stadium, home of the Cleveland Browns.

A huge man with blue Scandinavian eyes and ruddy cheeks, a bushy yellow beard streaked with gray, and blond hair down to his shoulders stood up as we entered Buzz's corner office, smoothing the trousers of his pin-striped, navy blue suit. The guy looked like a Viking banker. He was clutching a manila file folder that was stamped in red, "TS-SCI—Top Secret-Sensitive Compartmentalized Information."

"Cordell Logan, Arvid Hauksson," Buzz said by way of introductions. "Arvid's my X-O. He's from the teams."

"Your executive officer's a SEAL? Wow, Buzz, you must've really had to scrape the bottom of the barrel. I'll try not to hold that against you—or him."

Hauksson grinned. "I've heard good things about you, Logan. You've got quite the reputation in the community."

Commandos and government-sanctioned assassins tend to know each other, or *of* each other. As they say at Disneyland, it's a small world.

"Nice to be loved," I said.

He shook my hand like he was trying to break it. I guessed him to be about my age, but at six foot four and pushing two fifty, he had a good three inches and sixty pounds on me.

"There's one of those food trucks parked down the block," Buzz said. "Dude makes one badass breakfast burrito. Who's in?"

"Music to my ears," I said.

"You want extra chorizo on it?"

"You have to ask?"

"Arvid, burrito?"

"Not for me, thanks. The wife says I gotta drop ten pounds."

"And you listen to that noise?" Buzz was incredulous. "Did your wife drop into Pakistan and help grease bin Laden, too?"

"She cares about my well-being, Buzz."

"Your well-being? If she cared about your well-being, Arvid, she'd let you have a goddamned burrito once in a while. I swear to god, I'm calling Little Creek when we're done here. Your fellow frogmen, they're gonna want to hear about this."

Hauksson stared up at the ceiling and exhaled like he knew he couldn't win. "Fine. Gimme a burrito. Extra chorizo."

Buzz leaned out the door, ordered somebody to go get us three burritos with extra chorizo, closed the door, told us to sit, then dropped into his high-back leather chair behind his big executive desk. He propped up his feet and eyed me over the toes of his glossy black wingtips.

"So, Logan, I'm assuming you've heard of the Socialist Republic of Vietnam?"

"The name rings a vague bell."

He opened the belly drawer of his desk, got out a nail clipper, and began working on his fingernails. "What about the Hanoi Hilton? Ever heard of that?"

"By Hanoi Hilton, I'm assuming you mean the prison camp in Hanoi where the North Vietnamese tortured our downed pilots, not the actual hotel run by Paris Hilton."

"Paris Hilton doesn't run Hilton Hotels, Logan. She's like a model or something."

"Actually," Hauksson said, "no one's really sure what she is."

"I was being facetious," I said.

"Facetious?" Buzz clipped his right thumbnail. "What is that, Logan, one of your fancy air force words? Too bad you zoomies can't fight as well as you sip coffee and *vocabularize*."

He waited for me to fire back some equally insulting remark about the army, but I was long used to his incessant teasing and let it slide. Grizzled ground pounders like Buzz relish taking potshots at the air force—a "country club with airplanes," they like to call it. All of that name-calling ceases, of course, the minute they're being overrun by enemy infantry and screaming into their field radios for someone, anyone, to please come save them. On those occasions, as far as army infantrymen are concerned, the air force is the greatest invention since strip joints and chewing tobacco.

Buzz looked over at his second-in-command. "Okay, Arvid. Give him the dump."

Hauksson opened the file folder he was clutching and handed me a briefing paper. "Four days ago," he said, "a former guard from the Hanoi Hilton was murdered. His name was Pham Huu Chi, except our guys, the ones he guarded, didn't call him that. They called him Mr. Wonderful. Some civilians found his body floating in a lake in downtown Hanoi, stabbed to death. He'd been with three former American prisoners of war the night before. All three were pilots who'd spent time at the Hilton."

"The Vietnamese consider all three suspects in the murder," Buzz said.

I wanted to know what they were doing in Hanoi to begin with.

"Washington arranged a big, ceremonial 'kiss and make-up' dinner," Hauksson said. The administration wants to expand a multibillion-dollar, bilateral trade agreement with the Vietnamese. The hope is that both sides will sit down and negotiate revisions in import quotas and export restraints. Then, factoring in prevailing market pressures in the major commodity exchanges—"

"Arvid, for Chrissake, this isn't Econ 101," Buzz said, focused on his clipping. "We're burning daylight. Get to it."

Hauksson went on. "None of the POWs had seen the guard, Mr. Wonderful, since 1973, when the war ended and they were repatriated stateside. The dude had a reputation for being more sadistic than any other guard at the Hilton. He liked to beat 'em half to death with a tire iron just for fun. Hence the moniker, 'Mr. Wonderful.' The deal was they'd all meet for dinner in Hanoi with toasts and speeches, etc., etc., in the furtherance of international commerce."

"Old adversaries letting bygones be bygones, all that happy horseshit," Buzz said. He gathered up his nail clippings and dumped them in a trash can. "Things apparently were going along peachy keen until Mr. Wonderful showed up in that lake."

Two of the former prisoners, Hauksson said, were being held under house arrest at a hotel in Hanoi. The third had left Vietnam shortly after the guard's body was discovered and before he could be detained. Upon his return to the United States, he'd been briefly questioned by Defense Department investigators and had denied any knowledge of the murder. Vietnamese authorities were demanding his extradition, threatening to rescind the trade deal unless he was returned forthwith. The problem was that the United States has no extradition treaty with Vietnam. Both sides had been able to keep the story out of the press, but for how long no one could predict. Washington feared that once word of Mr. Wonderful's murder was made public, the trade deal would quickly unravel.

"We need boots on the ground over there," Buzz said, "somebody who can get in there quick and quiet, who can think on his feet and generate accurate assessments as to who might've stuck this asshole so that the White House can know how to respond appropriately. The other concern is the health of our two guys they're holding. The president's worried about them having to relive being in captivity, the whole POW experience. We know the name of the hotel in Hanoi where they are being held—the Yellow Flower. We think they've cordoned off an entire floor. If we can find a slick way to get them out of there before the whole thing turns into a bigger shit sandwich, so much the better. That's where you come in, *doctor*."

I looked at him, not fully understanding.

"You're going in as a psychologist," Buzz said.

As a humanitarian gesture, Vietnamese officials had agreed to let an American mental health expert into their country to assess and help manage the emotional well-being of the Americans being held there. I was to play that expert. The plan called for me to fly to the Vietnamese capital where I would pretend to be a psychologist while attempting to determine who really was responsible for Mr. Wonderful's murder and ideally figure out a way to get the two former POWs out of the country. Buzz and his crew had constructed an elaborate cover story for me, replete with faked credentials and an impressively extensive online history designed to counter any suspicions that I was anyone other than "Dr. Bob Barker, PhD."

"Bob Barker? Are you serious?" I tried not to laugh.

"What's wrong with Bob Barker?"

"Buzz, Bob Barker hosted *The Price is Right* for, like, two hundred years."

"The price is what?"

"It's a game show," Hauksson said. "On TV. Contestants guess the price of toasters and shit."

Buzz turned to his executive officer with an accusatory look. "Bob Barker's a *game show host*? Why didn't I know about this?"

Hauksson shrugged. "Do I look like I have time to watch game shows? I liked the name, that's all. It just came to me, boss. It was a coincidence, that's all."

Buzz looked away, thinking, exhaled, then turned toward me. "Well, it's too late to change it, anyway. We've already built the infrastructure online, your backstory. We'll just have to make it work, that's all. My guess is that nobody in Vietnam has ever heard of this show, anyway—what was it called again?"

"*The Price is Right*," Hauksson said. "It's still on."

"*The Price is Right*. And they guess how much toasters cost? This is what passes for entertainment these days?" Buzz shook his head. "Ridiculous."

"There are a hundred guys out there who could do a better job than me on this op," I said. "I pulled triggers, Buzz. I wasn't exactly a primo undercover operator."

"Don't sell yourself short, Logan. You operated undercover plenty. And you fly by the seat of your pants better than any operator I've ever known—except, of course, me." Buzz got up, leaned out his office door, and barked at one of his staffers to put a rush order on our burritos.

"But I don't know the first thing about how to play a psychologist, Buzz. I'd probably be better off seeing one on a regular basis, not pretending *being* one."

Buzz scoffed. "Like there's anything you really have to know to be a psychologist." He sat back down at his desk. "You wear sweater vests. You talk softly. You ask sympathetic questions. 'When did you decide you hated your mother?' 'If you were a tree, what kind would you be?' You'll be fine, Logan. Trust me. Piece of cake."

I told him about the commercial with Kiddiot that had found its way onto YouTube, how I'd achieved a certain degree of international notoriety because of it, and how I was concerned that such celebrity might blow my cover.

"Not to worry," he said. "They don't watch cats over there. They eat 'em."

"Actually," Hauksson said, "it's dogs the Vietnamese eat—in the north, anyway. It's considered a delicacy. In the south, they prefer rats."

Like I really needed to know that.

"Why wasn't the FBI assigned this mission," I asked, "or the State Department?"

"The State Department?" Buzz grunted. "State's a bunch of inept weenies. They couldn't investigate their way out of a lighted broom closet. And the FBI? Christ, Logan, the last thing the White House needs is a bunch of lawyers and accountants with guns who think they're real cops going in there big-footing everybody like they always do and pissing off the Vietnamese government even more than it already is."

"What about Langley?"

"Vietnam's been a backwater for those guys since we pulled out forty years ago," Buzz said. "Whatever human intelligence assets they maintain in-country are marginal at best. Under ordinary circumstances, believe me, the CIA could give a giant flying crap about what goes on in Hanoi."

My involvement in the operation, Buzz said, was expected to take no more than a week. Get in, find out what I could, and get out. That was my mission. He told me how much I could expect to be paid for my services. I didn't quibble. The money was more than generous, especially compared to my old government service salary with Alpha.

"There's something else you need to know," Buzz said, his tone turning somber. "One of the men they're holding is an old acquaintance of yours."

As if on cue, Hauksson pulled a three-by-five-inch color photo from the file and handed it to me.

The gaunt, dark-haired man in the picture wore the blue dress uniform of a United States Air Force lieutenant colonel, his blouse festooned with silver command pilot's wings and seven rows of ribbons, among them the Silver Star and Distinguished Flying Cross. He was sitting at an angle to the camera, posing for an official portrait shot with the American and air force flags behind him. His smile, which seemed pained, revealed stained, uneven teeth. His long thin nose looked as if it had been broken more than once, and his watery blue eyes radiated a tangible sadness. I recognized him instantly as Steven Cohen, my brilliant former philosophy professor from the Air Force Academy.

My cadet classmates and I were all well aware that Cohen had been a prisoner of war for three years in Hanoi, captured after his F-4 Phantom fighter was tagged by a Russian-built surface-to-air missile. He had a knack for languages and spoke several fluently, including Vietnamese, which he'd learned while in leg irons. The horrors he'd endured in the Hanoi Hilton were profound, none more so than when another captured pilot, badly injured, was rumored to have died in his arms. Cohen, however, refused to talk about any of it. Those days were behind him, he'd say, when we pressed him. Then he'd invariably change the subject by quoting some classic bit of philosophy, about how people can't change the past, only the future. It was Cohen who'd gotten me thinking about the virtues of Buddhism. It was, quite frankly, inconceivable to me that my gentle, soft-spoken professor could be suspected of murder.

"You knew him, right?" Buzz asked me.

"Been a long time but, yeah, I knew him. One of those people who change your life. Make you see things in a different light."

Cohen, Hauksson said, was still teaching part-time at the academy, living alone in a small cabin up in the mountains, west of Colorado Springs. I handed him back the photo.

"When do I take off?"

"You're booked on a flight out of Los Angeles tonight under the name, Dr. Bob Barker," Buzz said. "There'll be a native language speaker, an interpreter, waiting on station to assist you when you arrive."

"Who's the terp?" I asked.

Hauksson flipped through his file. "His name is Nguyen Phu Dung. Says here he flew combat during the war. Knocked down a couple of F-4s in 1971, before he got shot down himself."

I was speechless. Almost. "He flew for the *North Vietnamese*?"

"That's what it says here."

"An enemy pilot who's now working for us, and I'm supposed to trust him with my life?" I tried not to look as stunned as I felt. "What kind of shop are you guys running here?"

"Look," Buzz said, "the guy's been fully vetted, okay? Both DIA and CIA vouch for him. You're just gonna have to go with this, Logan. We don't have the luxury of asset shopping at this point. You're it. And so is he."

I ruminated for a couple of seconds. Buzz was right. Under the circumstances, time was of the essence.

"Where do I find him?"

"He'll find you," Buzz said.

Our chorizo burritos finally arrived. They tasted like they were from Cleveland.

~~~

Buzz drove me back to the airport in his personal ride, a gold Kia Optima with Virginia plates. Given the government's mileage reimbursement rates, he said, he preferred driving between Ohio and his home in suburban Washington rather than flying commercially.

"I put it on cruise control, crank up a little Placido Domingo, and boom, I'm pulling into the driveway six hours later. Hell, it takes me nearly that long just to get through security at the airport."

"Nice car," I said.

"Yeah, Kia does a pretty good job. They're building airplanes now, too, forklifts, buses, big-ass cargo freighters, you name it. I read the other day they build more ships than anybody in the world. They're gonna *own* the world someday at this rate, the South Koreans."

We crossed over a rusting bridge spanning the Cuyahoga River, heading south on Interstate 90. Sand and gravel pits lined both sides of the water. The sky was clear, the traffic light. Most of the other cars on the road looked like they hadn't been washed in months. There was no mistaking Cleveland for Los Angeles.

When we got to the airport, Buzz pulled into the passenger loading section, reached into the glove box, and handed me a US passport issued to Dr. Robert Barker. Along with the passport was a preapproved visa application letter that I'd need to gain entry to Vietnam, as well as copies of letters in both English and Vietnamese, signed by the Vietnamese ambassador to Washington, granting "Dr. Barker" permission to counsel and assess the mental health of the two Americans being held in Hanoi. Buzz also issued me a brown leather wallet containing a California driver's license and credit cards identifying me as Barker, along with six million Vietnamese dong worth about $300. Then he gave me an iPhone and charger.

The phone, he said, was encrypted. Installed on it were various relevant apps. There was a dictionary listing fundamental Vietnamese words—yes (vâng), no (không), thank you (cảm ơn bạn), and so forth. Another app served as English-Vietnamese translator. If worse came to worst and nobody spoke English, I could use it to make myself understood. Another app offered a guide to useful mental health terms (cognitive dissonance, associationism, etc.) so that I might familiarize myself with the vernacular of psychology and hopefully sound credible. The last app Buzz pointed out was the latest version of the kids' game, Angry Birds. In reality, it was a countersurveillance program that would allow me to detect electronic bugging devices. Also downloaded was a file with relevant background information on my mission as well as the bogus résumé of the fictitious Dr. Bob Barker that I was to memorize if I hoped to be convincing in the role. All of the apps would remain but the informational files would erase themselves as a security precaution, Buzz said, after being opened once.

"As always," I deadpanned, "should you or any of your I-M force be caught or killed, the secretary will disavow any knowledge of your actions. Good luck, Jim."

Buzz looked over at me like he had no idea what I was talking about.

"Who the hell's Jim?"

"Forget it."

"Just so you know," Buzz said, "nobody can track you on that phone. Nobody can listen in, not even the NSA. My direct number is on speed dial. So is my twenty-four-hour command post here in Cleveland. If you need help, hit zero."

"And what, the cavalry comes riding to my rescue?"

"You're pretty much out there on your own on this one, Logan. Screw the pooch, and we'll make all the necessary arrangements to have your remains shipped home with full honors."

"And I'm taking this assignment why?"

"Because you're a patriot. Because you owe it to all those studs who came before you. That includes the two they got locked up over there right now. Just do me one favor."

"Name it."

"Don't go looking for trouble over there. Get in, find out what you can, and get the hell out. The last thing the administration needs is having to negotiate the release of one more American. Copy?"

I nodded. We gripped forearms, gladiator-style—our old, premission routine from Alpha—and I got out of the car.

"I mean it, Logan. In, out, done. No trouble."

"Me?" I smiled. "Never."

When I looked back, he was watching me, frowning.

~~~

The Gulfstream was waiting where I'd deplaned earlier that morning. The cockpit door was still closed. For all I knew, both pilots were still inside, still cowering in embarrassment at that miserable excuse for a landing. The flight attendant, Best, welcomed me back on board with a chicken salad deli sandwich on rye, a bottle of fresh-squeezed guava juice, and a midsize rolling suitcase, black.

"The boss told me business casual," he said. "Hope everything fits okay."

Three pairs of Dockers slacks. Conservative dress shirts. Suede Rockport oxfords. Argyle socks. Two sweater vests. Your grandfather's boxer shorts. Buzz's definition of the well-dressed psychologist. I changed into slacks and one of the shirts, and stuffed my old clothes into the suitcase, along with my toothbrush and other toiletries. Best assured me my duffel bag would be waiting for me when I got back stateside.

"You'll need to leave your old wallet with me," he said, "and anything else that could identify you as anybody other than your operational cover. You'll get it all back after."

I tossed him my wallet.

"Anything else that could identify you? Monogrammed garment labels? Tattoos? Not that we could do much about the ink at this point."

"I'm not into body ink. And, fortunately, I left my mono-grammed bikini briefs at home." I laced on my new Rockports, which looked like the kind of shoes old folks slip on to walk the mall, sat back, and settled in for what would be an uneventful flight to Los Angeles.

Thinking about my old professor, Steve Cohen, gave me a welcomed respite from thinking about Savannah. I remembered that Cohen had a history of heart trouble—he'd been hospitalized briefly when I was at the academy for what was described as a "mild cardiac event" before returning to the classroom. I wondered to what extent his being back once more in Hanoi and under armed guard would cause him tumult. More than anything, though, I also wondered how the hell I was going to pull off this operation.

FOUR

The flight was a China Airlines red-eye with a short layover in Taipei, leaving at 0105 hours out of LAX's Tom Bradley International Terminal. I had plenty of time to kill before my scheduled departure.

After a sumptuous, two-entree dinner at Panda Express, I visited the international terminal bookstore. There, I perused an article in *Cosmopolitan* magazine about sixteen problems people encounter during drunken sex. I felt particularly fortunate that I don't drink anymore. After that, with still plenty of time to kill, I went window-shopping.

From Hermès to Gucci, the terminal's merchants catered to a clientele of which I surely was not a member and never would be. At one duty-free shop, I paused to admire a bottle of single-malt Balvenie whiskey on display behind glass. It's been years since I touched a drop of liquor, but I remembered the stuff was high-end. Two haughty sales associates stood nearby, arms folded, chatting with each other and looking bored.

"Mind me asking a question?"

One looked over like she was doing me a favor. She had dark hair and way too much lipstick.

"May I help you?"

I pointed to the bottle. "What's the price on that?"

"The Balvenie? It's $46,000."

I started laughing. She seemed offended.

"Sir, this is the absolute best scotch money can buy. In the world. Period. For, like, ever. It's nearly fifty years old."

"So am I, but I guarantee you, nobody'd pay that much for me."

At the Porsche Design shop, a sleek-looking, squared-away African American sales clerk dressed all in black tried to interest me in a $480 stainless steel pen that flexed like a snake. The technology, he said with pride, had come by way of NASA, where engineers required a "writing instrument" that would perform reliably in harsh, zero-gravity conditions of Earth orbit.

"The Russians came up with a similar writing instrument," I said. "It was called a pencil."

He forced a thin smile. Call it a hunch, I don't think he thought I was the least bit funny.

My seat was on the aisle, thirty-seven rows behind the nose of the China Airlines Airbus A330. The flight attendants were stylishly coiffed and all unusually statuesque for Chinese women. They wore their hair up in identical buns and went about their work with all the humor of Marine Corps drill instructors. If you deigned to leave your seatback even slightly reclined when they were coming down the aisle, serving a meal, they were only too eager to lean over, push the button on your armrest, and return your seat to its full and upright position without asking whether you'd like to do it yourself. They served us chicken and rice with a full-sized Almond Joy candy bar for dessert. Not bad.

"First time to Taiwan?" the guy in the middle seat asked me. He was Asian, midthirties, and spoke with an Asian accent. His aloha shirt was open to his navel, revealing a proliferation of gold neck chains, from one of which hung a two-inch rendition of the Buddha, carved from jade.

"I've been there a time or two," I said.

"On business?"

"More or less."

"So what is it you do?"

"As little as possible."

He smiled and seemed to know enough not to pry.

I ate

"Taiwan's awesome, dude," he said after a while. "Really hot chicks there."

"Is that right?" I forked some chicken into my mouth.

"Not as hot as Vietnamese women, though. That's where I'm from. Vietnam."

He told me his name was Tony and that he ran a filling station outside New Orleans. He was making a connection in Taipei and flying on to Ho Chi Minh City—what was once known as Saigon—to attend his mother's funeral.

I offered my condolences.

"Yeah, thanks. She's a great lady. Never wanted to leave the old country, though. It was home, you know?"

I nodded and told him I was headed ultimately for Vietnam myself, to Hanoi.

He shook his head. "Just be careful up there, man."

"Something wrong with Hanoi?"

He unwrapped his Almond Joy. "Bad things happen in Hanoi, that's all."

He dozed off after dinner. The young woman sitting against the window next to him, ensconced in a gray, hooded, oversized UCLA sweatshirt, had fallen asleep even before we'd taken off.

I dug out the iPhone Buzz had given me and studied the White House's executive summary of the crisis in Hanoi:

Being held in the Yellow Flower Hotel along with my former professor, Colonel Cohen, was retired Air Force Captain Virgil J. Stoneburner, 71, of Boca Raton, Florida., whose F-105 Thunderchief had been hit by ground fire while attacking a bridge south of Hanoi in May 1969. Stoneburner had been badly injured ejecting from his stricken jet. North Vietnamese doctors tried to reset his broken legs after he was captured, but he never walked normally again.

The third former POW who'd been prescient enough to leave Vietnam and return home hours before Mr. Wonderful's body was found, Clarence "Billy" Hallady, resided in Redlands, California. He'd flown propeller-driven Skyraiders off the carrier, USS Ticonderoga. Shot down in December 1965, Hallady held the distinction of having spent more time in North Vietnamese prison camps than just about any non-jet-driver in the fleet. He'd spent three years at Walter Reed and other VA hospitals upon his release, undergoing nearly twenty surgeries to repair the injuries he'd sustained to his arms and shoulders during countless torture sessions at the Hanoi Hilton, many of them at the hands of Mr. Wonderful. The records described the psychological trauma he'd sustained during those sessions as "profound."

"Coffee or tea, sir?"

I looked up from my phone into the flight attendant's perfect porcelain face. She was holding silver decanters in either hand and possessed the kind of body that generated recreational thoughts about which I immediately felt conflicted.

"No, thanks."

She moved down the aisle without so much as the hint of a smile. Say what you will about flight attendants on American commercial airlines these days. At least they smile. Occasionally, anyway.

I glanced over at my seatmate to make sure he was still snoozing—he was—and returned to my reading.

Cables from the US Embassy in Hanoi to the White House showed that officials had made repeated efforts to resolve the looming crisis by reaching out to Vietnam's Foreign Ministry as well as the Supreme People's Procuracy. The Americans had been essentially stonewalled.

The only pertinent bit of intelligence gleaned from these failed diplomatic efforts had been to confirm the identity of the man heading the investigation of Mr. Wonderful's murder. He was from the Ministry of Public Security—Vietnam's version of the FBI. His name was Truong Tan Sang. His photos were included in the briefing package on my phone. Open source analysts at CIA reported that Sang was a Vietnamese army colonel whose mother had been killed during US bombing raids on Hanoi in December 1972. The colonel by every indication was a rising star in the Communist Party. At fifty-two he was unmarried, a fluent English speaker and hard-line ideologue with no known personal vices and a seemingly limitless political future.

Some predicted he might one day even become prime minister. He had silver hair and conveyed the imperious countenance of a man used to giving orders and having them obeyed.

As for Mr. Wonderful, his sadistic exploits had been told and retold in memoirs published by various former American prisoners of war. It was said that he smiled and hummed pleasantly while torturing downed flyers. Intelligence reports indicated that in civilian life after the war, he'd married and started a small company selling used car parts in Hanoi. The venture had proven profitable, allowing him to buy up several apartment buildings throughout the city. Acquaintances described him as a kind and honest man who, like many veterans, never talked about what he'd done during the war. Allegations of his brutality were inconceivable to his family and friends. So, too, for that matter, were stories that any US prisoners of war had ever been mistreated in any significant way by any Vietnamese prison guards. The Vietnamese were a civilized people; the notion of torture was antithetical to their culture.

My curriculum vitae, or rather, Dr. Bob Barker's, was a creative amalgam of truth, half-truths, and flat-out fiction. Like me, he'd grown up in Colorado and enjoyed flying small airplanes in his spare time. But while one of us had gone to the Air Force Academy, flown more than one hundred combat missions, and eventually gone to work in the shadow world of covert intelligence operations, the other of us had dallied for years in the womb of academia, racking up two master's degrees and a doctorate. Barker had matriculated all over the country, from Purdue to Penn State to Carnegie Mellon, before setting up a private clinical practice in Rancho Bonita. He was a member of the American Psychological Association and innumerable other esteemed professional organizations, and had been honored for his clinical research in the area of post-traumatic stress disorder.

I felt honored knowing the guy.

I pocketed my phone and checked my watch. We still had another five hours to go before landing in Taipei. A one-hour layover there was followed by a two-hour connecting flight across the South China Sea to Hanoi. There was a small, high-resolution entertainment screen on the seatback in front of me and a remote control built into my armrest. I spooled up a preposterous action thriller in which the famous movie star I'd taken whale watching portrays a blind ex-Green Beret who teams up with a janitor (played by a wise-cracking, African American comedian) to save the Pentagon from terrorist attack. I made it through about ten minutes before nodding off.

~~~

There's an adage among Special Forces tacticians that applies to life in general: If it's stupid but it works, it isn't stupid.

I was convinced that the Vietnamese would never buy my slapdash psychologist ruse, and that I'd be arrested as a spy upon landing. Hanoi's stylishly steel and glass Noi Bai International Airport could've been just about any big city airport but for the fact that you could spot with a satellite the numerous counterintelligence agents posing as maintenance workers and airline ground crew. They surveyed my fellow passengers and me a bit too intently as we proceeded from the airliner, down a long narrow concourse, and into the terminal's customs and immigration area. To my surprise, no one stopped me. Nor did they try while I paid the required forty-five dollar entrance fee and waited, trying to look nonchalant, as they ran my visa application through their computers. After about ten minutes, a sharp-featured young man wearing a green, military-style uniform with red and gold epaulets slipped me back the passport through an opening under the glass partition behind which he was standing. Affixed to an inside page of the passport was a sticker, granting me in both English and Vietnamese a thirty-day stay in-country.

"Welcome to Hanoi," he said and smiled.

"Good to be here."

I grabbed my suitcase off the carousel and passed two government officials whose sky blue shirts and dark blue trousers reminded me of the uniforms I wore at the academy. They gazed at me sternly with arms folded. The younger of the two held out his hand indicating I was to stop. He asked me something in Vietnamese. I gave him one of those I-have-no-idea-what-you're-saying-I'm-just-a-dumb-foreigner kind of shrugs.

"He say do you have anything to declare?" the older official said.

"No."

The younger guy eyed me, then my suitcase for a long moment, apparently decided I was telling the truth, and tilted his head curtly toward the exit.

I was free to go.

Walking outside felt like someone had thrown a damp hot towel in my face. Not yet noon and the temperature was already well above ninety. The sky was hazy and the day thick with humidity. Taxis were cued up the length of the terminal. I climbed into the back of the first one in line.

The ride into downtown Hanoi took about forty minutes. The cab, like most cars seem to be in Vietnam, was a Toyota Tercel with manual transmission. The air-conditioning did little more than spit out lukewarm air. My driver couldn't have been more than eighteen, as thin as any waif you'd find in a Dickens orphanage. I handed him a slip of paper printed in Vietnamese that directed him to the hotel where I'd be staying. He uttered not a word.

The road was rutted and chaotic with small motorbikes, some transporting entire families, maneuvering wildly around the occasional truck or car. Every driver seemed to be beeping his or her horn all at once while appearing to disregard anything even remotely resembling Western-style traffic laws, yet none of them seemed to get the least bit upset at anything, regardless of how boneheaded the other drivers were around them.

Water buffalos grazed in rice paddies along the roadside where stooped old women in conical straw hats trudged along pushing rickety wooden carts filled with melons. Others walked with bamboo poles slung across their shoulders, balancing baskets laden with bananas and freshly cut pineapple. I saw lines of school children in their white shirts and red Communist Party neckerchiefs, some toting backpacks emblazoned with the American flag. I saw one kid on a bicycle wearing a Green Bay Packers jersey. Go figure.

We passed over the Red River, as wide and muddy as the Mississippi in springtime. In English, a large sign on the bridge said, "Hanoi, City for Peace"—a rich irony given the pounding the city had taken forty-plus years earlier from American warplanes, including one piloted by my former professor, Steve Cohen. I wanted to ask the kid driving my taxi about that, but he was no talker. Even if he had been, what insights could he offer me? He hadn't even been born yet when the war ended.

I sat back and watched two Vietnamese men whiz past on a motor scooter with perhaps two dozen chickens in wire cages draped over the handlebars. The passenger on the back was balancing a full-sized grandfather clock on his thighs.

~~~

My hotel was situated in Hanoi's Old Quarter, a neighborhood of narrow streets and three-story, tin-roofed shanties—apartments above, businesses below—stacked cheek-to-jowl, one to the next. The buildings had faded canvas awnings and balconies with wrought iron railings shaded by lush, broadleaf trees. But for the red Vietnamese flag with its yellow star hanging limply here and there, the place reminded me more than a little of New Orleans's Bourbon Street. Riding there in that cab with the windows open, nobody gave me so much as a second glance despite my face looking radically different from virtually every other face in sight. It was not lost on me the fact that their reaction to me was in profound contrast to what it must've been like during the war, when captured American pilots were paraded in chains through angry mobs before arriving at the infamous prison camp that came to be known ubiquitously and derisively as the Hanoi Hilton.

By all appearances, the Yellow Flower Hotel that would serve as my home away from home was a stylish and modern eight-story oasis in an otherwise frenzied, grossly overcrowded city. As we pulled up, I saw no signs of military or law enforcement presence, nothing to suggest on the surface that inside the hotel, two former American POWs were being held pending murder charges.

I paid the cabbie the equivalent of about twenty dollars for the ride in from the airport. A uniformed doorman with dark hair slicked back Elvis Presley-style fetched my suitcase from the trunk while another eagerly held open one of two big glass doors leading into the hotel. The air inside was pleasantly chilled. The floors were polished inlaid marble. Crystal chandeliers hung from a fifteen-foot ceiling over a compact but handsomely appointed lobby. Adjacent to the front desk was a reception area decorated with club chairs and ornate, fresh flower arrangements. As I walked in, the manager and two clerks on duty got to their feet from behind the front desk, smiling at me in welcome. The clerks were young women, slim and dark-haired and garbed in identical black slacks and yellow high-necked, thigh-length Vietnamese silk tunics slit up the sides. One wore glasses. With purple-tinted lenses. Her name tag identified her as Cara. The other, Nu, was about seven months pregnant. Big round clocks hung on the wall behind the front desk indicating the time in Dubai, London, New York, and locally.

The manager was about thirty and wore a dark suit, white shirt and yellow tie that matched the pattern on his clerks' tunics. His gold name tag said, "Dan." He looked more like a Duk or a Duong. His aftershave smelled like limes, or maybe it was the stuff he used to slick back his hair that smelled. His wide smile revealed flawless teeth.

"We have your reservation right here, Dr. Barker," Dan said, studying a computer screen. I discerned a hint of West Texas twang in his accent. "What brings you to Hanoi? Business or pleasure?"

"Hopefully a bit of both," I said, lying.

"And, may I ask, what sort of doctor are you?"

"A damned fine one."

"I meant your specialty. Heart? Lungs?"

"I'm a psychologist."

"I see." He seemed somewhat disappointed by my answer. "Well," Dan said, still peering at his computer, "it appears as though your room has been prepaid, and that you will be staying with us for seven nights. Is that correct?"

"Sounds about right."

"Very good, sir. All I need, then, is a credit card for incidental expenses and your passport, to make a copy for our records."

I gave him my Buzz-issued passport and Buzz-issued Visa card. He thanked me and gestured with an outstretched hand to the reception area. "Please, Doctor, would you be kind enough to make yourself comfortable momentarily while we finalize the necessary paperwork?"

I walked over and parked myself in a club chair. Nu, the pregnant desk clerk, brought me a steaming cup of sweet tea without my asking. She smiled graciously in response to my nod of thanks and returned to the front desk, leaving me with an unobstructed view of the hotel's main entrance and the street beyond.

Guests came and went—out-of-shape European and Australian tourists, mostly, clad in walking shorts and sandals. They lugged expensive backpacks and slung their camera bags across their chests so as to deter the pickpockets and all the many other thieves they'd no doubt heard populate the streets of Hanoi. Most of the tourists wore vaguely worried expressions—mouths tight, eyes peeled—the consequence, I suppose, of obtrusiveness, non-Asians in an Asian land.

I expected to see soldiers or police investigators milling about the lobby, but observed none.

After a few minutes, Dan came over and sat down beside me with my credit card and passport, along with an authorization form to sign that would permit the hotel to bill me should I decide to raid the minibar. Nothing in his demeanor suggested that his hotel stood at the epicenter of a looming international crisis. After I scrawled Dr. Bob Barker's name on the agreement, Dan handed me an electronic key card in a small envelope with the room number printed on it.

"We have you in 508, a deluxe room on the fifth floor. Your room key also affords you access to the exercise and business centers, both of which are located on the second floor. A buffet breakfast is served in the dining room downstairs each morning from seven until nine thirty A.M. Room service is available until eleven P.M. One of my staff has already taken the liberty of moving your luggage to your room for your convenience."

"I would have preferred to handle my own luggage."

"My apologies," Dan said. "I was merely trying to make your arrival a bit more pleasant after what I'm sure has been a very long journey."

"I appreciate the gesture. Next time, though, I'd appreciate you asking me first."

"Of course. May I ask, Doctor, have you been to Vietnam before?"

"First time."

"Ah, I see. Y'all might be pleased to know, then, there is generally no tipping in Vietnam."

The guy was accusing me of being tight with a buck, of trying to avoid having to tip the bellman. I won't lie: he was partially correct. But the real reason I didn't want anyone else touching my suitcase was that I was concerned about their planting an eavesdropping device. I couldn't very easily tell Dan that, though. I said nothing.

"We are honored you've chosen to stay with us during your visit to the lovely and peaceful city of Hanoi, Dr. Barker. If there is anything you require, anything at all, please do not hesitate to contact me directly. I will be only too happy to make your stay with us as comfortable as possible."

"I do have one question," I said.

"Certainly, sir."

"What's with the '*y'all*'?"

Dan beamed proudly. "Texas Tech. Bachelor of science in hotel management."

Vietnam's deified communist leader, the late Ho Chi Minh, would've been rolling over in his grave. That's what I wanted to say, anyway, but I didn't.

We shook hands, and Dan excused himself to return to his desk duties.

Somewhere above me in the hotel, unless they'd been moved to another location, two American heroes, including my former philosophy professor, were being held against their wills. I needed to make contact with them quickly.

FIVE

A pair of elevators stood in plain view of the front desk. I told Dan and his clerks that I wanted to check out the hotel's gym before heading to my room. If my intentions seemed suspicious, it didn't register on their faces. They smiled and all wished me a pleasant day. I stepped into the first elevator that opened and pushed the button for the second floor.

The Yellow Flower's "exercise center" was only slightly larger than the walk-in storage locker that served as my office in Larry Kropf's hangar back home. Like my office, it was far from lavish: a tired treadmill, an older Universal weights machine mostly for upper-body work, and a watercooler. I would've expected something a little more elaborate given how nice the rest of the hotel seemed to be, but whatever. I'm not real big on working out, anyway. With a surplus of lifelong orthopedic souvenirs to show for the four years I spent playing college football, the last thing I feel like doing on most days is grunting and groaning through repetitious, weight-bearing exercises.

The guest rooms on the second were aligned in a squared U-shape, eight rooms on the floor, with the two elevators at the top of the horseshoe. The halls were paneled in dark teak, the walls adorned with copies of French impressionist paintings hung every few feet in gilded frames. I walked from one end of the U to the other, the soles of my shoes treading silently on the marble tile. The door to each room was closed. The rooms themselves were quiet. There were no posted guards.

I climbed the stairwell to the third floor. Same floor arrangement. Same silence.

On the fourth floor, I encountered an elderly housekeeper transferring fresh linens from her cart to the room she'd been cleaning. She had a wrinkled face and looked up at me as I passed by. I wondered if I'd seen that same face in photo essays about the war—a rifle-toting, pajama-clad guerilla fighter. North Vietnamese women often fought alongside their men, battling the French and, later, American and South Vietnamese forces. I nodded my head in greeting. She smiled in a friendly way and said something in Vietnamese. I assumed it was hello. You get a good vibe from certain people and you don't really know why. A primal thing, maybe. She was one.

Waiting for the elevator on the fifth floor was an attractive Asian woman wearing five-inch stiletto pumps and a tailored, cream-colored pantsuit that highlighted her every curve. She was texting on her BlackBerry and barely seemed to notice me. I noticed plenty: early forties, almond eyes, full lips, dark, shoulder-length hair with subtle red highlights parted to her left, long fingernails the color of oxidized blood, no wedding band. Gorgeous didn't begin to describe her.

"Apparently, you didn't get the memo."

"What memo would that be?" she asked, not bothering to look up from her texting.

"The memo that said the BlackBerry is a dinosaur."

"Hmm." I couldn't tell by her pursed lips if she was annoyed by me or mildly intrigued. "And where did you see this memo?"

"Actually, it wasn't a memo. It was an article in an in-flight magazine. I read it coming over here."

"I see." She stifled a smile and looked up at me for the first time. "Well, I'll just have to look into that, won't I?"

The British influence in her accent suggested she was from Singapore, possibly Hong Kong. I was tempted to ask if she was staying in the hotel and whether she might be interested in getting together later for a drink or dinner so that I might share with her my vast knowledge of cellular technology, of which, in fact, I know nothing, but it wasn't the right time or the place. I was on a government assignment. And, besides, I still mourned Savannah.

"You have yourself a great day," I said.

"You as well."

I strode around the corner to my room and swiped the card key through the slot in the electronic door lock. The temperature inside felt like about forty degrees. I turned up the thermostat and introduced myself to the bathroom.

My suitcase was resting on one of those little folding luggage stands near the foot of the queen-sized bed. The furniture was rosewood. On the desk was a bamboo bowl with two bananas and a little sign that said, "Welcome, Compliments of the Yellow Flower." Inside the closet was a small safe with a digital lock. Room safes are essentially worthless, their combination locks easily manipulated. I'd stash my wallet and passport where I always kept them while staying in foreign hotel rooms: in a Ziploc plastic bag hanging behind the water tank of the toilet.

When I went up to the sixth floor where the two former POWs were being held, I found myself standing face-to-face with a young Vietnamese soldier clutching an AK-47.

Startled, he jumped up from the plastic chair he'd been leaning back in as I emerged from the stairwell and brought his assault rifle to bear, ordering me in a high-pitched voice to halt. That was how I interpreted his words, anyway. He spoke no English.

"I'm a psychologist. I'm here to see the Americans."

I could've just as easily told him I was a cosmonaut or the pope. I probably would've drawn the same response. He began shouting over his shoulder, summoning what I assumed were reinforcements. They arrived within seconds in the form of another young soldier, similarly armed, and a junior officer of about twenty-five. Given his age, I figured he was probably a lieutenant. He, too, was yelling at me in Vietnamese, gesturing that I was to return immediately to the stairway from whence I'd come.

I raised both hands, palms out, and offered my best soothing, mental health professional smile.

"I'm here to help."

The lieutenant had a pinched face and hair that looked like it'd been trimmed in a machete factory. "Who are you? What do you want?" he demanded in passable English.

"I'm a psychologist. I have permission from your government to visit the men you're holding, to make sure they're doing okay."

I started to reach for the letters of authorization from the Vietnamese ambassador that Buzz had given me, which were folded up in the right front pocket of my Dockers. The lieutenant didn't like that. He drew his pistol while his two soldiers raised their weapons to fire. All three were now screaming at me. Nothing, I've discovered, sends a chill down your spine faster than staring down the business end of three fully loaded firearms.

"Relax, boys. I'm just getting some papers."

Ever so slowly, I unpocketed the letters and handed them to the lieutenant. He skimmed the copy written in his native language and glanced briefly at the English version, then ordered me to wait downstairs in the lobby for further instructions.

~~~

They were waiting in the hotel's reception area for the housekeepers to finish cleaning their room so they could check in. He was ruddy with coal black hair shot through with gray, and high cheekbones, like he might've had some Native American blood. His wife approximated what Janis Joplin might've looked like had she lived past sixty. She engaged me in conversation the moment I sat down, one of those always chipper, outgoing types eager to share the intimacies of their personal lives with complete strangers.

"You look like you might be from America," she said. "We're Americans, too."

"Really? I would've never guessed."

"Born and bred. I'm Lydia Rostenkowski. And this hunka hunka burnin' love is my hubby, Leonard."

Leonard nodded an annoyed hello, not looking at me, like he was used to his wife doing all the talking.

"How're you liking Vietnam so far?" Lydia asked me.

"No complaints."

"Leonard wanted to drive to Albuquerque to visit his sister, like we do *every* year, but I said, 'Leonard, I love you from here to the moon, but we are *not* going to visit your sister this year, and we are not going to Alamogordo just because they have a KOA campground down there. For once, we're going on a *real,* honest-to-god vacation.' And he said, bless his heart, 'What about my cousin? He lives in Vietnam. We could go visit him.' So, here we are. Pretty wild, considering neither of us has ever had a passport before and never even been out of the country, unless you count Nogales, which really doesn't count because everybody from Mexico is now living in America." She leaned forward, a twinkle in her eye. "You know what notebooks have that Mexicans don't, don't you?"

"Actually, I don't."

"Papers and borders," Lydia said, cracking herself up. "Isn't that right, Leonard? Isn't that what you say all the time? 'Papers and borders.' Get it?"

Her laugh reminded me of a machine gun. Leonard closed his eyes and gripped both arms of his chair like he was wishing it were an ejection seat.

"We're from Phoenix," she said. "Well, actually, Leonard's from Phoenix. I'm from Chicago, but I couldn't stand those darned winters after a while. That lake wind. Goes right through you, especially when you get old. The blood thins. Where are you from?"

"Rancho Bonita."

"Rancho Bonita, California?"

I nodded, wishing the housekeeper would hurry the hell up so Lydia and Leonard could check in.

"Oh. My. Gracious. Rancho Bonita," she said. "That is *such* a fabulous place. I was there for a weekend once with my old boyfriend, right after high school. Drove his old VW out. He came down with this condition. The doctors said it was from surfing—not much surfing in Chicago, you know. All that water pollution out there, whatever. Talk about swelling. He couldn't get his pants off without screaming. It was absolutely horrible. I mean, can you even begin to *imagine*?"

"I'm trying hard not to."

She droned on about everything and nothing. The Buddha says that tolerance is letting others be different in their views and actions. I sipped my second cup of sweet tea of the morning, nodding politely in all the right places, and tuned her out.

Through the windows, amid an endless procession of motorbikes and foot traffic outside the hotel, I watched a haggard-looking street peddler trying with little success to interest tourists in Zippo cigarette lighters—designed to look like those used by American servicemen during the war—that he was selling from a tray strapped around his neck. Another young entrepreneur outfitted with a pair of scissors and a tiny plastic stool was having better luck, barbering hair on the street.

Approximately ten minutes passed before a top-of-the-line Lexus SUV, a black, RX 450, pulled up in front of the hotel. I automatically made a mental note of the license plate number—you never know when information like that can come in handy. Hey, it's what I used to do. The doorman with the Elvis hair approached the Lexus from the passenger side. The rear window came down. Casually, the doorman looked both ways as if to make sure no one was watching him, then reached into the vehicle with his right hand and quickly pocketed something small that someone inside gave him. As he strode back to his workstation a little too casually, the army lieutenant I'd encountered upstairs emerged from the hotel. He approached the same Lexus where he offered a subtly reverent bow, then handed my letters to whomever it was sitting in the SUV's right rear passenger seat. After about a minute, the passenger door opened and a hard-looking Vietnamese man stepped out.

He was short and trim, with silver hair, dressed in a dark green uniform identical to the lieutenant's—short-sleeved and open at the collar. Only this guy sported way more stars on his shoulder boards. I guessed him to be in his early fifties. The doorman held the door open for him and he strode into the lobby with the lieutenant following him at a respectful distance.

Lydia was yammering on about how much her last root canal hurt. Listening to her was like undergoing a root canal. I excused myself from her monologue and stood as the man with the stars approached me.

"Dr. Barker?"

"That would be me."

"I am Colonel Truong Tan Sang."

The name came as no bulletin. He was the same man in the briefing photos I'd seen on my phone. We shook hands. He smiled, but there was no warmth behind it. His teeth were narrow and crooked, like misaligned pickets on a fence.

"You are a psychologist?"

"I am."

"Where, may I ask, did you receive your doctorate?"

Intelligence operatives are taught to prepare their lies in advance, to have their cover stories down pat, in detail, thus reducing the chances of being caught off guard if their identities or motives are questioned. I knew I should've prepared more thoroughly, nailed down psychologist Barker's backstory before landing in Hanoi, but there had been little time and I'd more or less blown it off. Now, nervous and jet-lagged, I couldn't for the life of me remember where I'd earned my pretend PhD. I also knew that if I hesitated even a millisecond answering Tan Sang's question, he might well smell a fraud and my mission would be over before it even began.

"Penn State," I said, hoping my guess matched the trail of fake credentials that Buzz and his team had established for me online. Wasn't Penn State where his kid had gone to school? It was as good a gamble as any.

"Ah, yes, Penn State." Tan Sang raised his eyebrows a little too dramatically. "I myself studied a bit of psychology, Doctor. Are you familiar with the work in object relations theory by Professor Frost? He has been at Penn State for decades."

I was being tested. If I said I was familiar with Professor Frost and his work, and neither existed, my cover would be blown. If I said I'd never heard of Frost, and the professor really had taught at Penn State for decades, I'd similarly be toast. So I said neither. My old football coaches always said that the best defense is a good offense. At that moment, I was inclined to believe them.

"We can stand here all day talking shop, Colonel. I demand to see the two United States citizens you're holding. Immediately."

"This is the Socialist Republic of Vietnam, Doctor, not America. You are in no position to demand anything."

"Those letters I gave your lieutenant, duly signed by your own government, would suggest otherwise. If you attempt to deny me access to those men, Colonel, or to obstruct in any way my efforts to assess their psychological well-being, I'll be forced to take the matter up with higher authorities. I hope you're prepared to personally deal with the consequences."

Colonel Tan Sang wasn't used to being challenged by anyone, let alone a foreigner. He took a step back, but his hard gaze never left me as he conversed in Vietnamese with his lieutenant. The younger officer bowed his head repeatedly and kept saying, "*Vâng, thưa ngài,*" which I took to mean, "Yes, sir."

When he was done addressing his lieutenant, the colonel said, "Very well, Doctor. I have directed my comrade to allow you access to conduct your assessments, but for no more than thirty minutes a day. The criminals are to be transferred to a more secure facility for their own safety."

"You mean to a prison?"

Tan Sang ignored my question. We both knew what he meant. "We are preparing the facility to make the criminals as comfortable as possible in consideration of their advanced age. We have our own mental health experts who will ensure their continued well-being. You will not be allowed to see them there."

"Read the letter, Colonel. My authorization grants me full access. It says nothing about thirty minutes a day. It says nothing about where I'm allowed to do my job."

"I am aware what the letter says, Doctor," he said, his voice rising. "I am in command of this investigation and I am responsible for the two criminals."

"You realize, Colonel, that these men underwent almost unimaginable hardships the last time they were guests of your country. Putting them back in a prison cell could be catastrophic to their psyches."

"The death and hardships they subjected my people to before they became our 'guests,' Doctor, more than justified whatever treatment they received then. They will be treated fairly, as they were then. This is my decision."

"When do you propose to transfer them?"

"Four days hence, at which time, with no other purpose to serve, you will be escorted to the airport and leave Vietnam."

"You're kicking me out of the country? I just got here."

"Four days, Doctor."

I'd pushed him about as far as I could, but I wasn't about to stand idly by while he railroaded two old men who'd yet to be convicted of anything.

"I'd like to see my patients now," I said.

Six

The Vietnamese lieutenant and I rode up to the Yellow Flower's sixth floor. Neither of us spoke. The elevator doors opened. He turned right. I followed him around the corner, down the hotel's north side. There, facing each other across the hallway, were two pairs of soldiers holding their assault rifles at port arms, across their chests, standing guard on either side of two doors. At the end of the hallway, a fifth soldier stood guard at the entrance to the stairway. Though I couldn't see him, given the way the hotel was configured, I assumed that the soldier who'd initially confronted me on the southern end of the floor was guarding the stairs there.

The lieutenant searched me to make sure I wasn't carrying any weapons or contraband. Then he said, "Fifteen minutes, each criminal."

"I can't do my work in fifteen minutes."

"Fifteen minutes."

He swiped a card key, opened a room door, and stood aside. After I entered, he pulled the door closed behind me.

Virgil Stoneburner was lounging on the bed in his boxer shorts. He lowered the Tom Clancy paperback he was reading and squinted at me with suspicion. Room service trays with half-eaten plates of food cluttered the floor.

"Who the hell are you?"

"Washington sent me. I'm a psychologist."

"You don't much look like a psychologist."

"I get that a lot. How're you holding up with all this, Captain?"

"How am I holding up? I'll tell you how I'm holding up. Shitty, that's how." Stoneburner sat up and swung his feet over the edge of the bed to pull his pants on. "These little cocksuckers have me locked up in here. They won't let me talk to anybody. They've disconnected the phone so I can't call my wife. They say I'm under investigation for some kind of murder, but they won't say who I supposedly killed. Some limp dick from the embassy showed up yesterday. He won't tell me, either, but says they're doing all they can to get us out, and that's the last time I saw him. Now the government sends in some *psychologist*? Are you fucking kidding me?"

He was pallid and bespectacled. What little hair left on his scalp was gray and uncombed, and when he stood, buckling his belt, he wobbled. One leg was noticeably shorter than the other.

"Look, I just wanna get out of here," he said. "I already served my time in hell."

"That you have, Captain. No one could ever argue with that. You seem stressed. Have you tried listening to music?"

"*Music*?" He was looking at me like I was a guy pretending to be a psychologist. "You think that's what I need? Music?"

"Music alleviates stress. It soothes the soul. What do you say we practice some meditative breathing techniques while we listen?"

Stoneburner was incredulous. "What in the name of the Almighty are you even talking about?"

The remote control to the room's Russian-made, thirty-two-inch flat-screen TV was sitting on a lamp table beside the bed. I turned on the set, found what had to be the Vietnamese version of VH-1—an Asian Justin Timberlake dancing and singing his way through an up-tempo, hip-hop video—then cranked up the volume to drown out any listening devices that might've been installed in the room.

"Okay, pal," Stoneburner said, "now, you listen to me. Whoever or whatever you are, what I don't need right now is listening to crap like this and putting up with your bull—"

I held up a finger to quiet him, leaned over and whispered in his ear.

"They're saying you murdered Mr. Wonderful."

"The guard?"

I nodded.

He sat down slowly on the bed, stunned, his expression was one of disbelief. He started to say something. I sat beside him and pointed to my ear. He got the crux of what I was trying to do and leaned in close.

"He's dead? You know that for a fact?"

"They found his body in a lake after your big dinner."

"And they think *I* did it?"

"Or one of the others."

"Well, it wasn't me," Stoneburner said. "And it sure as hell wasn't Cohen or Hallady. I can promise you that."

"How do you know that?"

Stoneburner looked up at me. "You don't spend years in a prison camp with a man and not learn everything about him. I *know* Steve Cohen. I *know* Billy Hallady. Maybe they had thoughts like that back then, you know, to kill the sonofabitch—especially Billy. Billy got beat worse than any of us, believe me. Wouldn't tell 'em a damn thing and spit in their faces. They'd knocked hell out of him two, three times a week. Nearly killed him I don't know how many times. You couldn't blame him for wanting revenge. Hell, we all did. But not now, not today. We're all old men now. You don't live as long as any of us has still filled with that kind of hate."

With the music blaring, Stoneburner recounted how he, Cohen and Hallady had gotten dressed up to attend the dinner that evening with Mr. Wonderful in the grand ballroom of the Metropole, Hanoi's most elegant hotel, a holdover from French colonial days. He estimated that more than 200 others were also on hand—North Vietnamese veterans, Communist government dignitaries, and a handful of representatives from the US Embassy. The former POWs had been coached by embassy officials to be on their best behavior, and that much was at stake economically. Then Mr. Wonderful showed up. He was drunk, Stoneburner said.

"He stood up after everybody got done eating and read some bullshit statement, which they translated for us, about how America was imperialist and how we'd been taught a valuable lesson by them kicking the crap out of us, but that we were all now good friends. No apologies, no nothing. We shook his hand because those were our orders. They snapped some pictures of us standing around together, like we were all good friends, and that was it. I saw him leave the hotel alone, about ten o'clock or so."

"Saw who?"

"Mr. Wonderful. The three of us waited around for maybe fifteen minutes, talking to the State Department people, then came back here. I've been stuck in this goddamned room ever since." He wadded up a paper napkin and flung it across the room.

"I don't blame you for being upset, Captain. We just want to make sure you're okay."

"Lemme tell you something, sonny. I spent the better part of seven years sleeping in leg irons. I can do this standing on my head. It's my wife I'm worried about. I have no idea if she even knows what the hell's going on over here. She has a heart condition. I was supposed to be home three days ago."

I told him I'd try to make sure his wife was kept informed of his situation.

"We're gonna do everything we can to get you out of here, Captain."

"Who are you, really?" he demanded.

"Is there anything I can get you? Anything you need?"

"Yeah," Stoneburner said. "You can get me a time machine so I can go back and bomb this shit hole back to the Stone Age, like we should've done forty years ago."

"I'll be back when I can. You take care of yourself until then. Try to keep calm."

"Calm, my ass. You tell whoever you're working for that unless Cohen and I are out of here pronto, we will sue the living shit out of Washington for putting us through this nightmare again."

"I'll let 'em know."

I rapped on the door. The Vietnamese soldiers standing guard outside in the hall let me out.

~~~

The television in Lieutenant Colonel Steven Cohen's room was tuned to a taped broadcast from the nearby Hanoi Opera House. My buddy Buzz, the opera fan, would've loved it: A bejeweled soprano with big hair and even bigger pipes was performing an aria, hitting the kind of notes that can shatter crystal glasses. Cohen could've easily blown my cover, but he appeared not to recognize me as I walked in. I wasn't surprised. More than two decades had passed since I'd graduated from the academy. How many hundreds of other cadets had attended his philosophy lectures in the interim, absorbing his learned insights on Plato and Confucius, John Locke and Descartes?

Like Stoneburner across the hall, Cohen didn't buy for one second that I was a psychologist. Unlike Stoneburner, he seemed content to accept the ruse and quietly resigned to his incarceration. He sat at his desk, legs crossed, impeccably dressed in country club casual—polished oxblood loafers, no socks, cuffed, razor-creased khakis, a blue polo shirt that matched the color of his watery eyes. When I commended him on his squared-away appearance under difficult conditions, he joked that house arrest had afforded him "plenty of time to catch up on my ironing," then offered me a cup of tea.

"Sure."

"How's Virg doing?" he asked, plugging in one of those electric kettles that heat water to boiling within a minute or two. "They won't let us talk to each other, you know. Just like the good old days. Only in this case, unfortunately, we can't communicate by tapping code through the walls."

I turned up the volume on the television. Cohen seemed to understand what I was doing. "He's worried about his wife," I said, "anxious to get home, as I'm sure you are."

"This has to be much harder on him than me. I really have no one to go home to."

Cohen told me that his wife had left him shortly after he came home from Vietnam, and that he never remarried—something I didn't know anything about when we were both at the academy. He didn't elaborate on how he'd ended up single and I didn't ask. If he had children, he didn't mention them.

"How's your health, Colonel? I know you've had some issues with your heart."

"My ticker's just fine. You didn't tell me you were a cardiologist as well as a PhD." He winked knowingly.

I was tempted to tell him who I really was and how his philosophy class had opened up my mind in ways that would've been otherwise lost on me, a working-class kid who'd grown up bouncing from one foster home to another. But I was well aware that my purpose in Hanoi, the importance of the mission on which I'd been sent, eclipsed any walks at that moment down memory lane.

I passed along the same information I'd given Stoneburner, essentially how Mr. Wonderful had been murdered within hours of the dinner ceremony, and how Vietnamese officials believed that one or more of the former POWs were responsible.

Cohen gazed at the floor with those sad eyes of his, as if he were staring into the past. "Socrates said that it's not right to return an injury, or to do evil to any man, however much we have suffered from him."

"You don't seem all that surprised the guard's dead, Colonel."

"Can't say I am." The teapot chimed. He poured steaming water into a white china cup. "A man like Mr. Wonderful, his past almost always catches up with him eventually. In other words, what goes around, as they say, comes around."

He asked me if I wanted sugar. I declined. He handed me the cup.

"Maybe you can walk me through what you remember from that night," I said.

Cohen eased himself into the wooden desk chair and folded his hands placidly across his lap.

"Perhaps the better question," he said, "is what happened after all of us got back to the hotel."

Speaking quietly, he revealed information that Stoneburner hadn't, something I hadn't read in the briefing package from Buzz: Cohen, Stoneburner, and Billy Hallady had been accompanied on their trip to Hanoi by Hallady's adult grandson, Sean Hallady, a former marine who lived in Salt Lake City.

"Sean worships his grandfather," Cohen said. "Of all of us, he was the most outwardly contemptuous of the guard. Wouldn't even shake his hand."

Following the reconciliation dinner that night, Cohen said, he, Stoneburner, and the two Halladys all watched Mr. Wonderful stumble out of the Metropole through the hotel's front entrance shortly after ten P.M., drunk and alone.

"Did anyone follow him?"

Cohen shook his head. "To tell you the truth," he said, "by that point, having to sit there for three hours, looking at him across the table, remembering, we didn't want anything more to do with the son of a bitch."

The Americans, according to Cohen, all hired "cyclos"—three-wheeled bicycles whose drivers ferry tourists around Hanoi—to take them back to the Yellow Flower Hotel.

"When we got there, Stoneburner said he wasn't feeling well and went upstairs to bed. I have no reason to believe he went out after that, if that's what you're wondering."

"What about you, Colonel? What did you do?"

"Billy and I went upstairs with his grandson to have a nightcap."

Shortly before midnight, following a couple rounds of beer at the Yellow Flower's rooftop bar, Sean Hallady, who was bunking in his grandfather's room, announced that he was turning in and left, Cohen said.

"Billy and I sat around for maybe another half hour or so after that, reminiscing about old times. I was a little worried about him because I noticed he was starting to slip a little."

"Slip?"

"Mentally. He couldn't remember certain things. Dates. Names. I don't know whether it was the beer or something more serious. We're all starting to get to that stage of life, unfortunately."

"And after the beers?"

"I headed down to my room. Billy and his grandson were catching a flight back to the states early that morning. Virg Stoneburner and I were scheduled to fly out the next day. Virg wanted to see Halong Bay. It's supposed to be gorgeous, all those islands." Cohen smiled. "Neither of us really got a chance to see it during the war, needless to say, except from the air."

"What about Billy and Sean Hallady? Had they planned to go sightseeing with you at any point?"

"Why do you ask that?"

"I'm just wondering if they cut short their trip to get home sooner."

"You mean, because they murdered the guard and had to get out in a hurry?"

"You have to admit, Colonel, the timing of their departure is a little curious."

"The answer to your question, *Dr.* Barker, is no. Billy has a granddaughter—Sean's sister, I think—who is going to Tulane medical school. She was getting some big award. Billy wanted to be there for that. He told me he didn't sleep well overseas, which I can appreciate, believe me. He planned to stay up all night, do some reading. That way, he could nap on the flight home. We shook hands and wished each other well. That's the last I saw of him. I'm assuming he made it home okay."

"Did you tell the Vietnamese authorities any of this?"

My old professor's eyes turned flat and hard. "When I was at the Hilton, I eventually broke under torture," he said. "We

all did. Any man who says he didn't is a liar. But we never volunteered anything that they could use against any of us or our
country. That was our code of honor. We lived and died by that
code, Doctor. After surviving that, day after day, year after year,
would I voluntarily tell the Vietnamese *anything*?"

"My apologies for asking the question, Colonel. I meant no
offense."

He got up and gazed out at the office building under construction across the street. Hazy sun filtered in through the
window. "Such a vibrant city," Cohen said. "Amazes me that we
bombed these people as vigorously as we did."

"How would you describe your interaction with Mr. Wonderful the night of the dinner?"

"Interaction?" He thought for a moment. "I'd say it was
minimal at best. His government wanted him to be there for
the better good. We were only there out of a sense of duty. We
shook his hand, but that was about it. It seemed to me like he'd
been doing some drinking. He wouldn't look me in the eye. He
wouldn't look any of us in the eye. He remembered what he'd
done. There's no question in my mind about that."

"Had you forgiven him?"

Cohen watched with rapt fascination as Vietnamese labor-
ers with their pant legs rolled up hauled wet concrete in buckets
up ladders across the street. They reminded me of worker ants.

"Aristotle believed that there were five primary social virtues, Dr. Barker: courage, compassion, self-love, friendship and
forgiveness. I learned the first four in my years at the Hanoi
Hilton. The fifth, forgiveness, I learned in the years that followed." He turned to face me. "Not all of the guards were bad.
Some of them showed genuine compassion toward us."

"I didn't ask you about the other guards, Colonel. I asked
about Mr. Wonderful."

Cohen rubbed the back of his neck. "Until the State Department called, I had essentially blocked him from my memory.
Did I forgive him for all the pain he inflicted on my brothers

and me? If forgetting constitutes forgiveness, the answer is no. Some things you can never forget. But if your definition of forgiveness is distancing yourself from the kind of rage a place like that can instill in a man, I'd have to say yes."

My eyelids were starting to sag—jet lag creeping in. I thanked him for the tea even though I hadn't had a sip, told him I'd be in touch with any news, and got up to go.

"You look familiar to me somehow," Cohen said. "Have we met before?"

"A previous life, perhaps," I said.

~~~

The anti-eavesdropping app on my iPhone disguised as Angry Birds was designed to make an audible beep whenever it found a listening device within a three-foot radius. I ran the phone across the walls of my hotel room, along the baseboards and electrical outlets, around the table lamps, under the bed and over the thermostat, then stood on my desk chair and ran it past the smoke detector, fire sprinklers, and air-conditioning grates. The device never beeped. Either it wasn't functioning properly or the room was clean.

I pulled off my shoes, sat down on the bed, and called Buzz in Cleveland. He sounded groggy, like I'd rousted him from sleep.

"What time is it there?" he wanted to know.

"About two in the afternoon."

"Yeah, well, here it's almost two in the morning," Buzz said. "Thanks for nothing. I was dreaming about Halle Berry. We were just getting to the good part."

"Sorry."

"You should be, Dr. Barker. What's up?"

I told him that Cohen and Stoneburner appeared to be in good shape despite the rigors of house arrest, then filled him in on what I'd learned about Sean Hallady, Billy's grandson, having come along on the trip to Hanoi.

"The fact that Hallady headed home along with his grand-son just before Mr. Wonderful's body was found makes you wonder," I said.

"Where's the grandson live?"

"Salt Lake City."

"I'll have my shop do a full workup on him when I get in at zero-five."

"One more bit of intel you're gonna want to run by the chain of command."

"Go," Buzz said.

"I met Colonel Tan Sang, the guy running the murder investigation. They're planning to transfer Stoneburner and Cohen to a prison ahead of criminal charges being filed."

"When."

"Thursday."

"That's four days."

"Affirmative. I didn't tell Stoneburner or Cohen. I don't want them stressing out any more than they already are."

"Spoken like the true fake psychologist you are."

I passed along Stoneburner's concern that his wife be informed of his status. Buzz said he'd make sure she was briefed and told me to keep him posted immediately on any relevant developments. I assured him I would.

The bathroom counter was black marble, the plumbing fixtures polished brass. I dropped my clothes on the floor and stepped into the shower. The water felt like a warm caress.

I lay down on my impossibly firm mattress to catch a few hours' sleep. Thirty-five minutes later, my phone rang. I, too, may well have been dreaming of Halle Berry. I honestly can't remember.

"Hello?"

The voice on the other end was male, the accent Vietnamese.

"Your life," he said, "is in danger."

SEVEN

He wanted to meet at a bar called the Giddy-up. The address was on Tran Hung Dao Street, which he said was a ten-minute walk from my hotel. An exhausting, sweat-filled, half-hour workout on a ninety-degree afternoon with 90 percent humidity is more like it. Amid the Old Quarter's dizzying labyrinth of side streets that resemble alleys and crazy crowded avenues whose names can change literally from one block to the next, I quickly became lost. The good news, given the serpentine route I navigated, was that nobody could've possibly tailed me without my having spotted him.

The Giddy-up was Hanoi's version of a Western saloon, replete with a dime store wooden Indian out front. Inside, Vietnamese men wearing ten-gallon Stetsons sat at the bar throwing back shots of whiskey and nursing bottles of Saigon beer, while a four-piece Asian cover band belted out an earnest though somewhat erratic version of Hank Williams's "Cold, Cold Heart."

"Logan?"

Slits for eyes barricaded behind puffy lids. Thick lips. Skull shaved smooth. A jade likeness of the Buddha, big as a silver dollar, hung from a leather strap around his beefy weightlifter's neck. He strode toward me from the bar with a beer in his hand and a rock star's swagger, decked out in black combat boots, bloused black parachute pants, and a white, form-fitted muscle shirt that flaunted his powerful physique. For a man who looked to be pushing seventy, he was still definitely a stud.

"I am Nguyen Phu Dung," he said, "your interpreter."

We shook hands. His unassertive grip contrasted with the fierce warrior image he conveyed. Lashed to his left wrist was a big silver pilot's watch with buttons and dials galore. An ugly scar ran the length of his left forearm.

"You got any ID?"

I showed him my Dr. Barker passport. He gave it a quick glance and handed it back to me, glancing over my shoulder toward the door.

"Were you followed?"

"No."

"You sure?"

"Pretty sure."

"You want something to drink? Beer?"

"I don't drink."

"Good. More for me."

He led me to an unoccupied table near the rear of the saloon. A waitress came over in fringed leather chaps and a tank top with the actor John Wayne's face on it. Phu Dung polished off what was left of his beer, handed her the empty bottle and nodded for another. I asked for a glass of water. He translated my request and the waitress headed back to the bar. We sat.

"You told me over the phone I was in danger."

"They're checking on you."

"Who is?"

"The government." Phu Dung surveyed the bar's patrons like he was keeping an eye out for snipers. "They find anything, you're going to be here a long time."

"How do you know this?"

He shrugged.

"You know people inside the investigation?"

"I know many people," Phu Dung said, sipping his beer.

"How do I know you're not working for the government?"

He slowly swung his eyes toward me, like the guns on a battleship.

"If I was, you would be in jail by now."

The band started playing "Stand By Your Man," only it sounded more like "Stand My You Fan."

"I am told you were a fighter pilot," Phu Dung said.

"Not me, friend. I'm a psychologist."

His eyes disappeared into their slits as his thick lips slowly spread into a smile that told me he was onto me. Buzz's people had undoubtedly passed along my service record, the flying part of it, anyway, to help build rapport between the two of us.

"I heard you were a pilot, too."

Phu Dung nodded. "MiG-21."

"I also heard you shot down a couple of our planes."

He held up four fingers.

"Four planes you shot down?"

"Only credited for two."

I was entrusting my life to a man who'd done his best to blast American airmen like me out of the skies. The notion didn't sit well.

Phu Dung sensed my discomfort. "I defended my people," he said. "You would have done the same."

He was right, of course. He'd fought to save his homeland against what his political leaders considered foreign aggression. Had our roles been reversed, I wouldn't have hesitated to do exactly that.

"Why are you helping us?" I asked him. "The risks are just as great for you as they are for me. Possibly even more."

I thought he was going to tell me that the war had ended long ago and that he held no personal grudges, but he said nothing. Instead he held up his right hand and rubbed the tip of his index finger and thumb together. So that's what it was: he'd gotten involved not because of some humanitarian, we-are-the-world-type ambitions, but because the job paid, and probably paid well by local standards. And yet I wondered: Nobody who wears a big jade Buddha around his neck is in it strictly for the paycheck.

Our drinks arrived. I gulped my water. Phu Dung downed his beer like it was water. I told him I wanted to see the crime scene.

"Let's go," he said.

∼∼∼

The sidewalk in front of the Giddy-up was clogged with dozens of scooters and small, underpowered motorbikes parked close together. Virtually all of the sidewalks of Hanoi appeared to be similarly jammed as were the streets—endless streams of Vespas and underpowered, two-wheeled Hondas, their helmeted drivers all vying for space with each other and the occasional taxi, minibus or car. Phu Dung's ride was easy to spot as we emerged from the bar: a gleaming black Harley-Davidson Sportster with chrome pipes. Painted on the side of the gas tank was the silhouette of a silver MiG-21.

"Hop on," he said, pushing the ignition starter button and firing up his two-seat motorcycle.

"What about a helmet?"

"No helmet."

"I'm looking around, Phu Dung, and everybody else is wearing helmets."

"Are you a fighter pilot or a little girl?"

"Fighter pilots wear helmets."

"This is not a fighter jet. It is a motorcycle. If you want to go to where the body was found, I suggest you get on because I am not walking, not on these knees."

I sighed, straddled the Harley's rear saddle, and propped my feet on the hinged passenger pegs. In a throaty flash, Phu Dung had us rocketing through traffic in complete disregard of the posted speed limit—not that there are any apparent speed limits in Hanoi, not that are obeyed, anyway. We got to the lake in less than two minutes. I've flown airplanes on fire that induced fewer heart palpitations than that motorcycle ride.

∼∼∼

Hoàn Kiếm was the lake where Mr. Wonderful's body was found. The name in Vietnamese means, "Lake of the Returned Sword." As near as I could discern from Phu Dung's somewhat flowery explanation, an ancient emperor was boating there one day when a giant sacred turtle surfaced and demanded that the emperor return some magic sword the turtle had loaned him to help defeat China's Ming Dynasty. I wasn't so much interested in local Vietnamese legends, however, as I was in studying the location where Mr. Wonderful met his end.

Phu Dung pulled up onto the sidewalk, turned off the Harley's engine, and deployed the kickstand directly in front of a no-parking sign featuring the image of a motorbike in a red circle with a slash through it. As I dismounted, a scrawny policeman with a bullhorn who reminded me of a Communist Barney Fife strode toward us, ordering Phu Dung to move his vehicle. Phu Dung smiled and sweet-talked him in Vietnamese. Whatever it was he said, the cop seemed to apologize, then went on his way, barking at others to move their scooters.

"Very impressive."

"Let us just say I know a few people," Phu Dung said.

"What does that mean?"

He flashed an enigmatic smile and said nothing.

The lake was an oval, about a mile around, and sat squarely in the historic center of Hanoi. It was surrounded by manicured flower gardens and lush leafy trees under which young lovers strolled arm in arm and new brides posed in their gowns for wedding pictures. Kids chased each other, laughing. People sat on concrete benches, reading books and eating ice cream cones. A toothless street vendor tried to interest me in an assortment of cheap folding fans. Phu Dung gently shooed her away, but not before taking pity and slipping her some paper money.

My initial suspicions aside, I found myself starting to like the guy.

There was a gracefully arched foot bridge painted bright red that extended about twenty meters into the lake from the northeast shoreline where we'd parked, connecting the lakeshore to a tiny island upon which was built what Phu Dung said was the ancient Temple of the Jade Mountain. We didn't get into the historical specifics of the place; I didn't care one way or the other.

"Two old women found him there," Phu Dung said. He pointed to where the bridge's round, telephone-like supports, also painted red, extended into the water. "He wasn't in the water long. An hour, perhaps."

"Which side of the bridge?"

"North side."

"How do you know all this?"

Phu Dung smiled. "Let us just say I know a few people."

"What time did the old ladies find him?"

Phu Dung held up all five fingers of his left hand. Five o'clock.

"I'm wondering if he drowned or bled out, the actual cause of death?"

"Bled." Phu Dung patted his chest. "No water in his lungs."

"You've seen the autopsy report?"

He shrugged. "Let's just say—"

"—You know a few people. Do you know if the police have any witnesses?"

"That I do not know."

"Do they have any hard evidence tying any of the Americans to the crime?"

"That I do not know."

"Well, what else *do* you know?"

"I know they do not believe he was stabbed on the bridge."

"What makes them think that?"

"There was no blood on the bridge."

"So he was stabbed elsewhere and thrown in."

Phu Dung didn't say anything.

"Do they have an approximate location where the stabbing occurred?"

"Somewhere between the Metropole," he said, "and where we are standing now."

I did the math.

"He leaves the Metropole around 2200 hours. His body is found in the lake at 0500 the next day. He's been in the water about an hour. Where was he, what did he do, in the hours he was still alive?"

"I do not know."

A gauzy haze obscured the late afternoon sun but not the heat. The winds were warm and light, out of the north. I gazed at the water. A thought hit me.

"Which direction does the wind in Hanoi typically blow this time of year?"

Without hesitation, Phu Dung pointed north. Any good pilot is also an amateur meteorologist. He learns to read the sky and to study local weather patterns, because it's at whims of the weather gods that he can easily die or live to fly another day.

By Phu Dung's reckoning, the Metropole hotel, where Mr. Wonderful was last seen alive, was a half mile southeast of where we were standing beside the lake. Given the location of where the body was first spotted and the prevailing winds, the theory that Mr. Wonderful had been murdered somewhere south of the bridge made little sense. His corpse had been discovered floating on the *north* side of the bridge. A body dumped into the lake north of the bridge would have drifted south on the wind—directly to the location where it was found. In other words, the police theory of where Mr. Wonderful had been stabbed made no sense.

I headed north along the lakefront.

"Where are you going, Logan?"

"I'll be back shortly."

"I will wait for you here."

"Roger."

He got out his phone and made a call, straddling his motorcycle, while I walked on.

I wasn't exactly sure what I was looking for—some bit of evidence, I suppose, to confirm my theory that Mr. Wonderful had been killed in a location different than the one the authorities asserted.

Aside from the occasional Caucasian tourist taking vacation snapshots, mine was the only non-Asian face among the milling throngs of Vietnamese. I paused a few times, pretending to retie my shoelaces, checking to make sure I wasn't being followed, but discerned no tails. A street vendor approached me, offering bootlegged, first-run Hollywood movies for sale. Another tried to sell me counterfeit US military dog tags, circa 1968. Beyond those two capitalists, no one appeared to pay any attention to me.

I explored several hundred meters along the banks of the lake's north shore, as close to the water's edge as prudence would allow. I climbed over gnarled tree roots, scrutinized stains on concrete walkways, and studied the ground. I looked for fresh scars in tree bark and disruptions in the dirt, any anomaly that might suggest a violent scuffle had occurred there. I came up empty. The shoreline itself offered no overt forensic insights, either, littered as it was with discarded soda straws and coffee cups, tin cans and candy wrappers, and pieces of newspaper. The random, universal detritus of urban life. The only thing that caught my eye worth noting was a man's dress shoe trapped about three meters offshore in a stand of lily pads. Mr. Wonderful's shoe? It was impossible to know without knowing more about what he'd been wearing that night.

Phu Dung came roaring up the lakeshore on his Harley, deftly weaving through old people and families with small children.

"Let's go," he said.

"Go where?"

"To see the police officer."

"Which police officer?"

"One of the ones who pulled the body from the lake."

I didn't ask him how he knew the cop or where to find him. He wouldn't have told me, anyway. Maybe because we'd both flown fighters, or maybe because I was a stranger in a strange land and would've been lost otherwise, I let him call the shots. For the time being, anyway.

I climbed onto his Harley. We accelerated from zero to warp speed in about three seconds, rocketing through traffic. The guy knew how to drive a motorcycle, I'll give him that much. If he hadn't, we would have both been dead ten times over before we got to where we were going.

EIGHT

The cop was shirtless and head-lolling drunk, but seemed to sober up somewhat as soon as Phu Dung told him who he was. He came to attention, offering a clipped, respectful bow and nearly spilling the bottle of Tiger beer in his right hand. He said something in Vietnamese. Then he tried to shut the door in our faces. Phu Dung blocked it with his boot.

"The money," Phu Dung said to me, struggling to hold the door open.

"Say again?"

"Money. Give him some money. This is how it is done."

Quickly, I peeled fifty thousand dong off the cash roll in my front pocket and handed it over.

The cop grinned and let us in.

He was close to my height, tall for a Vietnamese. He didn't offer us a seat or a drink and I didn't mind at all, considering that the cramped hovel he called a home smelled like a landfill. Phu Dung said the cop would remain nameless for his own protection. He spoke no English. I'll call him "Pigpen," because that's what he looked like.

Money aside, the only reason he said he agreed to let us in was out of respect for Phu Dung, whom he regarded as a national hero. A "famous combat aviator who helped save the motherland from the imperialist pirates" is how Phu Dung, beaming, translated the cop's words for me.

I didn't much cotton to him using those kinds of terms to describe my fellow servicemen who'd honorably answered their nation's call to duty, regardless the merits of the war in which so many gave their lives. But standing there in that rancid-smelling apartment was not the place to engage in geopolitical debates.

Pigpen said he recognized Mr. Wonderful the minute he and his partner dragged his body out of the lake.

"We knew he was a big deal because he was in the newspaper," he told Phu Dung. "We knew we would have to work to find who killed him."

"Who do you think did?" I asked.

The cop polished off his beer, set the bottle on top of a dorm-size refrigerator already crowded with empties, and uncapped a fresh bottle. "Somebody who had planned it out," he said. "Somebody who knew he would be there, walking by, and was waiting for him."

"Ambushed him, you mean?"

Phu Dung translated. The cop nodded.

"Ask him if he thinks one of the Americans did it."

He guzzled his beer, wiping his mouth with the back of his hand.

"Americans like to shoot with a gun, not stab with a knife," he said. "To pull the trigger on someone is easy. To plunge the blade is not so easy. Stabbing is much more personal. Americans do not have the stomach for it."

"So he thinks the killer is Vietnamese?"

Pigpen shrugged noncommittally.

"Maybe yes, maybe no," Phu Dung said.

The place smelled of spoiled vegetables and raw sewage. The stench was starting to get to me. "Ask him who else we should talk to."

Phu Dung asked. Pigpen scratched his head, thinking. Finally, he said, "The guard's wife. She knows a lot."

"The guard. Does he mean Mr. Wonderful? Mr. Wonderful's wife?"

My interpreter nodded.

"See if you can get her address from him and let's get out of here," I said.

I waited outside where the smell was barely more tolerable. Piles of garbage were heaped on the street. Motorbikes slalomed around them like so many pylons. Phu Dung emerged from the building a minute after me.

"A famous combat aviator," I said, teasing him. "I didn't realize I was in the presence of greatness."

It was the one and only time I ever saw him blush.

~~~

Mr. Wonderful's widow, Giang, lived in a windowless, one-room apartment down a dank, covered passageway just off Hanoi's fashionable Bà Triệu Street with its high-end boutiques and coffee houses. As the crow flies, it was less than a mile from the lake where her husband's body was found. She was hunched barefoot in purple pajamas over a small, coal-burning hibachi, grilling chicken in the passageway just outside the industrial steel grate that served as her front door. If her cataracts and wrinkled countenance were any measure, the woman had led an exceedingly hard life. She was in her seventies, but appeared easily thirty years older than that. She didn't look up from her cooking as we approached.

Phu Dung addressed her softly, with obvious reverence, as the Vietnamese are inclined to do with the elderly, I came to discover. Mrs. Wonderful answered his questions in a high-pitched voice and never once made eye contact with either of us. I stood by impatiently for approximately three minutes, not having a clue as to what either one was talking about, before injecting myself in the conversation.

"What's she saying?"

He ignored my question and continued conversing with the old lady in Vietnamese. It might've been the Buddha who said patience is the greatest prayer, but I wasn't in the praying mood.

"You're the interpreter, Phu Dung. I'm the interrogator. I'd like to ask her a few questions."

He turned slowly toward me, perturbed by what he regarded as my intrusion.

"Would you care to know what she has said so far?"

"Read my mind."

"She says she has not lived with her husband for many years. She says she does not know where he was or what he was doing the night he died. She says he was a very good father, but a very bad husband."

"Why was he a bad husband?"

"He enjoyed the ladies. Too much."

"Ask her if she knows whether he had a current lady friend?"

He asked. Mrs. Wonderful flipped a sizzling piece of chicken with a fork and replied to the hibachi, her eyes downcast.

"She thinks the woman's name is Bach Tuyet," Phu Dung said, smiling.

"Why's that funny?"

"Bach Tuyet means Snow White, a popular singer many years ago."

"Ask her where we can find this Snow White."

Mrs. Wonderful professed not to know the woman's address. She said something else in Vietnamese, still squatting beside the hibachi, never looking up.

I waited for the translation.

"She says she thought we were from the insurance company."

"What insurance company?"

Phu Dung asked. The old lady responded.

"Cathay Life. She says he told her he would buy a policy about a month ago, but she has heard from nobody."

I told Phu Dung to thank the widow for her time and to tell her that if we found out anything relevant about the insurance policy, we'd let her know.

She nodded her thanks to the hibachi.

"You want to eat?" Phu Dung asked as we walked out.

My stomach was all turned around, what with the fourteen-hour time difference. I honestly wasn't sure if I felt hungry or not. But in the military, you learn to chow down appetite or no appetite because you never know when, or if, you'll ever eat again.

"Starving," I said.

∿

The restaurant was on Phố Hàng Thùng Street and anything but elegant. Six metal tables open to the busy boulevard. A wobbly ceiling fan. A trifold menu with thumbnail photos and mangled English translations of the eatery's many native dishes. My choices included "Corn Beef Spinach Dummy," "Flowers of the Ceiling," "Baked Fish With Fever Language," and something called "Rang Me."

Our waitress was about twelve and wore her dark tresses in a ponytail, pulled back with a pink Hello Kitty hair bow. She stood over us with pen and notepad in hand, waiting for us to order.

"Try the pho ga," Phu Dung said.

"The what?"

"Chicken soup. Hanoi is famous for it."

I took him up on his suggestion along with a Coke. Phu Dung went with a glass of Tiger beer and something that looked from the menu photo like crispy spring rolls with shrimp. We watched the traffic on the street go by.

"Mr. Wonderful tells his wife he's taking out a life insurance policy and gets murdered a month later?" I asked rhetorically. "Sounds to me like he knew he was in trouble."

Phu Dung said he knew an insurance broker out by the airport who was well connected.

"I will talk to him. He may know something."

I asked him who he thought killed the former guard.

He shrugged. "My job is not to know. My job is to help."

Our drinks came. Phu Dung sipped his beer and checked his watch.

"What did that thing set you back?"

He looked at me, not understanding.

"The watch. How much did it cost you?"

"Captain Jack Fincher. F-4 pilot. It was his watch."

"You took that watch off a downed pilot's body?" I could feel my pulse jump.

"You think I would do something like that?" Phu Dung responded, scowling at me.

"I have no idea. Did you?"

"Fincher fired three Sidewinders. Couldn't hit me. Fourth Sidewinder, boom. Big fire. I punch out. Fincher sees my parachute floating by. Many years go by. He always wondered what happened to me. One day, he writes to the Vietnamese embassy in Washington and says he wants to find me, but he doesn't even know if I am still alive. The embassy finds me. Fincher comes to Vietnam to visit. Now we are good friends. He gives me this watch, the one he wore that day."

"Is that where you got that scar," I said, nodding toward his forearm, "when you got shot down?"

"Broke both arms when I ejected. The one never worked good after that. Fincher told me he would have it fixed."

The American pilot who'd shot him down, Phu Dung said, paid for an airline ticket and covered the cost of reconstructive orthopedic surgery at the University of Kentucky Medical Center, then put his former adversary up at his horse ranch outside Lexington while he recovered from the operation.

"Heartwarming story," I said. "It'd make a great movie."

Phu Dung said nothing, still steamed over my insinuation that he'd stolen the watch.

"That's why you're doing this," I said, realization dawning on me. "It's not about the money. It's about you returning a kindness."

He stared out at the street and asked me about the types of planes I flew in the air force.

"Mostly the A-10 Warthog."

"No F-4?"

"They'd pretty much retired the F-4 by the time I got my wings."

He sipped his beer. "Who would have won? You or me?"

"In a dogfight, you mean?"

Phu Dung nodded.

"The A-10's a tank buster. It wasn't designed to be an air superiority fighter like the MiG-21."

"So you are saying I would win."

I smiled. When I was getting too cocky during air combat training, one of my flight instructors, a nervous little guy with big jowls and even bigger ears named Waylon Bixby whom everybody called "Yoda," asked me what I thought the difference was between God and a fighter pilot, then answered his own question before I could. "The difference," Yoda said tersely, "is that God doesn't believe he's a fighter pilot." Could I have told Phu Dung that, all planes being equal, I would've easily spanked his butt in the air? You bet. One doesn't strap in to a heavily armed warplane and set off to kill the aviators of other nations miles above terra firma without a surplus of self-confidence. But the truth was, I hadn't been in the cockpit of a single-seat fighter in more than fifteen years. I was also an aspiring Buddhist, and the Buddha was all about humility. Moreover I was on a covert intelligence-gathering mission; the last thing I needed, especially in a place as potentially dicey as Hanoi, was to get into a dogfight of egos with my interpreter.

"Whatever you say," I said.

"I think you would have won, Logan," Phu Dung said.

I'd forgotten: he was a Buddhist, too.

We clinked bottles. Our food arrived. With the possible exception of Mrs. Schmulowitz's secret family recipe, I have to admit it was about the best chicken soup I'd ever had.

~~~

Phu Dung dropped me off three blocks from the hotel. He said he wanted to maintain distance between the two of us as well as a low profile, which made sense and didn't. How can a man who tools around Hanoi on a Harley, looking like the

Vietnamese version of Kojak, ever hope to maintain a low profile? I said I'd check in with him the next morning, slipped off the back of his motorcycle and walked the rest of the way. The traffic in the Old Quarter seemed especially heavy, an endless procession of mostly motorbikes coming and going. Getting from one side of the street to the other was like being in one of those old computer games in which the cartoon frog gets killed if he mistimes his crossing from one lane to the next. Miraculously, I avoided getting splattered.

The doorman with the Elvis hair smiled while holding the big glass door for me. The clerks behind the front desk stood and smiled as I approached the elevators. Nothing in the lobby conveyed anything amiss, nothing to suggest that the whole sixth floor had been cordoned off by Vietnamese paramilitary personnel and that two former American servicemen were being held there against their wills. I pushed the button to the fifth floor.

Back in my room, I again swept for electronic bugs but found none. The red digital numbers on the nightstand clock read 7:46 P.M. It was bedtime somewhere. I secured my wallet, phone and passport in the plastic bag behind the toilet, undressed, climbed in between the sheets, and was soon fast asleep. Two hours later, I was just as soon fast awake. Consciousness returned to me with a violent start and I realized I was lathered in sweat even though the air conditioner was blasting. The nightmare I'd been having began to fade even before I opened my eyes, but I remembered enough to know I had been dreaming of Savannah and the moment I first saw her corpse. I tried to scrub the image from my head, went to the sink, and cupped cold water on my face. A glass door led to my room balcony, more of a widow's walk really, fronting Gia Ngu Street, five stories below. I wrapped a towel around my waist and stepped outside.

The night was warm but not excessively so. The damp, heavy air felt good on my skin and in my lungs. Long after the sun was done for the day, Hanoi remained alive with the pounding of hammers and the high-pitched whine of circular saws, an ancient, restless city constantly rebuilding itself, even as the rest of the world slept. I found odd comfort in the aural stew. It helped drown all the noise inside my head.

"Insane, isn't it, this city?"

I glanced to my left, at the balcony adjoining mine. A woman was leaning on her elbows against the wrought iron railing, taking in the night air and admiring the lights of the city as I was. I'd seen her earlier in the day—the same beautiful Asian woman with the British accent I'd teased about her dinosaur of a BlackBerry while she waited for the elevator. She'd since changed out of her dress-for-success suit and into jeans, spiked heels open at the toe, and a coral-colored tank top. Her long glossy hair reflected the lights of the city, while her eyes made their own light.

"Define insane," I said.

She smiled. "Chaotic. Unpredictable. A bit dangerous, perhaps."

"You forgot cognitively discordant."

"Pardon me?"

"It's a psychological term."

"Are you a psychologist?"

"Some people say so."

Her face conveyed mild amusement mixed with skepticism. "Quite frankly, you don't look like a psychologist to me."

"I find that psychologically intriguing. What do psychologists look like?"

"Well, for one, they tend to be appropriately dressed when they step outside their hotel rooms."

"Let's just say I'm a different kind of psychologist."

Another smile. She turned and took in the view. "Such a lovely evening, isn't it?"

"Very."

"I wouldn't mind a drink. Perhaps you'd care to join me upstairs?"

The last time a beautiful woman had asked me to join her for a drink was, well, I couldn't remember when. I found myself torn between intrigue and guilt. To accept her invitation would be disloyal to Savannah's memory—I wasn't really ready to be with another woman. But Savannah was gone and I was very much alone in the world. What ill could come of an innocent drink? Buddhists aspire toward mindfulness when faced with a decision—the ability to recognize signals in one's own body that can guide him to the correct choice. *How do you really feel, Logan?* I realized that what I felt at that moment, more than anything, was a kind of fluttering inside, the kind of butterflies you get before a first date.

"You seem conflicted," she said. "If you'd rather not . . ."

"Give me ten minutes to put something on other than a towel. I'll meet you up there."

"Lovely."

She went back inside her room, leaving behind the faint scent of perfume—some exotic flower, I'd probably never heard of.

~~~

Singapore was where she was from. Her name, she said, was Mai Choi.

"Beautiful name."

"And yours?"

"Bob Barker."

We were alone on the bar's outdoor veranda. She shook my hand with a firm confidence like the successful international businesswoman she appeared to be. I took the cushioned, fan-back rattan chair next to hers.

"Bob Barker. Your name seems oddly familiar to me."

"What a coincidence. Me, too."

Mai smiled and sipped white wine.

The bartender came over. Oversized ears. Middle-aged. White shirt. Black slacks. I ordered club soda.

"*Nước ép ổi*," Mai said to him.

The bartender nodded curtly. Mai finished off her wine and handed him her empty glass. He went to fetch our drinks.

I asked Mai the nature of her work.

"I'm an attorney."

"I'm so sorry."

Her smile told me she didn't mind being teased. "A *non*practicing attorney," she said. "I'm actually a regional vice president of sales and marketing for Kia Motors. We're hoping to build a new manufacturing center in Hanoi, near the harbor."

"Yet another coincidence. I have a good friend who drives a Kia."

"I hope he finds it suited to his taste."

"To the extent he finds anything suited to his taste."

The lights of the city sparked below us. A quarter mile to the south, a crescent moon shone down on the lake where earlier that day I'd searched the shoreline for clues in the murder of Mr. Wonderful.

"So, tell me," she said, "what brings you to Hanoi?"

"I came in to counsel a couple of clients."

"There are no other English-speaking psychologists living in Hanoi?" she said, her turn to tease me.

"None they apparently trust."

"You must be very good at what you do."

"What can I say? It's a living."

I gazed at the side of her face. Some women exude a kind of raw sensuality they're incapable of masking even if they tried. Mai was one of those women. I couldn't help but be drawn to her. She asked me how long I planned to be in Vietnam.

"A few days," I said. "You?"

"A few days." There was a pause, then, "Are you married?"

". . . Used to be."

She studied my eyes. "I believe you."

The bartended returned with her wine and my club soda. Mai watched him set the glasses down, waiting until he left.

"In case you were wondering," she said, "I was, too. Once."

"I believe you."

We finished our drinks, taking our time, saying little. Mai insisted on paying, saying she was the one who'd invited me out. I didn't fight her for the check. We bade the bartender good evening and rode the elevator down to the fifth floor. If she suspected anything amiss as we passed the sixth floor, where the two former POWs were being held, she didn't say. I walked her to her room, neither of us speaking. She slid her card key into the lock and turned the lever handle. I held open the door for her and she turned toward me, her head tilted upward, her lips within easy range of mine.

"Would you like to come in?"

We both knew what it meant. I wanted to go in, I really did, but I couldn't.

"It's not you," I said.

She reached up and kissed me softly on the cheek. "I understand, love. I'm free tomorrow evening if you are."

"I have no plans."

"Good. It's a date, then."

I smiled.

"Good night, Dr. Barker."

"Good night, Mai."

I walked down the hall to my room, undressed, got in bed, and turned off the light, thinking of Savannah, remembering the first time we made love, the way we made the walls sweat. An hour went by, maybe longer, before I finally drifted off.

NINE

My phone rang me from a dead sleep.

"What time is it there?" Buzz demanded.

"You're running a big-time, secret squirrel op and you don't know what time it is in Hanoi?"

"I can't be bothered with minor operational details, Logan. I'm running a big-time, secret squirrel operation."

It was too early in the morning to humor him. I glanced at the digital clock beside the bed. It was 0403.

He'd telephoned Virgil Stoneburner's wife in Boca Raton, he said, to personally assure her, based on an expert, onsite evaluation by psychologist Bob Barker, that her husband was in good mental health. Mrs. Stoneburner was greatly relieved by the news.

"But that's not the reason I'm calling," Buzz said. "My analysts spun up some good dope on the RFI we ran system-wide on your boy, Sean Hallady. I thought you might be particularly fascinated from a pretend psychologist's standpoint."

"Sean Hallady." I tried yawning the cobwebs from my brain.

"The kid who accompanied his grandfather to Hanoi," Buzz said impatiently. "Wake the hell up, Logan."

"I'm awake. Sean Hallady. Grandson of former prisoner of war, Billy Hallady. So what did your request for information come up with?"

"Seems young Sean got booted out of the Marine Corps for being *too* violent. I mean, let's face it, you gotta be pretty god-damned dysfunctional to get your ass kicked out of *that* organization for any reason."

"Not that you're biased, Buzz, being an old army guy."

"Laugh all you want, Logan, but it's the truth. You know what you get when you cross a jarhead with a gorilla, don't you?"

"An intellectually challenged gorilla. You've only told me that joke a hundred times."

"Okay, so sue me. I need a sit-rep."

"I'm chasing a few leads, hoping to have something more definitive for you by tonight."

"That's not a situation report, Logan. That's a blow job."

"I'm doing the best I can, Buzz."

"Yeah? Well, do better. We got three days before the commies ship Stoneburner and Cohen off to prison, and right now, I got exactly diddly-squat from you to pass along, up the chain. POTUS's people are breathing down my neck. They need answers, like, yesterday. I e-mailed you Sean Hallady's file. Get on it."

The line went dead.

I rubbed the sleep from my eyes and checked e-mails on my iPhone. They were all to Dr. Barker. There was spam offering fake Rolexes for sale and two promising the lowest prices on erectile dysfunction medications to be found anywhere. I wondered what sort of crazy demographic the good doctor and I had fallen into.

Also in Dr. Barker's in-box were the results of Buzz's request for information from various intelligence databases detailing Sean Hallady's personal history. I stretched, stuffed a pillow behind my head, and read.

Following a few minor run-ins with law enforcement in high school, Hallady had gone to Reed College in Oregon for about a year before being expelled following a fistfight in which he broke his roommate's jaw over a dispute involving whose turn it was to clean the bathroom. Under threat of jail time, he then enlisted in the marines. Adhering to requirements in basic training proved a challenge. He was recycled through boot camp after mouthing off to drill instructors, and eventually posted to a rifle company at Camp Pendleton where he was deemed to be a disciplinary problem. After assessments by marine psychiatrists determined that he was bipolar with borderline personality disorder, he was summarily discharged from military service.

A series of menial civilian jobs followed: busboy, construction worker, shopping-mall janitor, stacking shelves at a grocery store. At twenty-seven, he'd ended up moving to Utah to live with his then-girlfriend. Their relationship ended after they got in an argument in the parking lot of Salt Lake City's Gateway mall and he shoved her to the ground, an act for which he later pleaded guilty to misdemeanor battery and served five days in the Salt Lake County Metro Jail.

Records showed he'd also been fined $1,000 and sentenced to one hundred hours of community service after being found with half an ounce of marijuana. In his probation report, Hallady claimed that many of his emotional issues stemmed from the rage he felt over the way his beloved grandfather, a war hero, had been tortured at the hands of the North Vietnamese. An enlarged photo of Sean's Utah driver's license showed a heavy young man with angry brown eyes and blond hair that hung unkempt to his shoulders. Tattooed in cursive script on the right side of his neck was the Marine Corps' motto, *Semper fidelis*—always faithful.

I got up and took care of the normal morning ablutions, dressed, and went downstairs for a quick plate of eggs and rice noodles from the breakfast buffet before heading out. Elvis the doorman shot off of his stool and held the door open for me as I left the hotel, nodding pleasantly.

Outside the dawn was cool and fresh. Hanoi was awakening with the new day. Not that the Old Quarter ever really slept. Shopkeepers raised the metal grates of their stalls while restaurateurs stood outside their open-air eateries, haggling prices with pushcart vendors selling fresh vegetables and live chickens. No one seemed to notice me. Certainly, nobody followed me.

Even at that early hour, motor traffic around Hoàn Kiếm Lake was heavy. I picked my way lane-by-lane through the glare of motorbike headlights, all but daring drivers to hit me. Somehow, none did.

The lakefront itself was tranquil. Old folks dawdled along the shoreline, men and women, hands clasped behind their backs. Others practiced the exercise regimen known as tai chi. Their slow, graceful movements reminding me of ballet dancers. Not far from the bridge where Mr. Wonderful's body was found, I stopped to watch a fisherman try his luck.

He was about my age, with a full dark beard. You don't see much facial hair in Hanoi. His pole was bamboo and he cast his line with a practiced elegance, alighting his feathered lure on the water without as much as a ripple. He sensed my presence and glanced over his shoulder. I waited for him to reel in and cast out again.

"Catching anything?"

"No."

"You speak English?"

He smiled without looking at me. Dumb question.

"You come here a lot?"

"Yes," the fisherman said.

"This time of day?"

"Best fishing, this time of day."

"A man was killed near here a few days ago. His body was found floating below the bridge. It was about this time of morning, maybe a little earlier. You didn't happen to see anything, did you?"

His back was to me. He didn't respond directly, but the quickness with which he reeled in told me he'd heard my question.

"He was famous, the man who died."

The fisherman quickly secured his hook to the cork handle of his pole and gathered up the wicker basket that served as his tackle box.

"I don't see nothing." Jaw set. Eyes to the ground. He was a bad liar.

"What are you so afraid of?"

He left in a hurry and didn't look back.

I decided to walk the half mile or so to the Metropole, where the reconciliation dinner had been held that night. Maybe someone at the hotel had seen something.

On Hang Dau Street, I passed two blocks of shoe stores, each selling knock-off Nikes and other counterfeit name brands for a fraction of what they'd go for back home. The proprietors, mostly women, sat on impossibly tiny red or blue plastic stools out in front of their shops, some reading newspapers, unwilling to make contact, others staring off at nothing. A sinewy man in a green pith helmet pedaling a three-wheeled cyclo for hire pulled up beside me.

"Where you go, sir?"

"The Metropole."

"I take you." His smile was a testament to lifelong dental neglect.

"How much?"

He held up four fingers. Forty thousand dong.

I held up two fingers. He countered with three. The ride would cost me about a buck and a half.

"You England?" he asked as he pedaled.

"American."

"Ah, yes." He flashed bad teeth. "America number one."

"You give a lot of Americans rides?"

"America number one," he repeated.

I got out my phone and showed him the driver's license photo of Sean Hallady.

"Ever seen this man before?"

More smiling and nodding.

"You saw him, this man?"

Another pleasant nod. "America number one."

Logan, you must be living right. Hundreds of cyclo drivers in Hanoi, and I happen to run into the one who remembers Sean Hallady. I commended myself on my good fortune.

"Where did you see him?"

"America number one."

"Right. I got that part. I need to know where you saw him and when."

"Okay."

"Okay?"

"America number one."

That's when I realized my driver had no idea what I was talking about.

"Do you know what you get when you cross a marine with a gorilla?"

"Yes."

"What about a cow and a trampoline?"

"America number one."

I didn't ask any more questions after that.

Phu Dung, my interpreter, was waiting in the lobby of the Metropole when I walked in. He was stationed in a high-back armchair where he could keep an eye on all the approaches, sipping tea like he was a member of the landed gentry.

"What are you doing here?"

"I followed you," he said, eyeing everyone who came and went. "It was not difficult."

"My countersurveillance skills must be a little rusty."

"So it would seem."

He wanted to know what I was doing at the Metropole. I said I intended to hopefully find an employee or two who was there that night, who could help shed light on the timing of events that led to the murder of Mr. Wonderful.

"No one will talk to you," Phu Dung said.

"Sure they will. International hotel like this, everybody speaks English."

"Even so, you are an outsider. Outsiders cannot be trusted."

"I'll pretend I'm Vietnamese."

Phu Dung smiled and stood. "Let's go."

"Lemme guess: you know somebody."

We were going to see an acquaintance of his former brother-in-law. The man had served with Mr. Wonderful at the Hanoi Hilton.

~~~

Duy Van was the former guard's name. He lived on the other side of the Red River, in the northern Hanoi suburb of Long Bien. The rusting, cantilevered bridge spanning the river, linking the Vietnamese capital to the port city of Haiphong, had been bombed repeatedly during the war. Back then, it was among the most heavily defended targets in the world. I remember when I was at the academy seeing archival film footage of those attacks. It was one of the first times the air force had used so-called "smart" bombs—guided munitions. Riding across the bridge on the back of Phu Dung's Harley, I could see sections that still remained damaged forty years later. Had it been worth the cost in human lives: trying to save, and the other hoping to destroy, so unattractive a hunk of iron? In truth, I suppose I could've asked the same question about all the many fixed targets I'd blown up on bombing missions in later wars.

Duy Van and his wife resided in an apartment above a liquor store, along a narrow street flanked by tall, leafy trees. He met us enthusiastically at the door, a wizened, white-haired old man who grinned and pumped my hand like I was a visiting diplomat. He seemed pleasant enough. History compelled me to dislike him, regardless. Who knows what horrors he'd inflicted on Cohen, Stoneburner, Hallady and other captured American airmen?

He gestured hospitably toward a couch and two matching chairs covered in a floral fabric that had seen better days. Phu Dung and I sat on the couch. Cheaply framed photos covered the walls. The canals of Venice. Michael Jackson. A portrait of the Communist revolutionary leader, Ho Chi Minh. Van lowered himself gingerly into one of the chairs, wearing what looked to be a genuine gold Rolex on his left wrist.

I looked over at Phu Dung. "Does he speak any English?"

"No."

"Where'd he get the watch?"

Phu Dung inquired politely. Van responded in Vietnamese, pouring three shots of scotch from a bottle of Johnny Walker Red. It was not yet 0800.

"He says he bought the watch."

I couldn't help but wonder if he'd taken it from an American prisoner of war.

Van handed me a shot. I knew enough not to insult him by turning it down. When a man invites you into his home, friend or foe, and offers you a drink, you drink, even if you don't drink, and even if you don't like him—especially if you're there to get information.

He raised his glass and proposed a toast in Vietnamese. He and Phu Dung gulped down the scotch. I held the glass to my lips and pretended to sip. The aroma, the taste, it all came back to me. I wanted more than just about anything to throw that shot back, to pour myself another, and another. Somehow, I didn't.

A frail old woman—Van's wife, I assumed—shuffled in from the kitchen clutching a platter of food with both hands. Slices of cantaloupe, honeydew melon, and a gold-lacquered bowl heaped with salty spanish-style peanuts. She set the platter down on the coffee table in front of me and returned to the kitchen without so much as looking up. Van gestured: help yourself.

"Why's he being so chummy?"

"I told him that you are an important writer. That you have come to tell the truth."

". . . The truth?"

"How your captured pilots were treated with compassion and punished only when they did not obey the rules."

With compassion? Something sour-tasting rose up in the back of my throat and stayed there. The urge to grab the old man by his throat was almost irresistible. Somehow, I resisted that urge, too.

"What can he tell us," I said, "about Mr. Wonderful?"

Phu Dung asked. Van talked nonstop in Vietnamese for more than five minutes, hands gesticulating, voice rising and falling. I could've just as easily been a potted plant for all the attention he paid me.

"What's he saying?"

Phu Dung acted like I wasn't there and continued conversing with the former guard while he poured him another scotch. Van said something and they both laughed. I'd never heard my interpreter laugh before. It sounded vaguely like Kiddiot throwing up a hairball.

"What's funny?"

Phu Dung wiped tears from the corners of his eyes. "How many men does it take to open a bottle of beer?"

"I wouldn't know."

"None. A man's woman should already have the bottle open for him."

Phu Dung laughed again. I didn't.

"Ask him if he tortured any American servicemen during the war."

Phu Dung's smile faded. "We are guests. To ask this kind of question would be disrespectful."

"Ask him or you don't get paid."

Phu Dung gave me a hard look, then turned and asked.

The former guard gulped down his drink and poured himself another. "*Không bao giờ*," he said.

"He says no torture, never."

"What about Mr. Wonderful? Did he ever torture Americans?"

"He says nobody ever tortured anybody."

I glowered at Van. The old man couldn't meet my eyes. We both knew what had happened in that prison so many years ago.

He began speaking rapidly in Vietnamese, gesturing animatedly, while Phu Dung interpreted on the fly. The crux of it was that Van and Mr. Wonderful would get together every couple of weeks to kick back and reminisce about old times. After a few pints of *bia hoi*, the thin but deceptively potent drought beer popular in Hanoi, Mr. Wonderful would invariably begin boasting of his latest sexual conquest for Van's vicarious pleasure. He claimed to have bedded more than one hundred women, married ones among them. It was because of his indiscriminate catting around, Van speculated, that Mr. Wonderful may have met his end. The husband of one of those women, he said, was a thug with ties to both the Hanoi police and the city's vast criminal underworld. He went by the name, Jimmy Luc.

Van further suspected that Jimmy Luc must've known about his wife's infidelity because, in the weeks prior to his death, Mr. Wonderful had begun receiving hang-up calls at all hours of the night. One morning Mr. Wonderful found a freshly slaughtered chicken draped over the handlebars of his motorbike. He regarded it as both a threat and a warning.

"How concerned was Mr. Wonderful that this Jimmy Luc might actually come after him for sleeping with Jimmy's wife?"

Phu Dung translated my question. The two Vietnamese men conversed for nearly a minute. When Van was finished talking, he poured himself another shot.

"Not worried," Phu Dung said. "He says Mr. Wonderful had many friends to protect him."

"Mr. Wonderful was paying off the police?"

"Everyone in Hanoi pays off the police."

Van said Jimmy Luc owned a religious curio store in the Old Quarter and readily provided the address. It struck me as suspicious that the old prison guard would have that kind of detail at his fingertips, but I let it go. He asked Phu Dung to ask me when the article I supposedly was writing would appear and where he could get a translated version of it. Whatever Phu Dung said in response seemed to satisfy him. I thanked him curtly for his time, got up, and left.

As I climbed onto the back of Phu Dung's motorcycle, Van emerged from his apartment and insisted on giving me a coin. It was a gift, he explained in Vietnamese, a token of lasting peace between our two nations. The coin was a US nickel, minted in 1971. I wondered if he'd stolen that off of an American prisoner, too.

He waved, friendly as can be, and watched us drive away.

Merging into traffic, I tucked the nickel in my pants pocket, hoping the coin might bring me more than five cents worth of luck. Something told me I was going to need all I could get.

TEN

If you're a small merchant in Hanoi selling, let's say, miniature pagodas and tacky plastic statues of the Buddha, how do you eke out a living flanked by literally dozens of other small merchants, all selling basically the same junk? From an economic standpoint, it made no sense, but that's how it works in the Old Quarter.

Jimmy Luc, whose wife had allegedly been cheating on him with the late Mr. Wonderful, owned a shop at 81 Hang Quat Street. "Dất Thánh" was the name painted in yellow on the grimy canvas awning above the entrance. Phu Dung said it meant "Holy Land."

"I'd prefer to ask the questions this time, if you don't mind," I said.

"Whatever you say," Phu Dung said in a way that made it clear he minded plenty.

A girl with plain features and dark straight hair was dusting a shelf of copper incense burners. She wore glasses and glanced at us shyly as she went about her work. Phu Dung said something to her in Vietnamese. She responded softly.

"She says she would like for you to buy many expensive things so her family will not starve."

I picked out some incense, a plastic elephant, and a wooden Buddha that was about six inches tall. The girl tried to interest me in a larger, more expensive jade Buddha, but that Buddha sported a fiendish smile, the kind you'd see in a slasher movie.

"Tell her when it comes to religious icons, less is more," I said, smiling, as she rang up my purchase.

Phu Dung told her. There was no response. The total came to less than five dollars.

"Ask her how old she is."

"I am . . . nineteen," she said with an embarrassed smile, braces on her teeth, as she carefully rolled my new Buddha in bubble wrap. "My English, not good."

"Better than my Vietnamese. What's your name?"

"My name Linh."

"Linh. Lovely name."

She said she was a college student studying tourism and marketing. She asked if I was enjoying my visit to Hanoi. I said I was. She asked me if I needed someone to show me the sites and volunteered for the position.

"I already have a tour guide," I said, pointing to Phu Dung, who'd gone outside to make a phone call. "Otherwise I would. You're much prettier than he is."

She smiled demurely, pushing an errant strand of hair behind her right ear, and handed me a plastic bag containing my purchases.

"Actually there is something you can help me with, Linh. I'm looking for the owner of this shop."

"The . . . oh-ner?" Her expression said she didn't understand the question.

"Jimmy Luc. The owner. We're old friends. Is he around?"

She licked her lips. "Jimmy not here."

"Where can I find him? It's very important, Linh."

"I . . ." She shrugged nervously.

"Will he be in later today?"

Another shrug. She wouldn't look at me.

"When was the last time you saw him, Linh?"

"I work now. Please."

Eyes darting. Dusting shelves a little too vigorously. She was frightened. Of what, I didn't know.

"I heard he was having problems with his marriage, with his wife. Is that true?"

A shrug. She wanted nothing more than for me to leave.

I rubbed the back of my neck and turned my head slightly, wondering what good I was doing there. That's when I noticed them: the photos of various attractive men and women tacked to the wall behind the cash register. The majority were flashing smiles that were just a little too perfect, with teeth that were way too white, like the kind you see on lounge singers and soap opera stars. I guessed most of them to be Vietnamese celebrities. In each picture, the subject posed beside a short, fashionably attired Asian man with a winning smile, gold neck chains, and cold, hard eyes that looked like he'd slit your throat for pocket change. Thuggish Jimmy Luc, the alleged jealous husband. Had to be.

"Good old Jimmy," I said, peering closely. "The man never ages, does he?"

She shook her head almost imperceptibly, dusting a shelf without making eye contact. Definitely Jimmy.

I took a closer look at each photo if only to stall for time, hoping Jimmy might come waltzing in, unaware. One of the pictures showed him arm in arm with a redhead in a turquoise tank top. Loaded down with shopping bags, flashing a gap-toothed smile and wearing two-tone shades, the woman could've easily passed for the singer, Madonna. For all I knew, she was Madonna.

The picture hanging on the wall below hers, however, was the one that grabbed my attention:

Standing close beside Jimmy Luc was Colonel Truong Tan Sang of the Ministry of Public Safety—the very officer heading the investigation of Mr. Wonderful's murder. Jimmy and the colonel were holding hands.

~~~

"Men hold hands in Vietnam," Phu Dung said. "It does not mean what it means in your country."

"I'm not suggesting they're taking cruises and warm showers together," I said. "What I'm suggesting is, at a minimum, that they all apparently knew each other—Jimmy Luc, Mr. Wonderful, and Colonel Tan Sang."

"Many people in this world know each other."

"You don't find the connection curious?"

"Many things I find curious," Phu Dung said, "including why your country felt the need to declare war on mine. But I no longer dwell on these things."

I didn't feel like debating him. There would've been no point.

We were sitting on stools in a haze-filled, second-floor coffee house across the boulevard from Hoàn Kiếm Lake, surrounded by male college students pecking away on laptops and iPads. The joint was up a narrow flight of stairs behind a luggage store—out of the way and hard to find, which was how Phu Dung liked it.

"Look," I said, "you can't tell me it's all coincidence. People don't post a picture of themselves in their shop holding hands with the lead investigator in a murder they may well have committed."

He sipped his coffee and said nothing.

Tacked to the walls were posters of British soccer clubs. The air inside the café was blue with cigarette smoke. We sipped steamed coffee with vanilla, sugar, and a raw egg stirred in. I watched a bead of sweat roll off Phu Dung's hairless, bullet-shaped skull, down his nose, and into his cup. He seemed not to notice.

"You have a woman?" he asked me.

"No."

"But you did."

I nodded, looking away.

"She was beautiful?"

"She was."

Phu Dung sipped his coffee, eyeing me. "You seem sad to me, Logan."

"You're not exactly a barrelful of monkeys yourself, Phu Dung."

". . . A barrelful of monkeys. You Americans and your expressions."

"Forget it."

He cracked his knuckles. "Whenever I am sad, I remember that I am not a woman, then I am happy. The only good thing about being a woman is that a woman gets the last word in any argument. Anything a man says at the end of an argument is the beginning of a new argument."

"Works that way in Vietnam, too, huh?"

Phu Dung smiled. At least I think it was a smile.

There are, of course, other advantages to being born male. Generally speaking, you can open your own jars. You need only shave your face and neck. You also tend to know stuff about carburetors. We could've chatted indefinitely on the transcultural differences between men and women, but I needed to get back to the hotel, to check on Cohen and Stoneburner. Truth was, I was also tired, still jet-lagged. I finished my coffee and got up to go. Phu Dung said he'd work up some fresh leads in hopes of finding Jimmy Luc. We arranged to reconvene at 0730 the next day near the lake, by the bridge.

On the walk back to my hotel, a man with bug eyes and a major overbite pulled his motor scooter to a rolling stop and asked me if I was in the market for "number one boom-boom"— what I presumed to be female companionship. I declined and continued on.

Two well-groomed, put-together Vietnamese men were standing outside the hotel, smoking and pretending to converse, each covering the other's back. Midtwenties, pressed slacks, subtle bulges at the waist under their polo shirts, where their holstered pistols rode. One locked eyes with me. He said something, then the other turned and eyed me as well. The only other people who look at you that way on the streets of Hanoi are those trying to sell you something. I made them as either undercover cops or intelligence agents.

"Afternoon, gents."

They quickly, uncomfortably looked away and said nothing as I strode past them into the hotel.

~~~

A soldier on the sixth floor held me at gunpoint near the elevators while another telephoned his superiors to make sure I was cleared to see the two prisoners. I bided my time by pretending to study the guy guarding me, in a clinical psychologist sort of way. He didn't seem to appreciate that. A couple of minutes passed before my clearance was confirmed and I was allowed in to see Stoneburner. His first words were, "How much longer am I going to be stuck in this shithole?"

I cranked up the sound on the television—it was turned to BBC news—before telling him I didn't know. I wasn't about to divulge that Vietnamese authorities were planning to transfer him and Cohen to a prison in three days. The news would've only agitated him more than he already was.

"There is some good news," I said. "We got word to your wife and let her know you're doing okay."

"I'm *not* doing okay," he said, pacing the room in his underwear and wiping the sweat off of his face with a hand towel. "I'm going nuts in here. I should've listened to her and never come on this trip."

"You need to take a deep breath, sir, and relax."

"Don't you tell me what I need to do, sonny. You have no idea what I've gone through, what these sons of bitches put me through the last time I was here. I didn't murder that bastard. I did nothing wrong. I want out of here."

He stormed past me and tried to force open the door.

"Open this goddamned thing right now!" he said, pounding on it.

The door quickly opened inward, nearly knocking him off his feet. The two soldiers I'd dealt with earlier stood in the entryway with their assault rifles at their waists, fingers on triggers, yelling in Vietnamese. Stoneburner was yelling, too, vowing to kill them both if they didn't let him out. I clamped my arm around his chest and pulled him back inside the room, assuring the guards that everything was under control. They didn't comprehend a word I said, but they seemed to get that the old man, though upset, was no threat to them and that I was doing my best to ease the situation. One of the soldiers pulled the door shut. Stoneburner sat down on the edge of the bed and wept.

"Them and their goddamned gibberish. I. I just want to go home, can you understand that? I don't want to be here anymore."

"You are going home, Captain," I said, gripping his shoulder, "just hang in there."

We talked for a while, everything from airplanes to the weather. By the time I'd left, he'd fallen asleep, curled on the bed like an infant.

The soldiers let me out and escorted me down the hall to Cohen's room. His demeanor was placid. He'd overheard the ruckus in the hallway involving Stoneburner and expressed concern.

"The captain had a slight meltdown," I said. "He'll be fine."

My old professor gestured toward his balcony. I followed him out the sliding door. The cacophony of the city engulfed us.

"I couldn't quite put my finger on it at first," he said, talking low and close, "then I remembered. Cadet Logan. The smart mouth. Good to see you again."

"Always nice to make an impression. Good to see you again, too, Colonel."

"Now maybe you can tell me what you're really doing here in Hanoi."

I told him, the truth this time. If he was surprised, he didn't show it. He wanted to know what I'd learned in the course of my investigation that might help clear him and Stoneburner as well as Billy Hallady, who'd escaped Vietnam with his grandson and had made it home safely. I was reluctant to get into specifics involving Jimmy Luc, the jealous thug who may or may not have killed Mr. Wonderful for cheating with Jimmy's wife. The less Cohen knew, I figured, the safer I was and the easier it would be for him to plead ignorance if and when the Vietnamese pressed criminal charges against him.

"We're gonna get you out of here, Colonel," I said. "That's all I'm prepared to say at the moment."

"Understood."

The room door opened. One soldier stood guard in the hallway while another brought in a cheeseburger and fried noodles. He set the tray on the desk and left.

"One thing I can't complain about is the chow," Cohen said. "At the Hilton, you were always famished. We'd eat anything we could get our hands on. Maggots were considered protein."

He slid the balcony door shut behind me, turned up the television, sat at the desk and dug in, seeming to relish every bite. I remembered I hadn't eaten anything since the few peanuts and bits of melon I'd had at former guard Duy Van's house. Cohen noticed me staring at his plate and offered me some of his food.

"I insist," he said, slicing his burger in half. "Please."

He wouldn't take no for an answer. I sat on the edge of his bed and dug in.

"You mind me asking you a question, Colonel?"

"Please. Questions are the cornerstone of philosophy."

"And philosophy," I said, "is the cornerstone of man."

Cohen seemed pleased. "Well, I can see you weren't the only one who made a lasting impression. What's your question, Mr. Logan?"

"What was the worst part of being a POW?"

Cohen drew a deep breath and let it out slowly. What I remember most was not the story he proceeded to tell me. What I remember is the way he told it, the almost eerie dispassion of his words, as though he were recounting another man's ordeal, not his own.

He'd been in solitary confinement for several months, he said, his cell a sweatbox in which no light or air could penetrate, his ankles in leg irons bolted to the unpadded, concrete bunk on which he spent his days and nights, when the door suddenly opened and three guards entered, including Mr. Wonderful. He was big for a Vietnamese, pushing six feet and 200 pounds, with a nervous tick over one eye and a thin, hard mouth that could only be described as bestial. Other prisoners had come to know him as a master torturer, an innovator of few words who was always inventing new ways to inflict pain just short of death. Cohen had never met him before; he was about to discover just how good Mr. Wonderful was at his job.

"His English was excellent. He demanded that I sign a confession admitting my 'crimes' against humanity and the people of Vietnam. I refused. He punched right in the face. Broke my nose. I told him to go to hell. He told me, 'Cohen, you are a criminal. You will be punished.' That was the end of the conversation.

"They chained my wrists behind my back. Then Mr. Wonderful hauled me to my feet and beat me bloody for a solid ten minutes with a three-sided ruler—he loved the ruler. When he was done, the other guards dragged me to Room 18. We called it the Meat Hook Room. This time, he beat me with his fists. For how long, I don't know, because I blacked out."

When he returned to consciousness, courtesy of several face slaps, Cohen found that the guards had shackled a cement-filled iron bar about nine feet long across his ankles. They rolled him over on his stomach. Mr. Wonderful took a length of rope and tied each of Cohen's arms from shoulder to elbow. Two other guards then stood on either arm, tightening the rope until his elbows touched.

"The pain, no one can imagine it," Cohen said with a faraway look. "I tried to think of anything to take my mind away from it. The teachings of Sartre. The slow, seductive way my wife would undress when she knew I was watching her. What it felt like, my stomach, the first time I soloed an aircraft. But you can't escape pain like that. Nobody can. And they knew that, the Vietnamese. They were masters at it."

They left him lying there, bound that way, for what Cohen estimated was about an hour. The pain had subsided by then and his arms had gone numb. Mr. Wonderful returned and loosened the ropes. The blood flowed back into Cohen's limbs along with a burning so excruciating that he vomited and soiled himself. Again, a signed confession was demanded. Again, he said he refused. Enraged, Mr. Wonderful released the iron bar that had been chained to Cohen's ankles and laid it across his shins, then stood on the bar while the other guards jumped up and down on either end. When this failed to produce the desired results, Mr. Wonderful and his fellow guards raised Cohen's torso off the floor with his arms manacled behind him and began dragging him around and around the room by his handcuffs. Several times, Cohen feigned unconsciousness, hoping they'd stop. Each time, Mr. Wonderful would merely pull Cohen's eyelids up, smile, and the torture would continue.

Until Cohen finally gave in.

"I signed a confession that night. I couldn't even really tell you what it said. My eyes were too swollen from the beatings. Will you excuse me a moment?"

He got up from his chair and walked into the bathroom. I thought I might've heard whimpering, but it could've been the plumbing. The toilet flushed, the water in the basin ran, and my old professor reemerged. He was dry-eyed.

"You're a better man than I ever could be, Colonel," I said. "I'm not sure I could've forgiven him had I been in your shoes."

Cohen patted me on the shoulder and slowly eased himself back down into his desk chair.

"When I finally came home, my wife said I'd changed. She was right. There was no denying, I had changed. Started drinking too much and talking not enough. She hung on as long as she could. I couldn't much blame her for leaving." He gave me a sad smile. "You know, Kierkegaard was right when he said that life can only be understood backward, but it must be lived forward."

There was something palpably broken about him. One doesn't endure what Steve Cohen and men like him did without the totality of the experience taking an irreparable toll on their souls and on those who try as best they can to love them.

I said I'd stop in to see him again in the morning. The soldiers let me out. I took the stairs to my room. My hope was to catch a badly needed nap before going to dinner that night with Mai.

The day didn't quite turn out that way.

Eleven

Colonel Truong Tan Sang of the Ministry of Public Safety was waiting inside my room. He'd already helped himself to a bag of chips from the minibar, along with a mini bottle of Jack Daniels, and was stretched out on my bed, shoes off, arms behind his head.

I shut the door and tossed my card key on the desk.

"Make yourself at home, Colonel. Can I get you anything else? A robe? Slippers? A copy of basic privacy laws?"

"Why is it you only have seventeen friends on Facebook, and that they all became your friend only last week?"

"I don't understand your question," I said, stalling until I could figure out where he was coming from and how much he knew.

He took a sip of whiskey. "It's as if someone created a profile under your name online to make it appear as if you are a real person."

"As you can see, I'm clearly a real person, just not a very savvy one when it comes to social media."

"I see." Tan Sang's expression left little secret that he had his suspicions. "So tell me, Doctor, how in your professional estimation are your patients faring psychologically?"

"As well as can be expected under the circumstances, I suppose." I watched him slip his shoes back on. "These are old men. They were traumatized the last time they were in your country. Being under house arrest conjures no shortage of bad memories from the past that are never far below the surface."

"We all have bad memories, Dr. Barker. The night my mother was killed by your B-52s as she stood in her kitchen is a memory that also is never far below the surface."

"I'm sorry your mother was killed, Colonel. Sincerely I am. But to hold these men responsible for that, or for a crime they might not have committed, it's not fair."

He set what remained of his drink on the nightstand and swung his feet over the side of the bed. "What do you know of fair, of having bombs rain down on you? You, Doctor, don't know the first thing about fair."

"What makes you so sure one of them killed the guard? What if it was someone else? A Vietnamese. A random street crime. A disgruntled business partner. A jealous husband, maybe."

I studied Tan Sang's face, hoping for some reaction, a sub-conscious microexpression, that might tell me my own suspicions were not ill-conceived. His features, however, remained impenetrable. He got up and walked on my balcony. I joined him there. On the street below, two Vietnamese teenagers in high heels and tight jeans were walking arm in arm, laughing about something. Tan Sang watched them with what seemed like more than casual interest.

"You have been asking many people many questions," he said. "Questions that have no bearing on your job as a psy-chologist."

"Whatever questions I ask of anyone are all geared to ensure the emotional welfare of the men I've been sent here to take care of."

"You insult my intelligence, *Doctor*." He fixed me with a hard look. "We both know why your government sent you. To deflect blame and accuse the peaceful Vietnamese people of fabricating a criminal case against your 'innocent' old men. But let me assure you, there is no need to fabricate anything. One of them is guilty. Or all of them."

"How can you be so certain, Colonel?"

He dug out a folded sheet of paper from the left front pocket of his trousers, handed it to me, and watched with keen interest as another underage girl walked by on the street below.

The paper was a printout, a copy of a feature article from the *Riverside Press-Enterprise* that had appeared online about a month earlier. The story detailed how retired air force officer Billy Hallady, a resident of nearby Redlands, would be attending a gala, State Department-sponsored dinner in Hanoi where he and two other former prisoners of war planned to bury the hatchet with an ex-guard nicknamed "Mr. Wonderful" from the Hanoi Hilton. The story quoted Hallady as saying, "We took a blood oath back then that if we ever got the chance, we'd make him pay for what he'd done to all of us, but that was forty years ago. None of us would ever do anything like that today. It's long past time to forgive and forget."

"This is what you're hanging your case on? A story in some newspaper that may or may not have quoted an old man accurately?"

"The quote is accurate."

I followed him back inside. "Even if it is accurate, Colonel, it says right here, 'None of us would ever do anything like that today. It's long past time to forgive and forget.'"

"We have other evidence, I can assure you." Tan Sang plucked the article from my hand and strode toward the door. "I agreed that you could remain in Hanoi until the American criminals are relocated for their own safety. I will continue to abide by my word. But if I find out that you are continuing to go about, asking questions, I will have you arrested for espionage. If that happens, I can assure you, Dr. Barker, those old men will see their homeland long before you do."

~~~

Mai said she'd never had Mexican food. Easily understood, I suppose, considering where she was from. Probably not a lot of Taco Bells in Singapore. She'd done research online and found that one of the few Mexican restaurants in all of Hanoi was located a mere four blocks away from where we were both staying. The place had garnered decent reviews and Mai seemed game. As we headed out of the hotel and into the crowded streets, I spotted the surveillance almost immediately.

He seemed too old and too well fed to be the roving post-cards vendor he was pretending to be. The fact that he made no apparent attempt to sell anyone any postcards on the street was my first clue that he was likely an intelligence agent. The second was that every time I glanced back over my shoulder at him, he'd stop and turn away, pretending to look in shop windows. He could not have been a more obvious tail had he been wearing one.

The place was called Bueno! Inside the door hung an over-sized black velvet painting of a Mexican bandito smoking a cigar, ammo bandoliers slung across his chest. Sombreros hung from the ceiling. Colorful serapes decorated the walls. On the cashier's stand sat a plaster cast of a human skull wearing a World War II German helmet.

"This place is almost more Tijuana than Tijuana."

Mai smiled as if she got the reference, but I doubt she did.

We took a table overlooking the street while the postcard vendor took up station at a souvenir shop across the way. A Vietnamese waitress in a Mexican peasant top and flowery, floor-length skirt, who didn't seem especially happy about working at Bueno!, brought us menus. They were in Vietnamese, with corresponding photos depicting the usual Mexican fare.

"What tastes best?" Mai asked me.

"Tough to screw up chicken tacos."

"Chicken tacos it is."

I pointed out the picture of the chicken taco plate for the waitress, then pointed to what looked like a burrito smothered in chili verde sauce. She jotted down our order wearing a slightly pained expression and departed.

"As we were walking over here," Mai said, "you kept looking back."

"Did I?"

She nodded.

"Force of habit, I guess." I said. "Bill collectors. You can never get away from those guys, even abroad."

She smiled again, but the way she averted her eyes told me she suspected otherwise.

She wanted to know where I grew up. Her face brightened when I told her Colorado. She'd twice been skiing there, she said, Aspen and Vail. She seemed eager to tell me all about her own upbringing in Singapore, the eldest child of an international real estate investor from Seoul and his Chinese wife. Her parents had insisted she take fencing lessons; she'd become so good at the sport that she made her country's Olympic team as an alternate, but never competed in the games. She'd gone to law school in London and been married briefly to an investment banker, but the union didn't hold. I mostly listened and tried not to stare at her lips while she spoke, or think about what she looked like without her clothes on.

Our food arrived. Mai's tacos looked more like one large tostada garnished with what appeared to be rice noodles. My burrito resembled a cross between a Philly cheese steak and some sea creature washed ashore. It tasted that way, too.

"Not the tastiest burrito food I've ever had."

"No?"

"Definitely no. How're your tacos?"

"They're . . . different," she said, halfheartedly picking at her plate.

"Well, that's one way to put it." Now it was my turn to smile. When I glanced up from my plate, she was looking at me straight on, her eyes unwavering.

"I'd like you to make love to me," she said.

～～～

A vanilla-scented candle flickered on the nightstand. Her balcony door was open. Curtains swayed on the breeze. I awoke to the patter of rain outside. Mai was curled in my arms, our legs entwined.

"The woman in your life," she said, her eyes dark and warm, her voice barely above a whisper, "how did you lose her?"

"She died."

"And you blame yourself."

I didn't respond. Mai seemed to know. "You were having a bad dream," she said.

"Was I?"

"It's okay. You're here." She kissed my chest.

My dreams that night weren't of Savannah. They were of a sortie I'd flown during Desert Storm, back when I was still with the air force, before I'd been assigned to Alpha. Forward combat air controllers had spotted a platoon of Iraqi T-55s, maneuvering in broad daylight along the Euphrates River, just north of the Kuwaiti border. I rolled in and destroyed three of the tanks on my first run. The three-man crew of the fourth tank got wise to what was happening and started to bail out as I rolled in on my second pass, but not fast enough. The armor-piercing incendiary rounds of my Warthog's seven-barrel, 30-millimeter Gatling gun found them and literally chewed them to pieces in a savage maelstrom of sand and blood and body parts. I was low enough that I could see legs and arms arching through the sky like so many lawn darts. It didn't bother me then, all the carnage I'd wrought, and it really didn't bother me afterward. But somehow that night, for whatever reason, the images took on a kind of Technicolor, phantasmagorical surrealism, like a Peter Max painting that startled me awake, my heart thumping in my throat.

"Are you all right?"

"Yeah."

"Are you sure?"

I nodded.

Tenderly, she pressed her lips to mine. I could feel the kiss all the way down my spine.

I asked her if she knew what time it was.

"A little after three in the morning. Why? Do you have to go?"

"Not really." Savannah was on my mind, but not in a haunting way. That was a first. I couldn't remember the last time I'd conjured memories of her and not been consumed by a crushing sense of loss.

A wise man once said that the living are obliged by the dead to go on living. It's why the people bring over casseroles following funeral services. To eat is to go on living. In that moment, in bed with a woman whom I barely knew, in a city I knew not at all, it occurred to me that to live is not merely the process of taking nourishment and drawing one breath to the next. It's about constantly reminding yourself that you're still alive, still capable of feeling something beyond the pain and loss that invariably befalls the average existence. I owed Mai, I realized, a debt of gratitude more than she would ever know.

She caressed my chest with a gossamer touch, her breath on my neck. We made love languidly, unhurried, her eyes locked on mine. I felt more alive than I had in a long time, and afterward slept as deeply as I could remember. For a few hours, anyway.

~~~

Mai was up before the dawn. She said she had meetings all day. We made arrangements to reconvene that night for dinner. I threw on my pants and shirt, then she walked me to her door, naked.

"Thank you," she said in that British-Asian accent of hers.

She stood on her toes and we kissed, long and deeply. The taste of her lingered on my tongue. I held her close, struggling to find the right words, something that would express my gratitude for the comfort she'd provided me, the temporary respite from my demons and my past, but all I could think to offer in response was a mindless, "No, thank *you*." That didn't seem nearly adequate, but it was the best I could do.

When I returned to my room, I fully expected to find at least one eavesdropping device planted while I was away, but an electronic sweep found none. I showered, changed into a clean dress shirt and Dockers befitting my image as a pseudo PhD, and went to check upstairs on Cohen and Stoneburner. Neither man said they had any memory of Billy Hallady's alleged claim in the Riverside newspaper that the three of them had sworn revenge against Mr. Wonderful. Virgil Stoneburner was particularly adamant in denying the assertion.

"Blood oath? That's complete bullshit. Billy must be getting Alzheimer's," Stoneburner said, scarfing down a room service breakfast of scrambled eggs and hash browns in his underwear. "Hell, we didn't have a drop of blood to spare. I was down to 120 pounds back then, teeth falling out. My body was one big open sore. We were doing everything we could to conserve energy, not waste it. All of us. Billy Hallady included."

When I was allowed into Cohen's room, the tight set of his jaw told me that something had changed since I'd seen him last. Gone was his placid demeanor, replaced by a notable air of anxiety. He ushered me out onto his balcony where we couldn't be overheard.

"I'm afraid I was less than honest with you last time we spoke," he said in a tone that was at once guarded and guilt-ridden. "You asked me if I'd cooperated with the Vietnamese about what I knew about what had happened to that guard. I said I hadn't. In fact, I did, and I feel awful about that."

He said he'd been eating alone in the hotel dining room the morning after the big ceremonial dinner, waiting for Stoneburner to join him for breakfast, when three Vietnamese men approached. One of them was clearly in charge of the other two. The description Cohen gave me matched Colonel Tan Sang.

"He wanted to know when I'd last seen Billy and his grandson. I thought something bad might've happened to them on the way to the airport, and that they might have been in danger. I was concerned. I told them about seeing them in the bar that night, and about how they were scheduled to catch an early flight back to the states."

"Did he tell you that the guard had been murdered?"

Cohen shook his head. "All he told me was to go back to my room immediately, that I'd be safe there—from what, he didn't say. I asked about Virgil, was he okay? He said he'd already talked to him, and that he was back in his room upstairs. One of the men walked me back to my own room. I could see the pistol under his shirt. I thought for a minute they were going to kill me, that the whole thing was a setup."

"What made you think that?"

"The war. Hard feelings on their part—you know, 'the imperialist pilots who bombed us,' that sort of thing. I wasn't exactly sure. I just had this very strong sense that the best thing to do was to do what they said. It wasn't until I got back to my room and they locked me in that I realized I'd screwed up, said things I shouldn't have. Not that they couldn't have figured those things out themselves, talking to the hotel staff." He leaned his elbows on the railing, staring at his folded hands, guilt-ridden. "They took away my phone and cut off the room phone. That's when they told me we were all being accused of murder, and that we would be executed. They wouldn't tell me who was murdered, though. It was straight out of Kafka."

The early morning air was damp and clean and I filled my lungs with it. The streets below were wet from the rain that had fallen overnight. Three boys on their way to grammar school in matching white shirts and red neckerchiefs stomped each other wet in the puddles, laughing.

"I'm ashamed," Cohen said, watching them. "I should've kept my mouth shut and never said anything."

"You did nothing wrong, Colonel."

His eyes glistening. "Have you ever had a man die in your arms, Mr. Logan? Someone you loved?"

"I've lost friends," I said, "more than I care to remember, but never in my arms, no."

There was a pause, as if he had to will himself to go on. "I'd been in solitary confinement at the Hilton for the better part of a year," he said, his gaze far away, "when they threw this young kid in with me. Both arms broken, bruises everywhere. The goons had worked him over, busted him up like nobody's business. He was bleeding internally. There really wasn't much I could do for him."

"I can't imagine how hard that must've been," I said.

"He told me he had a son. He was so proud of that boy. Told me all about him. Made me promise that if I ever got out, I'd find his family and tell the boy that his father honored his oath and died a patriot. I promised him I'd look after his son. He only lasted a couple nights before he passed." Tears streaked Cohen's face. "I really can't talk about this. You should go now," he said, "before I embarrass myself further."

"I'm so sorry, Colonel."

"We can chat later if you'd like. I'm apparently not going anywhere anytime soon."

He engineered a smile. I marveled at his courage.

I'd been in my room a few minutes when the phone vibrated in my pocket. The voice on the other end was male, high-pitched and agitated. He identified himself as Carl Underwood Jr., a diplomatic officer assigned to the US Embassy in Hanoi. He said he needed to see me urgently. Actually, what he said was, "It's a matter of national security."

TWELVE

We made arrangements to meet west of downtown in Lenin Park on Dien Bien Phu Street, across from the Vietnam Military History Museum. The ride by taxi would've cost me about four dollars, but that was before I noticed another cab following us. I waved a ten-dollar bill under my driver's nose, pointed up at the rearview mirror, and made clear that the cash was his as long as he lost the tail. He grinned like it was easy money. A few quick turns down side streets and the taxi behind us disappeared.

Occupying a bench in the shadow of Lenin's statue, his arms slung across the back, trying to strike a casual pose, Carl Underwood Jr. was easy to spot. Other than me, he was the only non-Asian in the park. He was also the only man in sight wearing a coat and tie, albeit disheveled. Even at a distance, I could see his left knee bouncing with anxiety.

"The poppies bloom in spring."

Underwood, who'd been looking intently the other way, glanced up at me, startled, shielding his brown, hound-dog eyes from the sun. He was tall and lanky, all knees and elbows.

"Excuse me?"

I sat down beside him on the bench. "You're supposed to respond, 'And the leaves fall in autumn,' or something to that effect. It's one of those cornball movie lines spies exchange to establish their bona fides when they meet in public parks. They also signal each other by stuffing umbrellas in trash cans and leaving potted plants on their patios, but it looks to me like we're both fresh out of plants and umbrellas."

"You must be Dr. Barker."

What remained of his receding, sandy-colored hair was sweaty and finger-combed across his sunburned scalp like guitar strings. He had big ears and frowned a lot, leaving the impression, perhaps intentionally, that confusion was his default state.

"Got any ID on you, Carl?"

He looked left, then right, to make sure nobody was watching, while digging a battered State Department identification card out of his wallet, which he held out for my close inspection. The card identified him as a "senior international trade specialist." It and his over-the-top awkward countenance left little doubt in my mind that he was likely working under diplomatic cover for the CIA.

"Your turn," Underwood said. "I need to see some identification, too."

"You were the one who called me, remember? You know who I am."

"Actually, I have no idea who you are. I have no idea who you work for. You weren't vetted through proper channels, but you do have some kind of juice behind you. I do know that."

I gave him one of my Dr. Barker business cards. It was a pretty spiffy card, I have to say, embossed in three colors, very professional-looking. For once, Buzz and Uncle Sugar had splurged. Underwood studied it

"So, what is it I can do for you, Carl?"

"You can back off, that's what you can do. Look, we're doing everything we can here to resolve this crisis as quickly and quietly as we can before it blows up on CNN. There are literally hundreds of people at State in Washington and here on the embassy staff working this problem. The last thing we need is some loose cannon from some secret operation, the name of which nobody will even tell us, to come parachuting in here and muddy up the water."

Over Underwood's shoulder, toward the east end of the park, I observed a young woman in sunglasses and a floppy hat. She was down on one knee, pretending to take close-up photographs of the daisies and chrysanthemums. Only her camera lens was too long for close-up pictures. She was snapping pictures of us.

I waved at her. She lowered her camera and immediately started walking out of the park.

"Who's that?" Underwood said, turning nervously to follow my sightline.

"I thought you might know."

"I don't know who she is."

Was he lying? It was hard to tell. I asked him where he was from.

"Ohio. Dayton."

"Dayton, Ohio. Home of Wright-Patterson Air Force Base. I spent some time there myself, back in the day."

Underwood seemed to brighten. "I was born at Wright-Pat. My father was a pilot. Got the DFC."

"Nice. So, Carl, what was so life-and-death important you had to talk to me right away?"

Again he glanced around to make sure no one else was within earshot, then leaned closer, his right hand on his right knee. "Okay, look," he said. "First of all, I need to know who you're working for, no bullshit."

"The White House."

Underwood's mouth opened. "Seriously?"

"Yes, Carl. Seriously."

He sat back, nodding to himself, as if it made sense. "The White House. Of course, they would've *had* to get directly involved in this. This is a big deal—or could be if we don't contain the damage." He produced a roll of Tums, peeled off two tablets and chewed them. "I'm assuming you've already been in touch with Colonel Cohen and Captain Stoneburner?"

I nodded.

"They're being transferred to prison in three days," Underwood said.

"I'm aware of that. I'm also aware that once they're transferred, the chances of getting them home anytime soon drop radically."

"Then what are you doing about it? Because if you are, in fact, working for the White House as you say you are, the administration must have *some* expectation that you bring something to the table the rest of us can't."

He needn't have reminded me of the magnitude of the task I'd taken on, nor of the fact that time was fleeting.

"First off, I need to know what you know. Have you or any of your people identified any suspects?"

"Lemme put it this way," Underwood said, "Mr. Wonderful was a sadist, okay? He was an opportunistic asshole from everything we've been able to learn about him. There's no shortage of people in this city who would've wanted to kill him for any number of reasons. And that doesn't even begin to include the possibility that maybe he was simply the victim of a random street crime, an attempted robbery. It happens here a lot, believe you me."

"I need specifics."

"What? You mean like the names of sources, that sort of thing?"

"Yeah, Carl. That sort of thing."

He said he wasn't at liberty to disclose specifics, but suggested I might want to start with Mr. Wonderful's widow.

"She paints a pretty bleak picture of the guy," Underwood said. "To hear her tell it, he had plenty of enemies."

I didn't tell him I'd already talked to Mrs. Wonderful. "That's it?" I said. "That's all you've got? The widow?"

Underwood ran his hand across his face. "Look, don't know who you are. And if I don't know who you are, I can't help you."

"Then why'd you call me? You said it was a matter of national security."

He cleared his throat and glanced around. "The Hanoi police have been asking questions about you—who are you, who you work for—that sort of thing. When they start asking questions, sometimes people have been known to disappear."

"I appreciate your concern."

"The least I can do for a fellow American."

"I need to know what they know, the police."

Underwood looked at me like I was kidding.

"I need to see their investigative file on Mr. Wonderful, Carl. Think you can get me a copy?"

"Sure, no problem. Gee, maybe while I'm at it I should ask to borrow Ho Chi Minh's body so we can take him joyriding. Just *ask* them for their investigative file? Are you nuts?"

"You must have contacts with the authorities, Carl. What's the worst they can say, no?"

"It doesn't work that way around here," Underwood said. "Trust me, they don't just *give* you the file. They give you nothing. Vietnam is an authoritarian, communist state. There's no such thing as governmental transparency here. You're asking me to do the impossible."

"By asking the impossible we obtain the possible. Isn't that what they always say at Langley?"

Underwood looked away and wiped the sweat from his brow with the back of his left hand. "I don't work for Langley."

"Just get me the file, Carl."

"Fine. I'll ask, but don't hold your breath." He stood, then he said, "A friendly suggestion. If I were you, as long as you're in Hanoi, I'd watch my back."

I watched him walk away. He had a gawky, shambling gate that, for some reason, reminded me of a scarecrow. When he got to the boulevard, he flagged down a taxi, got in, and was soon gone. I checked my phone, hoping there might be a message from Phu Dung saying he'd tracked down the jealous husband and religious artifacts shopkeeper, Jimmy Luc, but nobody'd tried to reach me.

Sunlight dappled the trees. Flowers perfumed the air. Across the way, two old men were playing chess. Mothers pushed their babies in prams, chatting with each other. The capital of Vietnam definitely had its charms, if not its secrets. I glanced around to see if I was still under surveillance. If they were there, I didn't see them.

I recalled something Colonel Cohen had said during one of his lectures at the academy, how one could never truly appreciate differing philosophies without first attempting to understand their historical and cultural contexts. It dawned on me, sitting there, that if I hoped to achieve my objective in Hanoi, I had to know better what I was up against.

~~~

Maison Centrale were the words painted over the entrance of the French-built Hỏa Lò Prison, a seven-minute cab ride from the park and statue of Lenin where I'd met with Carl Underwood Jr. In English, the name meant "central home," a misnomer if there ever was one. To the captured American servicemen who were imprisoned there, "homey" was the last adjective they would've given the place. In mocking irony, they dubbed it the Hanoi Hilton for its less than hospitable accommodations. With its quaint stone exterior painted a cheerful mustard yellow, though, the place didn't look so much like one giant torture chamber as it did some elegant *maison de maître* transplanted straight from the French countryside. Only when factoring in the Medieval-looking iron grate hanging above over its arched entryway and perimeter walls topped with not only barbed wire, but rows of multicolored glass shards designed to shred any prisoner attempting to escape, could one begin to understand the building's true purpose.

The Hanoi Hilton was now a glorified tourist trap, mostly dedicated to heralding the story of how the Vietnamese were abused by their colonial French masters, rather than how the Vietnamese brutalized others. A ticket kiosk sat to the left of the entrance. Security guards in black slacks and short-sleeved sky blue shirts milled about, smoking cigarettes, looking bored. I paid the 10,000-dong admission fee—about fifty cents—and walked in. You didn't need to be clairvoyant to feel the spirits that haunted the building, or to hear their anguished screams.

Gone was the sprawling compound that once housed hundreds of downed US pilots. The prison yard and outlying buildings had been demolished to make way for an ultramodern, high-rise residential complex that accommodated mostly well-heeled foreigners, while the museum itself was a masterwork of propaganda. Nothing suggested that American prisoners had experienced anything other than civil if not cordial treatment at the hands of their North Vietnamese captors. Black and white photos showed POWs playing basketball and volleyball, even billiards on a makeshift pool table. Many wore strained smiles. They looked fit and well fed, if not tense. Had I not known otherwise, I might've convinced myself that the snapshots were of large boys at summer camp. I peered closely at them, wondering if any of the faces belonged to Cohen, Stoneburner or Billy Hallady, but I recognized none of them.

I paused to listen to a young docent, who could've been a graduate student, leading a tour of mostly older Europeans. He explained to them in English how, even after raining bombs down on innocent women and children, shot-down American airmen were treated with nothing less than dignity. The Vietnamese were too refined a people to have ever tortured anyone, the tour guide said straight-facedly; allegations to the contrary were all lies.

"This is why the Americans called it the Hanoi Hilton. Because it was like a hotel to them."

None of the tourists called bullshit on him. They snapped photos. They said nothing. I left before they did.

A true Buddhist wishes ill on no one, his enemies included, because harboring hateful feelings toward others invariably comes full circle. It's called karma. Still, I couldn't help but think that if Mr. Wonderful had done half the things he'd been accused of to guests at the Hanoi Hilton, he definitely deserved a knife in his chest. I didn't necessarily like myself for feeling that way, but I didn't dislike myself, either. Ice enough people who deserved it and eventually you don't even give their deaths a second thought except, perhaps, in the wee hours, when their faces come to you in dreams, the fear in their eyes when they realize you're about to end their lives.

~~~

Phu Dung texted me the address of a restaurant where he wanted to meet for lunch. He said he had fresh information, but said he wanted to save it until we were face-to-face. The restaurant was called Tran Thanh Tong, which also happened to be the name of the street on which it was located. When I told the taxi driver where I wanted to go, his eyebrows danced. I understood why the minute I walked in.

Tran Thanh Tong was a cross between a Czech beer hall and Hooters. Leggy young Vietnamese waitresses in short-shorts, tank tops, and push-up bras ferried overpriced drinks to mostly businessmen in suits. Wall-mounted, flat-screen televisions were everywhere. Each screen seemed to show a different fashion show, with haughty, scantily dressed European fashion models plying the runways.

Phu Dung was sitting in back, his back to the wall. With his shaved head and white mesh workout top, he wasn't hard to spot. He was working on a platter of spring rolls. He gestured: help yourself.

I sat and did, shouting over the disco music pounding out of the bar's sound system. "Interesting place."

"Beautiful women," Phu Dung said.

I agreed.

A waitress of about twenty-two glided over. Her long hair was straight and the color of midnight. Her angelic face was the kind about which men write poems. Phu Dung asked me what I wanted to drink. I went with water.

"No beer?" the waitress asked me.

"Just water, thanks."

She gave me a sad smile, like she felt sorry for me, and left.

"I found Jimmy Luc," Phu Dung said.

"Outstanding. Let's go sec him."

"Can't do that."

"Why not?"

Phu Dung calmly sipped his beer. "Because Jimmy Luc is dead."

Thirteen

Phu Dung said he had a hunch that the girl I'd talked to at Jimmy Luc's shop knew more about her boss's whereabouts than she'd initially let on. He'd gone to see her a second time. His hunch had paid off.

What Linh hadn't revealed to us the first time was that Jimmy's body had been fished out of the Red River three days earlier. Authorities were calling it a suicide: diagnosed with terminal cancer, Jimmy, they claimed, had chosen to end his life and spare himself the indignities of a slow, painful death.

"How did the girl find all this out? Who told her?"

Phu Dung sipped his beer. "She did not say."

"What kind of cancer?"

"This I don't know."

"How do they know it was a suicide?"

Phu Dung rubbed the back of his neck and looked away, watching the waitresses. He was growing uncomfortable, me asking him questions.

"How do we know Jimmy's really dead?"

"She is a young girl. She would have no reason to lie."

"Everyone has reason to lie, Phu Dung, even young girls."

~~~

I made him drive me back to Jimmy Luc's shop. The girl saw us coming and ran. The sidewalk was thick with pedestrians. She was easy to catch.

"Please," she pleaded, melting under my grip like a wild animal caught in a predator's jaws.

"I'm not going to hurt you, Linh. I just want to ask you some questions."

Tears coursed down her cheeks. She wouldn't look at me.

"Did you know Jimmy was sick, that he had cancer?"

She shook her head.

"Who told you Jimmy killed himself?"

"Please . . ."

She tried to pull free, sobbing.

"What are you so afraid of?"

"He tell me, 'No talk. Nobody.'"

"Who told you that?"

A white four-door Toyota bearing Hanoi police markings approached. The girl turned away, hiding her face from the three uniformed cops inside the car. They cruised past without seeming to notice either one of us.

"Was it the police who told you not to talk? It's okay, Linh. You can talk to me."

She nodded tentatively, wiping her eyes.

"Do you remember their names, who they were, which police?"

"Jimmy, his friend."

"That photograph I saw hanging in the shop, the one with Jimmy and the police officer. That was the friend you're talking about? He was the one who told you Jimmy committed suicide?"

". . . Yes. But I think maybe Jimmy, he not . . ." She shook her head, trying to find the words in English.

"You don't think he killed himself?"

"No." The girl was now trembling.

I gave her a reassuring hug. "I want you to do something for me, Linh. Think you can do that?"

A scared nod.

I wasn't sure what had happened to her boss, but I sure as hell didn't want anything happening to her. I peeled off two 500,000 dong notes and handed her the money. "I want you to stay somewhere safe. Maybe outside the city. Just for a few days. Will you do that for me, Linh?"

She stared at the money. "Okay."

"Good. Now, I want you to do something else for me, okay? My name is Barker. I'm staying at the Yellow Flower Hotel. If you think of anything else that might be helpful, anything at all, I want you to call me. Do you think you can remember that—Barker, the Yellow Flower Hotel?"

Slowly, she raised her eyes to mine. "You are not Jimmy friend?"

"No, Linh, I'm not."

"You lie to me."

"Yes. I did."

She ran, vanishing into the crowded streets of the Old Quarter. I walked back to Jimmy Luc's shop. Phu Dung was leaning against his motorcycle, talking on his cell phone. He quickly hung up as I approached, as if he didn't want me overhearing his conversation.

"Colonel Tan Sang," I said. "He was the one who told the girl that Jimmy Luc's dead. How convenient."

"Convenient?" Phu Dung's expression told me he didn't get the American concept of irony—my version of it, anyway.

"Tan Sang's convinced the American POWs killed Mr. Wonderful. So even if Jimmy Luc was the real killer, it doesn't matter much now because Jimmy's dead. Tan Sang can still pin the murder on the Americans."

"You make it sound like Tan Sang killed Jimmy Luc," Phu Dung said.

"Look, all I know is, Tan Sang's got it in for the Americans because his mother died in the war, and he blames them. He wants vengeance, not truth and justice. A guy with motivation like that will do just about anything to get what he wants, including murder."

"It could be what he told the girl is true. Jimmy was sick. He was going to die. He killed himself."

"Could be. I want to see an autopsy report."

Phu Dung shook his head. Bodies, he said, were fished out of the Red River all the time. Rarely were the victims of suspected foul play autopsied. Rarer still were arrests made in their deaths. Most murders in Hanoi went unsolved.

A kid with a severe case of acne tried to interest me in a selection of cigarette lighters that he carried in a tray strapped around his neck. Phu Dung said something sternly to him in Vietnamese. The kid moved on.

That's when the thought hit me.

"Duy Van, the other guard who worked with Mr. Wonderful, he was the one who told us about Jimmy Luc and how jealous he was that Mr. Wonderful had slept with his wife, remember?"

Phu Dung nodded.

"Duy Van also told us that Mr. Wonderful was tight with somebody in law enforcement, somebody who provided him protection."

"And you think it was Colonel Tan Sang?"

"Possibly."

"If it was Tan Sang," Phu Dung said, smiling to himself, "he did not do a very good job. Mr. Wonderful is dead."

I couldn't argue with his logic.

~~~

I took my time walking back to the hotel, purposely taking several wrong turns down twisting, narrow lanes where mom-and-pop merchants, operating out of open-air stalls, sold everything from baby clothes to French colognes. I loitered periodically, pretending to shop, checking to see if I was being followed. I wasn't.

Clouds were scudding dark and low over the city, taking the afternoon light with them. The air smelled of rain. Then, as if someone turned on a tap, the skies opened up and it poured. I was ducking into a little flower shop on Hang Hom Street to stay dry when Buzz called.

"The White House just woke me up. They want to know what the hell's going on over there. They want a full brief. I told 'em be patient, I've got my best man on the case, he'll give us a situation report when he's able. They don't care about any of that. They've got their own schedule and they want answers. So, my question is, Dr. Barker, what in the hell is going on over there?"

"It's raining."

"I don't give a damn if it's snowing cornflakes," Buzz said. "Why haven't I heard from you?"

"I've been busy, Buzz."

"We're all busy, Logan! I didn't send you over there to chill out and eat barbequed dog or whatever it is those people do these days. I need a detailed sit-rep from you. Did one of our guys do the deed or not?"

"I'm not sure."

"Well, when *will* you be sure?"

A short-haired, middle-aged Vietnamese woman with a cherubic face was making floral arrangements behind the counter. I gave her a friendly nod. She eyed me warily. The rain was coming down outside in sheets.

"I'm not in a position to talk specifics right now, Buzz. I'll check back in with you in thirty mikes."

"I'll be waiting. As will the president."

No umbrella. No coat. I ducked out the door and sprinted through the downpour. The hotel was about six blocks away. Given the intensity with which the rain was falling, in wind-whipped sheets, it really didn't matter whether I walked or ran; I'd be drenched all the same. I ran anyway.

Elvis the doorman saw me coming, deployed a big black umbrella that had a yellow sunflower printed on it, and held the door open with an empathetic smile. "Crazy," he said, looking up and shaking his head at the leaden skies. It was one of the few English words he seemed to know. Then he tilted his head subtly, as if to warn me of some impending danger awaiting me in the hotel lobby.

Colonel Tan Sang set his teacup down as I entered. Flanking him were two leather-jacketed toughs wearing their sunglasses.

Both could've come straight from central casting, heavies in a kung fu movie.

"Where have you been, Dr. Barker?"

"Sightseeing."

"I think not. I think you have been doing what I specifically instructed you not to do. Asking questions. Harassing people. Making trouble."

He snapped his fingers. One of the goons handed me a digital camera. In the camera's viewfinder was a grainy photograph of me sitting on a bench in Lenin Park with Carl Underwood Jr. from the US Embassy.

"How do you explain this?" Tan Sang asked.

Rainwater puddled around my waterlogged shoes. I was wet and cold and in no mood to cooperate. I tossed the camera back to Tan Sang. "I'm a United States citizen. I have every right to meet with a diplomatic representative from my nation's embassy. Even in Hanoi."

"You said you were sightseeing. Why did you lie?"

"Why are your people following me?"

"We both know why. You are no psychologist. You are an intelligence officer, a spy. In Vietnam, spies are shot."

A muscle twitched under his left eye. The carotid artery on the right side of his neck pulsed noticeably. Tan Sang was working hard at conveying an imperious, in-control air, but he was clearly nervous. Was it because he feared how much I'd learned of his ties to Jimmy Luc and the late Mr. Wonderful? I could've spelled it all out for him to make him back off, but a good fighter pilot locked in combat never uncorks his strongest moves until his weaker ones have come up short. I still had a few left, including bluster and bluff, before going nuclear.

"You're out of your league, Colonel," I said. "I have official authorization from your government to provide humanitarian assistance to two American citizens who you've all but tried and convicted without having introduced a single shred of incriminating evidence against them in a court of law. You want to arrest me on espionage charges? Fire away. But fair warning: it won't be me begging for any do-overs at the end of the day."

Then Mai walked in from the rain. She was wearing black heels and a short, peach-colored skirt suit that showed plenty of thigh. The top buttons of her black silk blouse were undone, revealing a décolletage ample enough to turn heads, specifically Tan Sang's.

"There you are," she said, shaking out her wet umbrella and walking up beside me to kiss my cheek. "My goodness, you're soaked to the bone."

Tan Sang seemed surprised she knew me. "You know this gentleman?"

"Who doesn't know this gentleman? Dr. Barker, the world-famous American psychologist."

"Miss Choi was kind enough to show me around Hanoi this afternoon before it started coming down," I said. "She had some business to attend to, so I came back to the hotel."

Mai didn't blink at my untruths. "I'm just glad you made it back, love," she said. "I was beginning to grow worried about you." She turned to Tan Sang with a disarming smile. "And who might these very serious-looking gentlemen be?"

Tan Sang flipped open his wallet and showed her his identification with a practiced flourish.

"Ministry of Public Security," Mai said, glancing at his silver badge and pretending to be impressed. "You must be very important."

He asked to see her identification. Mai retrieved her passport from a white leather shoulder bag. The colonel gave it a quick look and handed it back.

"I see you are from Singapore."

"Born and bred."

He asked if she was a guest of the hotel. She said she was. He asked the purpose of her visit to Hanoi. She told him. He asked if the two of us were sleeping together.

"None of your business," I said.

Tan Sang smirked. "It is unlawful in Vietnam for unmarried individuals to sleep together in the same hotel room."

"If I'm not mistaken," Mai said, "that particular provision of Vietnamese law pertains strictly to a foreign national who sleeps with a Vietnamese woman and is not married to her. As you know, looking at my passport, I am not Vietnamese."

"Better watch yourself, Colonel," I said, "she's an attorney."

Tan Sang was a man who didn't appreciate being schooled by anyone, especially a woman. Tersely, he told her he was conducting a homicide investigation and that I was interfering with his efforts.

Mai didn't seem the least bit surprised by his telling her that, which struck me as curious. "Well," she said coyly, looking straight at me, "perhaps someone should distract Dr. Barker sufficiently such that he's no longer a distraction to anyone."

The colonel glared at us both, then said something in Vietnamese to one of his goons, who promptly headed for the door—I assumed to retrieve his Lexus.

"I will not warn you again, Doctor," he said. "Continue to cause trouble and I will have you arrested." Then he turned and headed for the hotel exit, the other goon following close on his heels like some devoted dog.

As he was leaving, I watched Tan Sang slip Elvis the doorman some cash. It wouldn't have been a big deal anywhere else in the world where people tip the hotel staff routinely. But there was something about this exchange that didn't seem right. It wasn't like a tip rendered for good service. It seemed more like a payoff, swiftly and discreetly pocketed with no acknowledgment—in much the same way I'd observed what appeared to be a cash exchange three days earlier outside the hotel between Tan Sang and the same doorman. Let me put it this way: it looked like a bribe.

"Come on," Mai said, taking me by the arm, "let's get you out of those wet clothes and into something warmer."

What a fine idea, I remember thinking. First, though, I had to call Buzz. I told Mai I had to take care of some business and that I'd be by in a few minutes.

"Try not to be too long," she said.

Fourteen

I swept the room once more for electronic bugs, took a quick shower, and telephoned Buzz.

"Thanks for taking time out of your busy day," he said, irritated at having had to wait for me to call.

I laid out my suspicions about Colonel Tan Sang's possible involvement in Mr. Wonderful's murder. I hadn't ruled out the very real possibility that one or more of the Americans were responsible, particularly Billy Hallady and/or his grandson, but I made clear that the focus of my investigation had shifted and was aimed increasingly at Tan Sang.

Buzz expressed frustration at my lack of progress. Time, he reminded me, was waning: The Vietnamese government had cabled the State Department hours earlier, informing Washington that both Cohen and Stoneburner would stand trial within a week, and that Billy Hallady, safely back in the United States, would be tried in absentia. Vietnamese lawyers would be appointed to represent all three former prisoners of war.

"Does the term, 'kangaroo court' mean anything to you?" Buzz said. "Hallady's lucky as hell. Those other two guys are as good as toast unless we get something going A-SAP."

"If I could hunt up something more implicating on Tan Sang, get him more pregnant, we could turn the tables."

"What about that terp we hired, the MiG pilot. He doing you any good?"

"Phu Dung? The jury's still out."

Buzz exhaled audibly. "Okay, I'll let the White House know about all of this. Just keep me posted."

"Roger that."

I thought he'd hung up without saying good-bye, as he always did, but then he said, "It must suck, having the fate of two old men in your hands."

"Nothing like a little pressure."

"You do your best work under pressure, Logan."

The fate of two old men is in your hands. Buzz's words echoed inside my head like a tune you can't shake.

~~~

We called room service and ate dinner naked, listening to the sound of the rain thrumming against the glass of her balcony door. I tried not to think of Savannah, or the two men being held prisoner one floor above us. I tried living in the moment as all true Buddhists do—to taste, really *taste, t*he beef skewers in lemon grass I'd ordered, and to savor the company of the woman in whose bed I found myself. I'd be lying, however, if I said my thoughts weren't elsewhere. Who killed Mr. Wonderful and why? I was no closer to finding out than when I'd first touched down in Hanoi.

"Hey," Mai said, leaning over and kissing my shoulder, "are you okay?"

"Yeah, fine. Just thinking about work, that's all."

She sat back under the sheets, sipping a glass of French merlot and eyeing me with curiosity. "I'd love to know what that was all about down in the lobby."

I feigned ignorance. "Something happened in the lobby?"

She playfully tapped my foot with hers. "The man from the Ministry of Public Security, what was his name? Tan Sang? I don't think he much likes you."

"What gave you your first clue?"

She smiled. "So what are you, some sort of international criminal or something? A jewel thief, perhaps? A *wanted* man. That would be terribly exciting."

I debated how much of the truth to share with her. She needed some logical explanation as to what had gone down in the lobby, and I needed to maintain my operational cover, so I told her in the vaguest possible terms about the murder of Mr. Wonderful and about Cohen and Stoneburner, how they were under house arrest on the sixth floor. But that was as far as I went with the facts. I stuck to my psychologist story, that I'd been contracted by the government to monitor the mental health of the two former POWs and to provide to them whatever counseling they required. I told her nothing of the real reason I'd come to Hanoi.

"The police believe you're someone other than who you say you are," Mai said.

"I don't know why they would think that. I mean, look at this face. Is this the face of a pretender?"

"Well, as I pointed out when we met, you don't look like a psychologist to me."

"Yeah, well, you don't look much like an attorney or the vice president of Kia Motors to me."

She snuggled into me. Her hair smelled of lavender.

"Perhaps you could tell me," Mai said, "what precisely in your estimation an attorney or a vice president of Kia is supposed to look like?"

"Well, for starters, they don't usually have legs like yours."

"That's a rather sexist thing to say, don't you think?"

"We all have our faults."

She kissed me. Her lips were warm and I didn't want it to end.

"Who are you really? I promise, your secret's safe with me."

"I told you who I am."

"I don't believe you," Mai said, slowly kissing my shoulder and working her way down my chest. "If you tell me the truth, I promise you, you'll be amply rewarded."

Maybe it was her persistence, or the intoxicatingly seductive tone of her voice—breathy, intentionally alluring. Or maybe it was simply the cynic in me, the skepticism a covert operator harnesses and hones over the years, that voice in your gut that compels you to question the veracity of every word that comes out of everyone's mouth because everybody has a hidden agenda, and sometimes those agendas will get you killed.

"What kind of reward are we talking about?"

"What kind would you like?"

"How 'bout a new car? A Kia Ambassador, like my friend's I told you about."

Her fingers stroked the inside of my thigh, inching closer to more sensitive anatomical turf. "I'll see what I can do," she said, still kissing.

Buzz didn't drive an Ambassador. To my knowledge, Kia has never made a car called the Ambassador. A Kia vice president would've likely known that and would've just as likely corrected me. Was I being played? Was Mai a plant working for the Vietnamese government? I was beginning to wonder—but that didn't make me stop her hand from wandering, or doing everything that came so naturally in the hours that followed.

~~~

She snored. Not offensively. Not in a sawing-of-logs sort of way. More feminine than that. A soft, almost melodic whistling. Shortly after 0500, I extricated myself from Mai's embrace as gently as I could and slipped from her bed. She stirred briefly, rolled over on her side, and fell back asleep. Her shoulder bag rested on the floor near the desk. I carried it into the bathroom and quietly closed the door.

The average woman's purse is a wonder of both utility and chaos. How Savannah ever located anything in her bag, crammed as it always was with everything from lipstick to pepper spray, was always beyond me. Once when she'd insisted on taking me shopping because she said my shabby but comfortable wardrobe embarrassed her, she reached into her purse to get out a credit card and I saw two pairs of pliers in there along with a pair of yellow dishwashing gloves. Mai's bag was different.

Everything was neatly arranged, compartmentalized, in its place. Her passport, issued to Mai Kwan Choi, had her photo. In her wallet was a driver's license issued in her name by the Singapore Traffic Police Department. There were also Kia Motors Corporation business cards with a Singapore address that said, "M.K. Choi, vice president, sales and marketing, Southeast Asia Division." Either my suspicions about the woman I'd just slept with were misplaced, or her handlers had done a masterful job in establishing her cover.

"What are you doing?"

I looked up in the mirror over the sink. Mai was standing behind me in a white terry cloth robe.

"I asked you a question," she said, folding her arms. "What do you think you're doing?"

"Regretting that I didn't lock the bathroom door."

She stood there with her mouth open.

"Who do you work for, Mai?"

"Please leave."

"Colonel Tan Sang? Is that who you answer to?"

"I'm asking you nicely to leave. If you don't get out of my room immediately, I *will* call the authorities and I *will* have you arrested for theft."

"I didn't steal anything, Mai."

"My trust. You stole that."

I handed her the bag, threw on my pants, and gathered up the rest of my clothes. She stood aside as I opened the door.

"I thought we had something," she said. "I was wrong."

The door slammed behind me.

A real Buddhist believes that all people are inherently trustworthy and good. I was a long way from that. I'd just ruined what could have been a very good thing. Part of me wanted to kick myself. But another part was patting me on the back, that part where you wall off your heart from the vulnerability that comes with trusting anyone. As pleasurable as my brief time with Mai had been, the fact was, I didn't need her. I didn't need anyone. That's just how things go when you choose this line of work, or it chooses you.

I got dressed in the hallway and decided to take a walk down to the lake where Mr. Wonderful had met his end. The sun was coming up as I left the hotel. Almost immediately, I noticed I was being followed—the same postcard vendor who'd tailed me two nights earlier, when Mai and I had gone to eat Mexican food.

I turned and strode straight at him.

"What's going on, chief?"

Caught off guard, he tried to ignore me at first, acting like he was rearranging his tray of postcards. When he realized confrontation was inevitable, he pivoted to face me, his stance defensive.

"How much for one postcard?" I said, digging out the wad of dong in my front pocket.

Mr. Postcards looked at me blankly.

"I want to buy a postcard. How much?"

"Twenty."

"Thousand?"

He responded with a nervous nod.

"You speak English?"

He held his thumb and finger a half-inch apart. A little.

"You got any postcards showing the lake?"

He thumbed through the selection like it was the first time he'd seen them himself.

I picked one out and unfolded a 500,000 dong note. He stared at the bill like a heroin addict in need of a fix.

"Do you have a wife?"

He nodded, still staring at the money.

"Good-looking young dude like you, I'm sure she's a knock-out. Listen, why don't you take her out for a nice breakfast, just the two of you? That way, I can take a little stroll by myself and enjoy a little early morning solitude without you shagging after me everywhere. Deal?"

He glanced around to see if anyone was watching us, then snatched the bill out of my hand, stuffed it quickly in his pocket, and hurried away. Money may not buy everything, it's true, but not, apparently, in Hanoi. He disappeared around the corner. It would be awhile before I saw him again.

~~~

With the sun came rising humidity. People around the lake were getting their daily exercise in early. A roller-blading teen-ager with spiked hair dyed purple zipped past me going back-ward, carrying an honest-to-god boom box and rocking out to what sounded like the singer, Rihanna. The lyrics were in Eng-lish, something about how love is like checking into drug rehab. Not exactly Donnie and Marie Osmond material.

My acquaintance, the bearded fisherman, was casting out near where I'd seen him the first morning I'd visited the lake. I watched him reel what looked like a perch. Gently, he unhooked the wriggling fish, knelt at the water's edge, and released it.

"Any trout in this lake?"

He glanced over his shoulder, seemed to recognize me, and turned away, saying nothing.

"We catch trout where I come from. Rainbows, mostly. A few browns and cutthroats. You can always tell the native fish from the stockers. They're smarter, harder to catch. Plus, their meat's a lot firmer."

He cast without looking at me. His demeanor, the vibe he gave off, told me he wasn't merely being shy or standoffish. He knew something, had *seen* something relevant to the murder of Mr. Wonderful, something he wasn't telling.

"Trout have more bones than perch, but they're worth it," I said. "Better fighters, and better eating."

No response.

Rapport is the key to interrogation. No matter their cul-tural backgrounds, people are almost always more willing to give up the information you're looking for if you gently cajole them rather than by, say, removing their fingernails one by one. The name of the game is finding common interests that you can discuss without conflict.

"I bet there's some pretty good saltwater fishing in Vietnam. I wouldn't mind doing some while I'm here. Know anybody I could talk to about that?"

More silence. He appeared to have zero interest in talking to me. So much for my expert, rapport-building techniques.

"Well, anyway, I hope you catch the big one."

I was starting to get hungry for breakfast. I turned to go when he said, "You are American?"

"Yes."

"Other American. He come. Like you. He talk to me."

"About what?"

The fisherman pointed to the water, then made a stabbing motion toward his stomach.

"About the man they found in the lake?"

He nodded.

"When was this?"

He held up one finger, then another. I told him I didn't understand what he was trying to tell me. He pointed once more to the water, again pantomimed a stabbing motion to his own stomach, this time more animatedly, then pointed to his wristwatch.

"One or two hours?"

He nodded.

"You're saying this American, he talked to you one or two hours after they found the man in the lake?"

"No." The fisherman gestured sharply, his hand like a flat blade across his throat. "He not talk to me. He say *no* talk."

"He told you not to tell anyone about the man in the lake?"

The fisherman nodded.

"Why? What did you see?"

"Him."

"Him?"

The fisherman nodded.

"You mean, the man, the American? He didn't want you telling anybody you'd seen him?"

"Yes."

"This American, what did he look like?"

The fisherman stroked his chin, mulling the question. "Family," he said, "very hungry."

He wanted to be paid for his information. I peeled off 500,000 dong from the cash roll in my pocket.

He shook his head and indicated he wanted a million.

"Seven hundred and fifty thousand," I said. "That's as high as I'm prepared to go."

Granted, it wasn't my money. It was the taxpayers'. But it's been my experience over the years that if a man knows you're prepared to drive a hard bargain, even in the middle of a crisis, he's also inclined to realize that the information he gives you better be worth the money, or you'll come find him later.

The fisherman considered my counteroffer, then responded with a quick, single nod of his head.

Seven hundred and fifty thousand dong. About thirty–seven dollars.

As near as I could decipher, given our language differences, the American who'd told him to keep his mouth shut about what he'd seen that night was tall and balding, with oversized ears. He wore a coat and tie.

The man he described sounded a lot like Carl Underwood Jr. from the US Embassy.

"This American, he spoke Vietnamese?"

A nod.

I dangled another million dong.

"Tell me what you saw that night."

The fisherman took the money eagerly. Then, as best he could, he told me.

FIFTEEN

It wasn't so much what the fisherman saw that night. It was what he said he heard.

He'd just caught a nice-sized perch and was reeling it in when, from where he was standing along the water's edge, perhaps no more than fifty or sixty meters to the north of his position, came the discordant strains of two men shouting at each other—an argument that swiftly turned heated. Flowering bushes and the branches of an overhanging tree obscured his view of the fight, the fisherman said, but not the sound of it.

An anguished scream. A loud splash. The footfalls of someone running away, fast.

"Do you remember what the two men said to each other?"

He didn't understand the question. I rephrased it several times. He still didn't get it. Then I remembered the translating program Buzz had installed on my phone. I typed in my question, hit translate, and showed him the screen. His eyes lit up and he smiled in recognition, then typed a response. We were off and running.

He couldn't make out the gist of the argument; the yelling lasted only a few seconds, but each combatant's parting words, he said, were unmistakable. One of the men shouted, "Die!" This was followed almost immediately by the different male voice yelling, "*Không! Không! Không!*"—the Vietnamese word for no.

Afraid that he might be next, the fisherman said he dropped his pole and ran south, toward his apartment on Hai Ba Trung Street. He didn't stop running until he got home. An hour or so later, after he'd caught his breath, he chanced to retrieve his gear. That's when he crossed paths with the American who told him in Vietnamese to keep his mouth shut about whatever he'd seen if he knew what was good for him. Police officers swarmed the area. The fisherman said he spoke to none of them.

"Why didn't you tell the police all of this?"

I hit translate and handed him the phone. He typed his response and hit translate.

"Because South Vietnam I am from. Police not trust."

"You are not a member of the Communist Party?"

He chuckled when he read this.

"Only some people Communist Party. Not many."

The fisherman was convinced that the man who'd repeatedly shouted "No" was the same man he would later read about in the newspaper—the former prison guard who'd watched over captured American pilots forty years earlier.

"Could the man who yelled, 'Die,' be the same man you saw later that morning? The American who told you to keep your mouth shut?"

He typed on my phone and hit the translate button: "I certain cannot be."

I thanked him for his time and his candor. He wanted to say one more thing, typed some more and again hit the button. "I take want one day go my children Disneyland," it said on the screen.

"Bring lots of money," I said. "You'll need it."

There was a boulangerie on the north side of Hoàn Kiếm Lake, about a five-minute walk. Fronting the street inside the shop was a display case filled with fancy french pastries to rival any I'd ever seen in Paris. I ordered a custard-filled éclair because you've gotta die of something so it might as well be custard, and a cappuccino instead of my usual black coffee. After I was comfortably settled at a table outside, I called Phu Dong. There was no answer. Almost immediately, my phone rang. Caller ID indicated it was Buzz.

"I was just about to call you," I said.

"Great minds."

He said his people back in Cleveland had dredged up some new and potentially troublesome information about former POW Billy Hallady's grandson, Sean Hallady, the ex-marine who'd left the corps for psychiatric reasons, and who had accompanied his grandfather to Hanoi.

"Figured you might be interested," Buzz said, "given your extensive training in clinical psychology."

"More than interested," I said.

What Buzz passed along was troubling. Sean Hallady had gotten loaded inside a Salt Lake City bar the night after he got back from Vietnam. Words were exchanged followed by blows between Hallady and several patrons. Police were summoned. One of them happened to be of Asian ancestry.

"So Sean starts calling the guy names—gook this, slant-eyes that. Then he starts talking about how he would 'set things straight' for his grandfather, the big war hero, against all the 'gooks' of Vietnam who'd done gramps wrong. He ended up spending the night in the drunk tank."

"'Set things straight.' What does that mean?"

"You're a college graduate, Logan. What do you think it means?"

"Sounds to me like he was bragging about taking out Mr. Wonderful."

Buzz concurred. He said his people were working with authorities in Utah to locate Sean Hallady, in hopes of questioning him in greater detail. The problem was, nobody had seen him since his release from jail. The guy had disappeared.

"Anyway," Buzz said, "you were about to call me?"

I filled him in on the fisherman who'd likely heard Wonderful being stabbed to death, possibly by an American, and how the fisherman alleged that he'd later been told to maintain his silence by another American who resembled in description possible CIA operative Carl Underwood Jr.

"Just because the guy heard somebody yell, 'Die,' does not mean the killer was an American," Buzz said. "He could've been a Brit, or an Australian. They speak English, too, you know. More or less."

"What I want to know is why would an intelligence operative tell the potential witness in a murder to keep his mouth shut, unless it was to protect an American suspect?"

"Or maybe his own ass."

"Yeah. That, too."

The General Services Administration's Federal Citizen Information Center maintains a list of all US government employees whose e-mail and mailing addresses are available to the general public. Those employees working in classified assignments, needless to say, don't appear on the list. What's not commonly known is that all Tier One intelligence agencies have instant online access to all employee résumés, as well as the results of all background security investigations. Buzz had already spooled up Carl Underwood's package without my even asking for it.

The records showed that Underwood had grown up outside Dayton, Ohio, home of Wright-Patterson Air Force Base, where I'd once been assigned to the Air Intelligence Agency. He'd majored in international relations at Ohio's Oberlin College, one of those small, quaint liberal arts colleges that serve as a fallback for kids whose SAT scores won't get them into the Ivy League. Oberlin had a reputation as a feeder school to the intelligence community, its students not uncommonly recruited by the CIA and the National Security Agency, furthering my suspicions that Underwood was a spook operating out of the embassy in Hanoi under diplomatic cover. His seventeen-year career with the Foreign Service also gave me pause. Prior to his posting in the diplomatic backwater that was Hanoi, he'd been stationed in a half-dozen hotspots around the world, including Russia, China, Pakistan, and Yemen. But that wasn't all.

"Check this out," Buzz said over the phone. "It says here in the questionnaire he filled out for his last security clearance renewal that he was twice questioned by detectives from the Russian Ministry of Internal Affairs after he was posted to Moscow, back in 2006. They were looking into the disappearance of a drug dealer. The dealer and Underwood lived in the same apartment building. Underwood said he didn't know the guy. Claimed to have never met him."

Underwood's second contact with Russian authorities, Buzz said, involved a $1,000-a-night Moscow call girl who went by the name of Nastya. She claimed that Underwood refused to pay her fee after she serviced him, and then beat her up when she threatened to tell his wife. The case appeared to have been quietly dropped because of Underwood's diplomatic standing.

Despite the evidence, Buzz said he had his doubts that Underwood was CIA. "If this guy really does work for Christians In Action, how come I don't ever remember running into him when I was in the field? I mean, I ran into *everybody* when I was out there."

"I don't know, Buzz. Your guess is as good as mine."

He reminded me that my assignment was no guessing game. Conjecture didn't factor into the equation. If Carl Underwood had anything to do with the death of Mr. Wonderful, whether he did or didn't work for the CIA, the White House was still obliged to know ASAP. I assured Buzz I'd do my best to find out.

Another call to my interpreter, Phu Dung, proved fruitless. He didn't answer. Again. I left another message on his voice mail, alluding to the new leads I'd developed and that I required his assistance in pursuing them. Then I set out for the US Embassy.

As I stepped to the curb to hail a cab, a woman piloting a Vespa motor scooter angled through one-way traffic on the boulevard to stop beside me. High-collared, long-sleeved white blouse, black slacks, spiked black heels. A hennaed ponytail hung down the back of her pink helmet. Her skin was luminous. She couldn't have been older than twenty-two.

"You need ride? Come on, I take you," she said in more than passable English.

A beautiful young thing just happens to see a foreign national standing on the street and offers to give him a ride out of the goodness of her heart? Doubtful.

I looked past her. There were no taxis in sight. "I'm good," I said. "Thanks anyway."

I walked on. She persisted, smiling, keeping up with me. "Where you go? I am excellent driver. I take you. Cheap. Hop on. You see." She patted her backseat. "You will see."

"Cheap, huh?" I decided to play with her just for grins. "How much?"

"This depends. Where you go?"

"The American embassy."

"You are American?"

"Yes."

"America number one."

"I'm glad somebody thinks so."

"A very long walk, American embassy. Half-hour. I take you there for . . . four dollars."

"Who do you work for?"

"I am student."

"A student. Right."

She reached into a little red purse slung like an ammo bandolier across her chest and proudly showed me a photo ID, supposedly from some university, the name of which was printed in Vietnamese.

"I am study to be pharmacist."

"And I'm an astronaut."

"What?" She seemed genuinely starstruck. "You are really *astronaut*?"

"No, not really."

I tried flagging down an approaching taxi. The cabbie speeded past.

"Okay, okay," the girl said, almost pleading, "three dollars."

I stopped and looked at her. Her eyes conveyed a persuasive innocence. Some men will do just about anything for a pretty face. I suppose I'm one of them.

"Okay. Three dollars."

I climbed on behind her and we took off, the inside of my thighs straddling her hips, my hands locked around her exquisitely thin waist. If she was an intelligence operative, she was among the most convincing I'd ever met. If I was sitting too close, she never complained.

Don't ask me her name. She gave it to me as we drove, but I didn't catch it; Hanoi's incessant sound track of honking horns and tinny, two-stroke motorbike engines drowned out her words. She dropped me off around the corner from the embassy and asked if I needed someone to show me around the city, a tour guide. When I declined the offer, the corners of her mouth dropped.

"You are married?"

"Used to be."

"You have girlfriend?"

"No."

"Vietnamese girl make very good girlfriend," she said. "Very loyal. Cook very good. Ten dollars a day."

I handed her five dollars instead of the three we'd agreed upon. "Good luck with college."

She tucked the money in her back pocket, disappointed at not having landed the more lucrative gig, and zoomed away.

The US Embassy in the Ba Dinh district south of downtown Hanoi was a six-story fortress of prestressed concrete surrounded by an imposing, eight-foot security fence topped with concertina wire. I handed my fake Dr. Bob Barker passport to a Vietnamese police officer standing guard behind the fence. He eyed it, then me, then the passport again, then unlocked the gate and pointed to the lobby.

"May I help you?"

The receptionist, a blousy, big-boned African American woman, was sitting at a desk on the other side of a bullet-resistant Plexiglas window with a two-way speaker built into it.

"I'm here to see Carl Underwood." I slipped my passport through a slot at the bottom.

She picked up the passport and looked at it like it took effort on her part. Her acrylic nails were long and shiny purple, their squared-off tips painted white.

"Purpose of your visit?"

"It's confidential."

"Sir, I'm sorry, but it doesn't work that way around here. Y'all gotta state a legitimate reason for the purpose of the visit or it isn't happening. Simple as that, okay? Those are the rules."

"Okay, if those are the rules."

"So, the purpose of your business is . . . ?"

"To speak with Mr. Underwood about his many illegitimate children. It's time they knew their father."

She gave me one of those snarky, oh-no-you-didn't-just-say-that kind of looks. Then she snatched up her phone and swiveled her chair away from the window so I couldn't overhear her conversation. When she was done talking, she hung up and wheeled back to face me.

"I spoke with Mr. Underwood's assistant. Mr. Underwood's out of the office."

"Any idea when he'll be back?"

"No."

"Today?"

"It's hard to say."

"Sometime this century, you think?"

She gave me that look again.

"I'll wait."

Across the lobby was a sitting area with two rows of metal folding chairs, six chairs to a row, flanked by anemic and wilting potted plants. Seven people occupied the chairs—four Caucasians, two Asians, and a guy in a brown Nehru-style jacket who looked to be Pakistani—all waiting, apparently, to be admitted inside the embassy itself. Two stout US marines, both Latinos, stood guard in Kevlar and camouflaged combat utilities, cradling their M-16s, scrutinizing people entering and exiting the building. The jarheads were chuckling about something and paying little attention to me as I took a seat behind a man I quickly recognized: Leonard Rostenkowski, whose overbearing wife, Lydia, had chatted me up days earlier in the lobby of the Yellow Flower Hotel. He was engrossed in a tattered copy of *National Geographic* and rubbing his right ear, which I noticed was not small.

"What're you doing here, Leonard?"

He glanced back at me over his half-glasses and blanched, obviously nervous. "Me? Oh, I was uh, just here to, uh, meet somebody . . . " He got to his feet, said something about having forgotten he was supposed to meet his wife somewhere, and quickly left the building.

Definitely strange behavior.

On the chair beside me was a week-old copy of the *Viet Nam News*, an English-language newspaper published in Hanoi. On the front page was a story about the collision between a train and a taxi in which two people were killed, and another about a Vietnamese amateur photographer winning some prestigious photo contest in Uruguay. There was also a piece on the People's Court having handed down harsh prison sentences under the government's new zero-tolerance policy on human trafficking. Four defendants had all been found guilty of kidnapping girls from rural villages and forcing them to work as prostitutes in Malaysia. One defendant got sixteen years. I remember reading intelligence cables back in the day, describing how peasants from rural villages in Southeast Asia were often prime victims of ruthless traffickers who hustled them out of the country and into lives of sexual exploitation or hard labor in places like China, Malaysia, and even the United States.

"Mr. Barker?"

It took me a second to realize that the receptionist behind the Plexiglas was curling her finger, beckoning me. I got up and walked over to her window.

"I was able to reach Mr. Underwood. Unfortunately, he will not be in for the rest of the afternoon. If you want to leave me your number, I will make sure he gets it."

Determining when people are lying is rarely easy. Much depends on knowing how they behave when they're telling the truth—using their habits as a comparative benchmark when you suspect they're being evasive or deceitful. My new friend, the receptionist, had used contractions when we first spoke, before she let me know that she'd spoken with Underwood and that he was gone for the day. During our second conversation, she avoided contractions altogether—"He'll" became "he will"; "y'all" became "you all." Some of the best interrogators around contend that liars are more inclined to avoid contractions, as if using the King's English somehow makes them sound more convincing. My gut told me the receptionist was being less than honest about Carl Underwood's availability.

"Tell him I'll meet him outside in five minutes."

"Maybe you didn't hear me," she said.

"Maybe I did."

I headed for the exit. When I glanced back, the receptionist was on her phone.

Across the street from the embassy was a stall open to the street. An old woman was stirring a large metal pot and serving up chicken soup. I handed her 20,000 dong and she ladled me out a bowlful. Carl Underwood emerged from the embassy about five minutes later and strode toward me with a grimace on his face.

"We can't talk here," he said. "Let's take a walk."

"Gimme a minute." He waited impatiently, biting his left thumbnail and glancing anxiously down the street—at who or what I couldn't tell—while I spooned out the last bit of broth. "Okay, lead the way."

The sidewalk was crowded with Vietnamese. We towered above them.

"What do you want?" Underwood said.

"I want to know why you told the fisherman to keep his mouth shut."

Underwood looked over at me like he had no idea what I was talking about. "What are you talking about? What fisherman?"

"You threatened him if he told anybody about what he saw that night."

"Okay, look," Underwood said, "I seriously don't know who you are or what you *think* you know, but whatever it is, you're wrong."

"You were seen that night, Carl," I said, bluffing, hoping to get a reaction.

A look came over his face, something between dawning realization and horror. "If you think for one second I had anything to do with what happened to that guard," Underwood said, "you're out of your mind."

I asked him how long he'd worked for the CIA. He denied working for the agency. I smiled like I knew better.

"Look," he said, "even if I did, you know as well as me I couldn't tell you."

At least I knew that much to be true.

We passed by a gelato shop, the likes of which you can find at any shopping mall in America, where teenage employees in pink uniforms scoop Italian-style gelato into paper cups. Customers were lined up. Gelato. In Vietnam. The concept for some reason was hard to get my head around.

Dodging motor scooters, I followed Underwood across the street and inside a small convenience store. The shelves were crammed to overflowing with myriad canned goods and packages of dried noodles, all labeled in Vietnamese or Russian. The only items I recognized readily were bottles of Coca-Cola and a broad selection of American-made hair products.

"We can talk here," Underwood said.

He told me he'd intended to call me that day, to let me know that Vietnamese authorities had refused him access to their files on the death of Mr. Wonderful.

"That's the bad news," he said.

"What's the good news?"

Underwood glanced around to make sure we were alone. We were. "The good news," he said, lowering his voice, "is that I was able to obtain information from other channels on the knife that was used to kill the guard."

Lacking sophisticated spectrometers, officials in Hanoi had had the murder weapon flown to Moscow for analysis at the Russian Interior Ministry's famed Forensic Science Center. Russian experts had determined that it was a knockoff of the most popular hunting knife ever produced, an American-made Buck Model 110 with a wooden handle and a folding blade measuring almost four inches in length when unlocked. Based on the amalgam of the metal used to forge the blade, the Russians had concluded that the particular knife in question was either Chinese in origin or made in Taiwan.

"Any prints?" I asked.

"No prints." Underwood shook his head. "There was one thing, though. They found a tiny speck of paint on the handle. Oil-based. Waterproof. It had a high lead content, apparently."

What that told me was that the paint hadn't come from the United States, where lead in manufactured goods has been outlawed for decades as a health hazard. Most likely, Underwood said, the paint was Chinese-made, but that didn't help narrow down where the knife was from, considering that paint manufactured in China is distributed worldwide.

"What color was the paint?" I asked.

"They described it as aquamarine."

Aquamarine? He might as well have been speaking Swahili for all I knew. Beyond the basic shades—red, blue, green, et al—I'm lost when it comes to envisioning colors. I'm not colorblind. You can't legally fly an airplane if you are. But for whatever reason, I have trouble equating names to fancier colors. I couldn't tell you the difference between periwinkle and puce to save my life.

"What color is aquamarine?"

Underwood looked at me funny. "It's a cross between blue and green."

"Good to know."

"There's one more thing I found out," Underwood said. "You know Colonel Tan Sang, who's heading the investigation? He's an avid knife collector."

"The knife belonged to Tan Sang?"

Underwood shrugged noncommittally. "I'm just telling you what I heard."

"Where'd you hear that?"

"I'm not at liberty to say."

It defied logic that a man suspected of murder would willingly confide classified information about his crime to someone obviously investigating that crime—unless he was purposely trying to be deceptive. Carl Underwood Jr. didn't seem bright enough to be deceptive. But, as the old saying goes, sometimes you never know about people; sometimes, the dumb ones turn out to be not so dumb—with the possible exception, perhaps, of former US presidents.

"How long have you been in Hanoi, Carl?"

"Too long. I'm tired of the food, tired of the smell. I'm tired of the way these people are always correcting the way I speak."

"You speak Vietnamese?"

"Enough to be understood, I suppose."

The iPhone vibrated in my pants pocket. The name on the screen said Phu Dung. I told Underwood I'd be in touch, walked outside, and took the call.

"I've left you messages," I said. "Where the hell have you been?"

Phu Dung seemed surprised that I was agitated.

"Working," he said, "for you." In the background, I could hear the whine of jet engines.

As near as I could make out, Phu Dung had gone drinking the night before with a former MiG squadron mate-turned-insurance broker named Cuong. Phu Dung said he confided to his buddy, without revealing any sensitive information, that he'd been hired to help look into the widely reported murder of Mr. Wonderful. Cuong, he said, was very familiar with the case. He was now calling me from outside Cuong's office near Hanoi's

Noi Bai Airport, from which both pilots had taken off hundreds of times to attack inbound American warplanes.

"He told me, 'Phu Dung, I know this man. I read about him in the newspaper.'"

Phu Dung said his friend had told him that another agent from his office had sold Mr. Wonderful a life insurance policy about a month before his death. It paid 100 million dong—about $4,600. Two people were listed as beneficiaries. One of them was his wife. That didn't surprise me, even if they were estranged.

The other person named on the policy, who would share in the proceeds from Mr. Wonderful's demise, was a stunner.

SIXTEEN

The death benefit paid 100 million dong—about $4,600. Phu Dung's insurance broker friend had provided him a photo-copy of the signed policy. Under a heading that Phu Dung said translated to "Beneficiaries," I could make out the name of Mr. Wonderful's widow, Giang. Directly under her name was that of Truong Tan Sang—the purported knife-collecting colonel from the Ministry of Public Security directing the Vietnamese gov-ernment's investigation of Mr. Wonderful's murder. The policy stipulated that Tan Sang and the widow were to split the pro-ceeds from the policy fifty-fifty.

I slid the copy back across the table of the outdoor cafe where Phu Dung and I had arranged to rendezvous, a few blocks south of the embassy. There was more: records showed that Tan Sang had paid the policy's premium himself with a check drawn on his personal account at Asia Commercial Bank.

"Tan Sang pays for an insurance policy on the guy, then bumps him off. He's a big knife collector, according to the guy I was talking to from the embassy."

Phu Dung wore a puzzled look. ". . . Bumps him off?"

"Murders him. Or had him murdered."

"There is that possibility," Phu Dung said.

Call me naive, but I couldn't rationalize why someone would risk his freedom by murdering someone else for half of a $4,600 insurance policy. Granted, $2,300 was probably a considerable sum for the average Vietnamese worker, but Tan Sang was a respected, senior public official. He was undoubtedly well paid, relatively speaking. If he was complicit, there had to be another, more logical explanation.

"Mr. Wonderful sold car parts after the war and invested in apartment buildings. He and Tan Sang had to have known each other exceedingly well for Tan Sang to pay for an insurance policy. What if they were in business together? Tan Sang eventually decides to get rid of him and take over. Happens all the time, bad blood between partners."

"If that is true," Phu Dung said, "why kill him now, after so many years?"

"Who knows. Could be somebody tried to screw somebody out of some money and somebody got royally torqued." My mind raced with theories. "What if Tan Sang found out that American prisoners of war are coming back to kiss and make up with the guy who guarded them way back when—it's all over the news, right? Tan Sang decides it's the perfect two-for-one: he can knock off his partner and pin it on Americans, whom he hates. And, hell, why stop there? Why not kill Jimmy Luc while he's at it?"

"Why would he kill Jimmy Luc?"

"Look, he knows I've been going around town asking questions. He knows I'm looking for anything that would clear the Americans, or at least cast doubt on their having had anything to do with what happened to Mr. Wonderful. Could be he knows that a jealous husband like Jimmy would be a prime suspect in the death of Mr. Wonderful because Mr. Wonderful was sleeping with Jimmy's wife. That's a problem for Tan Sang. He wants to pin Mr. Wonderful's murder on the Americans. So Tan Sang kills Jimmy, too, and calls it a suicide."

Phu Dung frowned, mulling my theory.

"Look, I don't know if they're connected, either," I said, "but it's worth exploring."

"Let's just eat," my interpreter said. "We can think later."

My lunch was a flaky, deep-fried pastry shell called *banh goi* stuffed with minced pork and vermicelli. Phu Dung had insisted I try it. I regretted that I had. Delicious as it was, within a half hour, I felt like a fragmentation grenade had gone off in my stomach. After Phu Dung dropped me off near my hotel, it was all I could do to make it upstairs and into the bathroom. Whether I'd been followed was the last thing on my nausea-addled brain.

I was paying homage to the porcelain gods ten minutes later when the wall phone next to the toilet rang.

"Yes, hello, Dr. Barker, this is Cara at the front desk. Your friend is—"

"—Hang on a second, Cara." I set down the phone, pried myself off the floor, rinsed my mouth in the sink, splashed water on my face, and grabbed a towel off the rack. I felt better, but not by much. "Sorry, Cara. You were saying . . ."

"Your friend is here."

"My friend?"

"Yes, sir. Your friend. She said she will meet you outside."

I thought she might've been talking about Mai. She wasn't.

Linh, the girl who worked at Jimmy Luc's religious artifacts shop, was waiting for me across the street. I had the presence of mind this time to check for surveillance before approaching her. There was none so far as I could see.

Behind her glasses, her eyes were rimmed red. She'd been crying.

"Jimmy, he—"

"Not here," I said, taking a page from Carl Underwood's playbook. "Let's take a walk."

Off Gia Ngu Street and right on Cho Cau Go, I found a narrow alley, more of a passageway, really. It dead-ended at an iron gate and what looked to be a retirement home. An old man missing his lower left leg camped in a wheelchair inside the doorway, his bony hands folded across the tartan blanket that covered his lap, watching us with a blank expression. He was too far away to hear us.

"I thought I told you to go away for a few days."

She nodded, wiping away tears, barely holding it together.

"What's wrong, Linh? Is it about Jimmy? I still want to talk to him. Is he alive?

She shook her head no.

"How do you know that?"

A pink plastic purse was slung across her chest. She reached into it and handed me an envelope. Inside the envelope was a severed human ear.

The short black hairs protruding from the flap of cartilage protecting the canal indicated that the ear was most probably male. The way the ear had been cleaved from the scalp, without jaggedness in the surrounding flesh, told me a straight blade, rather than a serrated one, had been used to do the cutting. The swollen cartilage, spongy to the touch and virtually drained of pigment, suggested that the ear had been submerged in water for several hours at a minimum. The thing you learn tracking bad guys for a living.

"Jimmy's?"

Linh nodded, refusing to look at it. The envelope and its grisly contents, she explained as best she could, had turned up overnight outside the apartment where she lived with her parents.

"Do you know who sent this to you?"

She shook her head no.

"Do you know *why* they sent it?"

"To say . . ." She couldn't find the word in English and finally gestured instead—slashing a finger across her throat.

"To say nothing?"

A downcast nod was her response.

"Talk to me, Linh. What didn't they want you to say?"

"Jimmy very, very bad man."

That would've been putting it mildly given what she described were Jimmy's other business activities beyond selling statues of the Buddha and incense burners to mostly tourists. I got out my phone. We conversed by typing via the translator, passing the phone back and forth. Jimmy, she said, was also into money laundering, fencing stolen motorbikes, and may have had a minor hand in the heroin trade. But her late boss's bread and butter, the girl said, had been in human trafficking.

"How do you know Jimmy was doing these things, Linh?"

She pointed to her eyes.

"You saw with your own eyes?"

She nodded.

"What did you see, Linh?"

"Jimmy. He show me."

"I don't understand."

She took the phone and typed. Jimmy, she said, had blind-folded her one night and driven to a house where several Vietnamese women were being held. He told her that she would be going with them unless she did what he wanted her to do.

"Which was what, Linh?"

She hung her head in shame. Her cheeks were wet with tears.

"Jimmy forced you to have sex with him, didn't he?"

She nodded, trying to hide her face with her hand and the shame that consumed her. I asked her if she recognized the name, Pham Huu Chi, better known as Mr. Wonderful. She didn't. I asked if she knew whether Colonel Tan Sang was Jimmy's silent partner in running young women like her to Cambodia and Thailand. She didn't know that, either. Then she wept. I held her and comforted her as best I could, while the old man in the wheelchair watched us, his lips curled in a slow, lurid grin. I stared him down and he looked away.

"Linh, I want you to listen to me. I want you to leave Hanoi for a few days, until the heat dies down. Do you understand? Leave. Can you do that?"

"Yes."

She said she had an aunt who lived in Hue. She would go there.

"Outstanding. There's one more thing I want you to do for me, Linh. I want you to call me if there's anything you need, anything I can do for you. If you run into any trouble, I want you to call me. Okay?"

She nodded, then asked for the envelope back, and hurried on like some small, frightened animal. What she planned to do with that ear was anyone's guess.

A shortcut led back to the Yellow Flower, a narrow alley crowded with open-air stalls offering mostly baby clothes for sale. Through the crowds, ahead of me, I could see two men watching me. One was the postcard seller who'd followed me before. The other guy I didn't recognize. He had a horse face and was wearing a Bruce Lee T-shirt. The two men stood intentionally in my path. I thought one of them was going to say something along the lines of, "Colonel Tan Sang wants to speak with you. Come with us or we're going to beat you to a pulp," but no words were exchanged.

As I closed the gap, Horse Face flexed his neck side-to-side like he was preparing for war and assumed an almost comically dramatic martial arts pose, apparently having watched too many Bruce Lee movies, then swung his left foot at my head in a high, roundhouse kick. I went low, came up underneath him, and landed a solid uppercut to his jaw while shoppers screamed and scurried, grabbing their children. The guy dropped to the pavement like he'd been deboned. I followed through, using the momentum of my punch to pivot within range of the postcard seller, but he'd already bugged out.

Horse Face wasn't moving. I stooped and checked his pulse to make sure he was still alive—he was.

"Why'd you come after me?" I got no response. I grabbed him by his hair. "Answer me."

He couldn't. He was out cold.

~~~

On the sixth floor of the Yellow Flower, where Steve Cohen and Virgil Stoneburner were under arrest, the mood was mixed. Both men had been apprised that they were being transferred to jail: one more night enjoying the relative comforts of hotel living before being shipped off to hell.

Sitting calmly at his desk, Cohen was predictably professorial, befitting an old fighter pilot who'd set aside his warrior ways to teach philosophy.

"Everything is determined," he said, "the beginning as well as the end, by forces over which we have no control. Human beings, vegetables, or cosmic dust, we all dance to a mysterious tune, intoned in the distance by an invisible piper."

"Albert Einstein's theory of determinism. Every event, every decision, every action in one's life is predetermined by an unbroken chain of prior events, decisions, and actions."

Cohen beamed. "Perhaps I haven't been merely talking to myself all these years, standing up there in front of that blue sea of cadets. You actually absorbed something."

"I absorbed many things in your class, Colonel."

He sipped his tea. "I'm afraid there's nothing you or I or anyone can do at this point that hasn't already been done. What will be has already been."

I didn't share with him what I'd learned about Colonel Tan Sang's possible involvement in the murder of Mr. Wonderful. I figured that would only get him needlessly agitated.

Down the hall, Stoneburner was already plenty agitated by the time the soldiers standing guard outside his room let me in to see him. He paced the floor like a man condemned to death row, wiping the constant sweat from his forehead and ranting about our current president.

"You know what the problem with America is today?" he asked.

I might have offered any number of theories if only to lighten the mood, from too many bacon cheeseburgers to the detriments of major league baseball's designated hitter rule, but I doubted that making light of his predicament would've done him much good.

"What's that, Captain?"

"Nobody's afraid of us anymore," he said, shaking a finger at me. "I guarantee you, had Ronald Reagan been in the White House, he'd have deployed a carrier battle group by now. He would've issued ultimatums that these people would've by-God known he was serious about, and Cohen and I would be home right now. Instead, I'm getting hauled off to prison and none of you incompetent dipshits seem to be able to do a goddamned thing about it!"

The Buddha believed that being angry is like grasping a hot coal with the intent of throwing it to somebody else; the person who ultimately gets burned is the angry one. Stoneburner didn't want to hear that, though. Enraged, he punched the wall, then immediately groaned in pain and clutched his hand. I told him he needed to calm down. He told me rather loudly to perform an anatomically impossible act on myself.

Alarmed by the commotion, the soldiers out in the hall stormed in, ready for action, shouting all at once in Vietnamese and apparently demanding to know what the noise was all about. I pantomimed how Stoneburner had accidentally tripped on a shoe and fallen into the wall, trying to steady himself. I'll admit it was a pretty lame excuse.

"His hand, he needs a doctor," I told them.

"I don't need a goddamned doctor," Stoneburner said. "What I need is you to get the hell out of here and don't come back."

"I'm sorry you feel that way, Captain. I came here to help, not make things worse."

"Just get out."

Calling Buzz, to fill him in on Jimmy Luc, he of the severed ear, was next on my list of things to do. Back in my room, I had just stashed my valuables in the plastic bag behind the toilet tank when the door opened wide. In came Mr. Postcards and Horse Face.

Behind them was Colonel Tan Sang. He was pointing a 9-millimeter pistol at my chest.

SEVENTEEN

I'd been hauled off more than once by the police on other continents, so I was already generally familiar with the indignities one could expect while being paraded under escort through a hotel lobby, this one crowded with members of an Australian tour group who looked to be checking in.

"What the hell, mate?" said a paunchy man with a florid face as Horse Face and Mr. Postcards herded me toward the exit.

"My sentiments exactly."

"No talking," Tan Sang said, his pistol leveled at the small of my back.

The two desk clerks on duty and their manager, Dan, didn't seem surprised to see me being led away with my wrists zip-tied behind my back. Nor did Mai Choi, whose bed I'd shared the night before.

She was standing with her suitcase outside the hotel in stiletto heels and a tight-fitting skirt suit that might have been mauve in color had I known what color mauve was. Tan Sang's gleaming black Lexus SUV was idling at the curb. She gave him a fleeting glance as he strode past her, toward the car. He pretended not to notice her at all. Mai was impossible not to notice. Their purposeful lack of eye contact convinced me that they were more than passingly acquainted.

"Heading out?"

Mai regarded me icily. "I'm waiting for a cab to the airport."

"Why not bum a ride with us? I'm sure your comrade, the colonel, would be only too happy to give you a lift."

She smirked. "I haven't the *foggiest* idea what you're talking about, love."

I wanted to ask Mai what she'd hoped to gain by having seduced me. Before I could, though, Horse Face shoved me into the backseat next to Mr. Postcards. Tan Sang got in on the front passenger side. Horse Face, whose breath reeked of bad fish, threw a coarse, burlap sack over my head, and climbed in on my right. Off we went.

A man forcibly held against his will can deduce one of two things when a bag is pulled over his noggin, preventing him from seeing. One is that he's being taken to a location his captors wish to remain secret; the bag is both a tool of intimidation and an implicit assurance that he'll eventually be released, unable to tell anyone where he's been. The other reason you bag a man's head is to keep him subdued and in the dark until you can take him somewhere remote and put a bullet behind his ear. That Tan Sang was going to kill me made no sense. Several people had witnessed my arrest—the desk clerks, the hotel manager, the Australian tourists checking in. He knew that if I went missing, my government would come looking. Call me dumb, but I wasn't especially worried. In hindsight, maybe I should've been.

"If you don't mind my asking, what am I being arrested for?"

"Public disturbance and assault," Tan Sang said, "and espionage."

"Covering all the bases, sounds to me."

"Silence."

Not to speak badly of my captors' tactics, techniques, or procedures, but there were enough gaps in the weave of the burlap bag they'd put over my head that if I turned a certain way, I could make out some details along our route—sort of like looking through a pinhole. The Lexus wended along a series of side streets before crossing over Red River on the Long Bien Bridge, heading northeast, away from the Old Quarter. We passed a Mercedes dealership, two karaoke bars with neon signs out front, and what appeared to have been a brick tenement building recently torn down. Scavengers picked through the debris like ants on a dirt pile, looking for anything salvageable to sell.

A series of turns down narrow residential streets took us to a dead end outside a small house with old tires and the hulks of dead motorbikes strewn about its walled front courtyard. I was hustled inside where hands pushed me down hard onto an unpadded, straight-backed chair. The bag over my head was removed, but not the restraints binding my wrists.

Slumped opposite me, chained to a chair in the middle of the kitchen where we were sitting, was my interpreter, Phu Dung. He was barely conscious. His right eye had been blacked. His nose and lower lip were swollen. His orange mesh muscle shirt was wet with the blood from various scrapes and gashes on his face. Somebody'd worked him over pretty good. I had a fair idea who.

"Is there something you'd like to tell your colleague?" Tan Sang asked me.

I wanted to hurt him for doing what he'd done to Phu Dung. I wanted to make him scream, beg for mercy, watch his eyes bulge as I slowly crushed his windpipe in my fingers, but I knew that reality, at that moment, trumped fantasy. To acknowledge a connection might well spell the former MiG pilot's death warrant, and mine.

"I've never seen this guy in my life."

"It is pointless to lie. We know he is working with you. We know he works for the CIA." Tan Sang nodded to Horse Face who wedged his thumb under Phu Dung's chin and held his head up so I could take a better look. "Perhaps you recognize him now."

Phu Dung's eyes came into focus if only for a few seconds and he gave me a faint, almost imperceptible nod, as if to tell me he understood what I had to do.

"I'd remember that face anywhere," I said, "and I don't."

He mumbled something. Whatever it was so enraged Tan Sang that the colonel drew his pistol and jammed the barrel into Phu Dung's right ear, screaming at him in Vietnamese. Phu Dung's lips curled ever-so-subtly in a smile, knowing he'd gotten the colonel's goat. Then, slowly, with the gun still in his ear, he turned his head, looked up at his tormenter, and spit in the bastard's face.

Stunned at first by this act of defiance, Tan Sang conveyed his fury in a primal yowl and raised his arm to pistol-whip him.

"Enough!"

Tan Sang stopped in midswing and looked over at me. "You will tell me the truth, all of it," he said, "or I will beat him to death."

Winning at poker isn't always the result of holding a good hand. Sometimes it's a matter of bluffing and playing poor cards well. The same goes for air combat. As a fighter pilot, you're taught that keeping your opponent in front of you at all times literally is a matter of life and death. The "three-nine line," it's called—the span from the three o'clock position of your right wingtip to the nine o'clock position of your left. I had to find some way of reversing the field, getting Tan Sang off my tail and me onto his. Even if that meant bluffing.

"You're not going to lay another hand on him," I said, "because if you do, there won't be enough pieces left of you to stuff in a garbage bag."

"*You* are threatening *me*?" He scoffed at the audacity of the notion.

"Yuck it up all you want, Colonel. You won't find it quite so funny when that Predator up there launches a Hellfire missile and blows your ass away."

Tan Sang blinked like he still didn't understand.

"There's a CIA drone orbiting this location as we speak. You know those two old men you have locked up in that hotel? Before I was sent over here to tend to their psychological needs, the State Department microchipped me, so they could know my precise location at all times. If they don't hear from me at regular intervals, their instructions are to immediately notify the Joint Special Operations Command and the agency's Special Activities Division. And those guys, as anybody who watches television news knows, are only too happy to fire missiles and vaporize anybody who looks like they're even sneezing funny."

I laid it on thicker than I probably should have, letting slip how the intelligence community had perfected technology that allowed third-generation guided munitions to sniff out and destroy targeted individuals like him using facial recognition software.

"What I'm saying, Colonel, is that big bug in the sky already has you in its sights. All I have to do is fail to call in when I'm supposed to, and you're as good as dead."

Was I making it up on the fly? Does Dolly Parton sleep on her back? The amazing part, though, was that Tan Sang appeared to actually be buying it—at least to the extent that he ordered Mr. Postcards to go outside, to see if I was telling the truth about the drone.

"You're wasting your time, Colonel. The Predator flies too high to be seen or heard."

"How would a clinical psychologist know such things?"

I smiled. "Let's just say I'm well read."

The way he ran the palm of his hand across his mouth let me know he was spooked. His attention was now fully turned toward me and not Phu Dung. I smiled inside. Advantage Logan.

"Why did you attack my men?" the colonel demanded.

"I didn't. They attacked me. I was only defending myself."

"You are a spy." Tan Sang pointed to Phu Dong. "He is a spy. We have all the evidence we need."

"What evidence would that be?"

"Photographs."

The images, Tan Sang said, provided incontrovertible proof linking Phu Dung and me to certain "nefarious individuals." He wouldn't reveal who those individuals were or the nature of their alleged nefariousness. When I told him I had a right to see the photos, he kicked my chair over with me in it.

"This is not America." He sneered. "Here you have no rights. Here you are nothing. Do you understand? *Nothing.*"

"You've got nothing on me, Colonel," I said, lying there on that greasy linoleum floor with my hands bound behind me, "and you know it."

Mr. Postcards returned from outside. I couldn't tell what he was saying but it was clear by his gestures that scanning the skies had detected no drones.

"Like I was saying, they're too high to spot. So here's how it's gonna go down: either you cut me loose and I walk out of here in the next five minutes so I can check in with Washington and take care of those two old men like your government authorized me to, or you better start finding yourself a good bomb shelter."

"There is no drone," he said. "You are lying."

"Okay, I'm lying. Or not. Believe whatever you want, Colonel. Only you better believe it quickly, because my deadline's about to pass, which means your clock's about to expire."

After about ten seconds of pacing back and forth and giving me the evil eye, Tan Sang reached into his pocket, flicked open a folding knife, and walked behind me. The blade looked to be about four inches in length. I couldn't tell if it was a Buck, but based on Carl Underwood's description, the knife was not dissimilar in design or size to the one that had been used to kill Mr. Wonderful. For a couple of anxious seconds, I thought Tan Sang was going to stab me in the back with it. Instead he stooped over and cut the plastic zip tie binding my wrists.

"If I you choose to remain in Hanoi, and I find out tomorrow morning that you are still here," he said, collapsing the knife and returning it to his right front trouser pocket, "you will not be as fortunate as you are today."

I got to my feet and nodded toward Phu Dung. "He comes with me."

"Why should he matter to you? You have never seen him before, remember?"

"He either comes with me, or I'll have no choice but to report you to the appropriate authorities."

Tan Sang translated for Mr. Postcards and Horse Face what I'd said. The two thugs laughed.

"I am the appropriate authority," he said with no trace of humor.

I realized my ultimatum sounded trite—threatening to send Tan Sang to the vice principal's office would've sounded only slightly less menacing—but I'd run my bluff about as far as it would go. Besides, saving Phu Dung was never my first priority. He might've been a fellow combat pilot and decent human being, but he was still a contract operative, and a foreigner to boot. In the world where I come from, that meant he was expendable. He had to have known that and the inherent risks before he took the job.

My primary mission all along had been to gather intelligence on Mr. Wonderful's murder and to determine what role, if any, the three former American POWs had played in his slaying. That mission remained largely unaccomplished. Warnings to get out of Dodge aside, I'm not in the habit of quitting any job before it's done.

"Okay, Colonel," I said, "name your price."

He stared at me. ". . . Price?"

"Dong. Dollars. Euros. Whatever. How much would it take for you to release the two Americans and let them come home with me? I'm sure my government would be willing to come to some financial arrangement."

I wasn't sure at all Washington would pony up a penny for Cohen's release, or Stoneburner's. More than anything, I asked the question to confirm my suspicions that Tan Sang was as dirty as they come.

Attempting to bribe a ranking official of the Vietnamese Communist Party, he said with his eyes narrowed and far too much righteous indignation, was grounds for long-term imprisonment.

"I will pretend you said nothing. Now get out. Before I change my mind."

"What makes you so sure it was the Americans who killed the guard?"

Slowly, deliberately, he said, "We have witnesses."

"Witnesses. Right. You mean like that doorman at the Yellow Flower I saw you paying off? You think anything he has to say will hold up in the court of public opinion? He'd testify the moon's made out of spring rolls if you paid him enough. The rest of the world will see right through your little witch hunt, Colonel, and do you want to know who the real victim will be in all of it? Vietnam. It'll be your country's economy that takes it in the shorts if you put any of those old men on trial. How many billions of tourist dollars will be lost?"

I was trying to goad him and it was working. He was clenching his teeth. Tersely, in Vietnamese, he said something to Postcards who threw the burlap bag back over my head once more. I caught Phu Dung's eye before he did. He was slumped, chained and motionless, in the chair. I wanted to offer encouragement, to tell him I'd try to figure a way to get him out, but I wasn't at all certain at that point I could. I gave him a wink. I thought I saw him smile before the burlap obscured my vision.

~~~

Night had descended. My view under the bag, from the backseat of the SUV, was an indistinguishable blur of storefronts, restaurants, and nightclubs. I knew we'd crossed back over the Red River into Hanoi proper because of the rumbling sound the tires made on the bridge. After a couple of minutes of disorienting turns and stops, the right front passenger door opened, Mr. Postcards with his fish breath exited, opened my door, pulled me out, and got back in. I removed the bag from my head as the SUV's red taillights disappeared into traffic.

My phone was back in my hotel room along with my money. I had no idea where in Hanoi I was beyond a street in a residential neighborhood that could only be described as dodgy. Rundown tenement buildings six stories high towered on either side of me. The street itself was littered with garbage and reeked of urine. Five young, hard-looking Vietnamese dudes were hanging out on the sidewalk, sitting on little blue plastic stools about twenty meters to my left, swigging bottles of Tiger beer and eyeing me the way lions do a gazelle.

" 'Evening, gents."

They seemed a bit taken aback that anyone, let alone an obvious foreigner, would deign to address them the way I had, and commiserated in low tones among themselves as if they weren't sure how to respond. Finally one of them got up and strode over with a decided hip-hop hitch in his stride, gangsta-style. Oversized white T-shirt, jeans sagging, wallet chain dangling, cigarette tucked behind one ear, Los Angeles Kings cap pulled on backwards, the brim comically flat, the sales stickers still on—Hanoi's version of some African American rap artist he apparently admired and whose mannerisms he was trying hard to emulate. With a distinctly Asian inflection and decidedly inner-city attitude, he said, "What up, my nigga?"

I wanted to laugh but knew that would only provoke him.

"Ain't nothin' but a thang, my brutha," I said.

"You America?"

"California."

"California? No way. You know my man, Snoop Dog?"

"Can't say I've ever met the dude."

"Got any bread on you?"

"By 'bread,' you mean money?"

He got up in my face, bad ass-like. All 120 pounds of him. "Whatchu think I mean, turkey? C'mon, now, gimme what you got. This be real. I ain't got all night."

"Sorry," I said, "I don't have a damned dong on me."

"Well, you better come up with some, player, right quick, if you knows what be good for you." He backed away a couple of feet and inched up the bottom of his T-shirt, showing me the green boxer shorts billowing over the top of his baggy jeans, along with the Medieval-looking dagger wedged down the front of his pants. The handle was wrapped in black electrical tape.

"Check that guy out," I said, nodding behind him. "He looks just like Snoop Dog."

He turned to look. In a flash, I reached out and snatched the knife.

He stood there with his mouth open, hands wide, not sure of his next move. His buddies weren't sure either. They all jumped to their feet, looking at each other, waiting for somebody else to take the lead.

"You should be careful with this bad boy." I flipped the dagger around and handed it back to him, hilt end first. "You could hurt yourself."

"My man." He grinned gold-lined teeth, then turned and shouted something to his homeboys in Vietnamese. They all eased up and sat back down.

He wanted to know why I'd been dropped off in the middle of the street with a bag over my head. I told him I was on a scavenger hunt. He had no idea what a scavenger hunt was and I didn't elaborate. I asked him where I was. The Dong Da district—the "South Central" of Hanoi, he said with obvious pride.

"I'm staying at a hotel in the Old Quarter, on Gia Ngu Street. How far is that from here?"

"Too far to walk it, you know what I'm saying?"

"I do. You think you or one of your homeboys over there could give me a lift? I can run inside when I get there and get you the money."

For a hundred thousand dong, he said, he'd drive me personally.

"Done."

I followed him down the block. His motorbike, a mud-splattered Honda Air Blade, was parked on the sidewalk. Two little boys watched us approaching and ran away—from him, me or both of us, I couldn't tell.

"What's your name, dude?"

"They call me Hammer."

They, whoever "they" were, could've just as easily called him Spartacus and it would've sounded no less preposterous.

I climbed on the back of his bike and we were off like a rifle shot. Opposing traffic was coming at us from every conceivable direction as we circled through a busy roundabout yet, somehow, nobody collided. The Vietnamese, I decided, had to be among the best drivers in the world.

Hammer was asking me something about Snoop Dog.

"Say again?"

"All the time, on TV, Snoop Dog, he, like, smokes weed, man," Hammer said, turning his head and shouting at me over the tinny roar of his motorbike's engine. "How's he do it, man?"

"I wouldn't know. Pot's not my cup of tea."

"In Vietnam, you smoke weed, go to jail long time. Too much weed, they hang your mo-fuggin' ass. I mean, kill you, man, you know what I'm talkin' bout? But if you Snoop, it's cool."

I could offer no explanation as to why some American celebrities can flaunt their illegal drug use with virtual impunity while the common man goes to prison. At that moment, however, I was distracted. Laser-focused might be a more apt description.

Ahead of us on Thong Phong Street, a black Lexus RX450 was pulled to the curb, parked in front of a small, intimate-looking restaurant called the Bouche Bistro. Colonel Tan Sang was standing on the sidewalk beside the SUV with his arms folded, facing toward the entrance. He seemed to be waiting for someone. As we passed by unnoticed, I observed a man emerge from the restaurant. I recognized him:

Carl Underwood Jr. from the American embassy.

He and Tan Sang shook hands warmly, like they were old friends, then Underwood got in the Lexus with him. The head of a high-profile murder investigation, socializing with a man who might well be a suspect in that murder.

Something about the arrangement didn't sit well.

Eighteen

"How'd you like to make a million dong?"

Hammer looked back over his shoulder at me as we rode on his motorbike past the Bouche Bistro.

"Say what?"

"We just passed a restaurant. There's a black Lexus in front, about to pull out. I want you to follow it—only I don't want the people inside the Lexus to know they're being followed. Think you can handle that?"

"For a million dong? Hell ya, dawg."

He guided his Honda to the curb, braking in front of a vegetable market. The parking area was thick with other scooters and milling shoppers, making it difficult for motorists passing by to see us. We didn't have to wait long. Tan Sang's SUV cruised past after no more than half a minute. Hammer gunned his engine and we were soon in trail.

I thought I might have to school him in the fundamental rules of a rolling surveillance—always maintain your distance and keep at least two other vehicles between you and the subject you're shadowing—but the kid seemed to know instinctively what to do. For once in my life, I was happy to find myself in heavily congested traffic. Engulfed as we were in a slow-rolling sea of mostly motorbikes, Hammer and I were hardly noticeable.

"That Lexus dropped you off with your head in that silly-ass bag."

"Affirmative."

"So, who are you, anyway, man? Some kinda Ice T-Shaft mo-fo or what?"

"I'm the guy who's paying you a million dong when this is all done."

"Damn. I heard dat."

What was a spook like Carl Underwood Jr. doing tooling around Hanoi with a corrupt Communist bigwig like Truong Tan Sang? I didn't know, but I had every intention of finding out.

After less than a mile, the SUV came to a stop across the street from a public park. Hammer hung back and pulled over around the corner without me asking him to—close enough that I could maintain eyes-on, but far enough away that we weren't noticeable. The kid was a natural.

Several older badminton players were smacking shuttle-cocks back and forth across a rope they'd strung up between a pair of streetlights. Skateboarders wearing kneepads and color-ful safety helmets were jumping concrete stairs, sliding down handrails. They looked like American skateboarders in Santa Monica and Rancho Bonita. On the other side of the park, four shirtless soccer players in a loose circle were laughing and prac-ticing their passing. One of them spotted Tan Sang's SUV and trotted across the street to where it sat, idling at the curb with its lights on.

It was too dark to make out much detail and I was too far away to hear what was said. The soccer player reached in through the left rear window, which was open, and received something small, which he quickly stuffed into one of the front pockets of his red, knee-length gym shorts. He nodded ada-mantly to whoever he was talking to inside the SUV, the way one nods when acknowledging a set of instructions, then trot-ted back across the street to rejoin his soccer-playing buddies.

"You wanna go talk to that dude?" Hammer asked gesturing toward the players as the SUV merged back into traffic.

"Stay with the car."

"You got it, bro man."

Past the grandiose concrete mausoleum where Ho Chi Minh's body lay in perpetual state, then west, we followed Tan

Sang's Lexus. On our left, just past a golf driving range, was what looked like some sort of military museum with various MiG-21 fighter jets and surface-to-air missiles displayed on its spacious grounds. If Tan Sang suspected he was being followed, he never let on. Sharp, abrupt turns and U-turns are among the most basic of countersurveillance methods, but the SUV's driver was hardly evasive—until he put on his signal, slowed, and made a sharp right between two apartment buildings.

"Kill your light."

"Say what?"

I reached forward and flicked off the motorbike's light switch.

"I can't see where I'm going, man!"

"Just drive."

By the time we made the same right turn, I'd lost sight of the Lexus. The road ahead was a twisting lane with apartment buildings on either side, barely wide enough to accommodate one vehicle. Twice, we nearly sideswiped parked motorbikes as Hammer struggled to maintain control in the dark.

"Faster, Hammer."

"I go any faster, man, we gonna die."

"We're losing them." Again I leaned forward and reached around him. Clamping my right hand on his, I goosed the throttle. "Faster or no dong."

"You crazy, man."

"Yeah, I get that a lot."

The kid accelerated despite his better instincts and fear. As we rounded yet another bend, I caught sight of the SUV's tail-lights turning down a narrow alley, the mouth of which was all but obscured by the densely packed apartment buildings that lined either side of the lane we were negotiating in virtual blindness. Two seconds later, and I would've missed the turn completely.

"Keep going straight."

"You don't want me to follow him no more?"

"Straight."

I could see driving past the alley that it dead-ended after about twenty meters in front of a single-story, fortress-like structure constructed of concrete blocks that had been painted a disarming lime color. The roof was flat. Heavy security grates barred the front door and two large front windows. It looked like a crack house.

Once we were safely past the mouth of the alley, I instructed Hammer to pull over and got off the back of his motorbike.

"Wait here."

"Where you going, man?"

"Don't worry about it. I'll be back in a bit."

I could smell fear on the kid.

"Look, man," he said, "I don't know what this is all about, okay, but you messin' with some freaky shit. Somebody fixin' to get killed, and I don't want that somebody to be *me*, so if it's cool wit' you, I be on my way."

I wondered how many hours of MTV he'd watched in his short life. MTV. America's greatest contribution to modern popular culture. That and Lady Gaga. You're welcome, earth.

"Wait here for me and I'll double that million dong I was going to pay you."

"Two million? Straight up?"

"Yeah, Hammer, straight up."

We shook hands on it.

The apartment buildings were decrepit and jammed close together. Collectively, they formed a funnel, flanking the approach to the house. There was nowhere for me to hide, no way to advance under concealment of cover. I'd faced similar situations with Alpha. The difference then was that I typically went in as part of a well-armed team, equipped with state-of-the-art night optical devices that gave us a definite tactical advantage against the high value targets we were hunting. Now I was alone, unarmed, and not at all sure what I was looking for. Instinct told me there was definitely something there. How to see without being seen, that was the catch.

All armies prefer high ground to low. Special operators are no different. The elements of concealment and surprise almost always are better maintained when advancing on the enemy from above; people tend to look down more often than they do up. Which was why, ultimately, I elected to sneak up on the house where Tan Sang's SUV was parked by hopping from the rooftop of one tenement to the other.

Climbing up was easy, even for a guy with a gimpy football knee approaching middle age. I found an old ladder lying against a wall, used it to reach a darkened second-floor balcony and, from there, climbed an iron railing to haul myself onto the third floor. From there, I grabbed on to an overhang and hauled myself up, then over the edge of the roof of the apartment building. Crouching low in the dark, I waited for any movement or sound that might indicate I'd been spotted, but saw or heard nothing alarming.

Jumping from one rooftop to the next was about as challenging as playing hopscotch. A few steps back, good running start and launch myself blindly across the void. Piece of cake. Unfortunately, on my third leap, I crashed rather loudly into some sort of knee-high vent pipe. The collision rattled my fillings and produced a major league bruise on my left shinbone, but left me otherwise intact. A dog barked somewhere below me. Again I crouched and waited. No one came running.

Two more leaps across space and I reached the end of the alley. Slowly, feeling my way in the dark, I crawled to the edge of the roof and peeked over. Three stories down and there it was: Tan Sang's Lexus. *Logan, you're such a pro.* I was feeling fairly special about my vast sleuthing talents until it occurred to me that I couldn't see inside the house from my vantage point on high. Nor did I know how the hell I was going to get down off of that roof without being seen and/or heard and drawing attention to myself.

Peering over the edge, I could see directly below me a couple and their three small children inside their apartment. They were all sitting around a TV inside the living room. Whatever they were watching must've been wildly hysterical because they were all laughing. Bolted to their balcony, as was the case with many apartment balconies and rooftops in Hanoi, was a small satellite TV dish. The dish offered a solid handhold. All I had to do was reach down and grab it, use my weight as a pendulum to swing myself onto the railing of their balcony, shimmy down, snag the dish on the second-floor balcony directly below it, then repeat the process to the first floor. But there was no way I could reach down and snag that first dish without being seen, unless the people inside were somehow momentarily distracted.

Directly above me, protruding from the rooftop by about three feet, was a weather head—a thick metal pipe from which six electrical power cables hung, swaying precariously on the evening breeze. Like petals on a flower stem, all of the power cables connected to a central telephone pole down on the street and a precarious-looking jumble of at least two dozen other lines, each one feeding a surrounding apartment building. I took off my shirt, draped it over either side of one of the lines to avoid electrocuting myself, and pulled. The line gave way with marginal resistance, sparking as it landed on the roof. The effort, however, didn't produce the result I'd hoped for. The lights in the apartment below me stayed on.

I repeated the process, draping my shirt over another line and yanking it down. No joy. A third line. Nothing. A fourth line. Nothing. After my fifth attempt, in an instant, all of Vietnam seemed to go dark. I could hear shouts of frustration from all over the neighborhood while the kids in the apartment below me whined in complaint.

Quickly, I reached out, snagged the satellite dish, and, like Tarzan swinging down from the trees, descended from the third to the second floor, strained to catch the second dish, and missed it.

Damn.

The fall was about twenty feet, long enough for me to remember proper parachute-landing techniques I'd learned nearly a decade earlier at Fort Benning where I'd gone through airborne training with Alpha: legs bent slightly at the knees; chin and elbows tucked in; and a sideways roll as you hit to distribute the shock on the body upon landing. I also remember thinking, "This is gonna hurt."

It did. And then some.

My right shoulder felt like I'd gone one-on-one with a freight train. The back of my skull throbbed where it had smacked the street. I was woozy and ached, but nothing felt broken. I quickly shook off the cobwebs, got to one knee, and then to my feet. In the blackness, I crossed the gap between the apartment building from which I'd plunged to the house where Tan Sang's Lexus was parked, and took cover beside it. The vehicle was empty. Time to advance on the house itself.

The number, 22, was painted in white on the wall beside the front door. Crouched there, I could hear the low, angry murmur of a male voice inside. A second or two later came the sharp, unmistakable crack of a human palm smacking human flesh. This was followed instantly by the wail of a woman crying out in pain, and the terrified screams of other women. Somebody in that house was getting a beating.

With the power out, flashlight beams danced behind the front windows but thick curtains prevented me from seeing inside. There had to be other windows in the back or along the sides, maybe even a way to get inside without being observed.

I was crossing in front of the house when the door suddenly opened and two young men armed with AK-47s came barging out looking like they were in a hurry to kick somebody's ass. With nowhere to hide but behind a spindly little bush that came up to my calves, I assumed the ass was mine.

Nineteen

All day. That's how long my fellow Alpha operators and I once were compelled to sit in a classroom, learning how the eye detects motion in low light. The instructor was a nerdy Yale University ophthalmologist with a profusion of nose hair who droned on for hours about cones and rods, peripheral drift illusion, and something called the Pulfrich effect. The only thing I remembered from that day was that cavewomen were gatherers and that cavemen learned it was much easier to spot prey when it's moving. This explains why men today can never find anything in the refrigerator while women can find everything. It was a lesson I tested when the two-man security detail bolted out of the house with their AKs.

Had they turned, they would've seen me. To my amazement, they didn't. As the Buddha said, it's better to be lucky than good. Okay, maybe the Buddha didn't say that, but he could've, because it's the truth. Sighting down the barrels of their assault rifles, the gunmen scanned the street and the surrounding apartment buildings, looking every which way but behind them—where I was crouched, motionless, doing my best to become one with the bush.

Carl Underwood emerged from the house and hurriedly piled into the SUV. Tan Sang shut the door of the house and joined him in the backseat. The gunmen then jumped into the front seats. How none of them saw me, I'll never know. Maybe it was the Pulfrich effect, whatever that is.

I watched the SUV drive away and didn't move a muscle until I could no longer hear its engine. Inside the house, meanwhile, I could hear crying and whimpering. I got up, hugged the wall, and found a window covered by a metal security grate. There were no curtains or blinds, affording me a view inside. It was one I won't soon forget:

I was looking into a bedroom that had been stripped of furniture. Through the security bars, in the light of a single, flickering candle, I counted nine Asian women sitting on the concrete floor. Shabbily dressed, like peasants, they were barefoot and chained together by their ankles.

A window about three meters to my left revealed a second bedroom with eight more women inside, similarly restrained. One of them was crying inconsolably. A guard with a pistol in his belt appeared in the doorway and yelled at her threateningly. The woman sitting on the floor beside her clasped a hand over the woman's mouth, muffling her sobs.

I already ducked under the windowsill to avoid being seen.

Linh, the girl who'd worked for the late Jimmy Luc, had confided to me that her boss was involved in the business of buying and selling women. Jimmy and Colonel Tan Sang were acquainted—a photo of the two of them hung in Jimmy's shop. Clearly, Tan Sang was deep into human trafficking as well, a modern day slave trader. Why Carl Underwood was palling around with such a monster, I couldn't say, but I intended to find out.

~~~

Hammer, my Asian wanna-be Tupac, was leaning against his motorbike and talking on his phone, waiting. That he'd stayed surprised me.

"Where you been, dawg?" he said, hanging up on whoever he was talking to. "I be trippin' out here all by myself, man, you know what I'm sayin'? All the lights went off. I was *freaked*, yo."

I nodded to his phone. "Does that thing come with a camera?"

"Yeah. Good one, too."

"Mind if I borrow it?"

"More like 'rent,' you mean. A brutha's gotta make a living, y'know what I'm sayin'?"

"Okay, how much?"

Hammer tapped a forefinger to his lips. "One hundred thousand dong," he said, like I might balk at the price.

Less than five bucks. Such a deal. "Fair enough. Put it on my tab. You'll get your money when we get back to my hotel."

He showed me how to take pictures with his phone. The procedure seemed pretty straightforward. I told him I'd be back soon and began walking back to the house where the women were being held, passing a sign that indicated the name of the street: Cao Bac Son.

The entire block and the area immediately surrounding it remained blacked out thanks to my electrical handiwork. A girl of about twelve stood outside the apartment building where I'd disabled the lines, playing with a flashlight, shining the beam all over, including at me. I did my best silly Wolfman imitation— teeth bared, growling, hands raised like claws—trying to get her to smile, but I frightened her instead and she fled inside. So much for my endearing way with children.

I wanted to take a quick series of photographs documenting the abuses. But when I got to the window, raised up, and tapped the shutter release button, the flash went off. Nobody was more startled than me. The women inside spotted me and began pleading loudly. I didn't have to speak their language to know they were begging for their lives. Unarmed as I was, there wasn't much I could do immediately to save them. I took off before the guard with the pistol showed up.

~~~

Back at the Yellow Flower, I had to persuade the two desk clerks working the night shift that I was still a guest of the hotel. Their records indicated otherwise, that I'd checked out of the hotel earlier in the day. My clothes had been gathered up, they said, and placed in a storage room for safekeeping.

"If I checked out, why would I leave all my stuff?"

"I don't know, sir." The gold name tag pinned to his white dress shirt identified him as Lap. He had red cheeks and licked his lips frequently.

After much conversation and a call to Dan, the hotel manager, who was at home but who fortunately remembered me, Lap issued me a new passkey to my old room, which fortunately had not been rebooked in my absence. My wallet, phone and passport were still where I'd left them in the bag behind the toilet tank.

Hammer waited for me outside on the street. He'd already uploaded to my phone the photo I'd taken of the women in the house.

"Thanks for the help, my brutha," I said, handing over the dong I owed him.

"Thank *you*, man." He stared at the money like it was more than he'd ever seen in his life.

Shaking hands good-bye was a production. Grip. Pull. Bump shoulders. Tap knuckles. Make your fingers like a starburst. I followed his lead and had no idea what I was doing.

"Take care of yourself, Hammer."

He tucked the cash in his sagging jeans and pimp-strolled back to his motorbike, the way somebody might who's seen plenty of blacksploitation films but never been outside Vietnam. You couldn't help but like a kid that innocently impressionable.

Standing outside the hotel with no surveillance in sight, I forwarded the picture of the women in the house to Buzz. Once upon a time, the old school, analog me would've had fits sending the most basic e-mail. Now here I was, downloading and uploading and sideways loading and doing whatever else one does as a participant in the digital age. I smiled to myself.

Buzz called me back almost immediately.

"What the hell is this?" he demanded.

"What the hell is what?"

"This. The picture I'm looking at that you just sent me. A bunch of women sitting on the floor? Lemme just say, Logan, your photographic skills leave a bit to be desired. What's this got to do with anything?"

"Potentially nothing," I said, "or everything."

I started walking, updating Buzz on what I'd learned of Tan Sang and what appeared to be a human trafficking ring, and Carl Underwood Jr.'s potential participation in the operation.

"You're saying Underwood's directly involved?" he asked.

Across the street from me was a hole-in-the-wall eatery doing a brisk business. Patrons were lined up outside the door, waiting to eat dinner late. Stacked up outside in four wire cages were eight small hairless dogs, listless and forlorn-looking, two dogs to a cage. The culinary reason they were there outside that restaurant was not lost on me. Something sour welled up from deep beneath my sternum and lingered in the back of my throat. I tried not to think about it.

"What I'm saying is that Underwood was there tonight with Colonel Tan Sang. At a minimum, Underwood has to have direct knowledge. Whether he's helping run the thing or profiting from it, I couldn't tell you at this point."

"If he is involved, he's going to Leavenworth—assuming the agency doesn't save itself the expense and embarrassment and just cap his ass. But what I still don't understand is what all this has got to do with them holding Cohen and Stoneburner. And, I guarantee you, the president's people will be asking me the same question."

"I don't have the answer, Buzz. What I need from you right now is to make happen what I'm about to ask for. They're moving Cohen and Stoneburner tomorrow morning to prison. We're rapidly approaching the two-minute warning and I'm basically down to one play. This is either gonna work or it's not."

He sighed and exhaled, letting the air out slowly. It sounded like a snake hissing—a sure sign my old battle-buddy-turned-supervisor was losing his patience with me.

"Well, maybe if you told me what *it* is," he said, "I might be able to help you out."

"It's called extortion, Buzz."

~~~

My ambition was simple: blackmail Tan Sang into releasing the two Americans by threatening to notify his government and international law enforcement officials of his apparent predilections when it came to abducting and selling peasant women. I planned to show him the picture I'd taken, to persuade him that I had him over the proverbial barrel. I knew that one grainy photograph would likely not be persuasive enough to convince him that setting Cohen and Stoneburner free would be in his best interest. I needed more damning and definitive evidence to throw in his face, something that he couldn't explain away. That's where Buzz would hopefully come in handy.

For years, special operators hunting terrorists have commonly relied on digital imagery from Advance Crystal KH-12 satellites operated by the National Reconnaissance Office. Envision a massive camera orbiting 200 miles above the earth that can look down through clouds to photographically capture with stunning clarity objects as small as six inches across. That's the KH-12. You might ask, do such satellites have infrared capacity allowing them to see inside buildings, through roofs and walls? If I said that, in fact, they do, I'd be either fibbing or violating the sworn confidentiality agreements I signed years ago before going to work in the intelligence community under threat of imprisonment or execution. Such oaths are like homicide; there are no statutes of limitations. So I'll just say, "Well, you never know," and let it go at that.

I could've asked that Buzz file a formal tasking, directing that the NRO fly one of its birds over Hanoi to shoot high-resolution pictures of the house where the women were being kept. We both knew, though, that even on a priority basis, it would take several days to run the request up the chain of command, write computer code to shift the satellite into position, take the pictures, review and enhance them, then have the NRO forward them to Buzz's Cleveland operation so he could forward them on to me. By then, the women would likely be gone, shipped off to whatever hell they'd been consigned. So, too, would Cohen and Stoneburner. Transferring the two old pilots from the hotel to prison in advance of a murder trial would surely make the news. Once the story got out, the chances of getting them out were sure to decline exponentially as officials in Hanoi, unwilling to bow to US pressure, would surely dig in their heels amid the crush of international media attention.

We needed to fabricate harder evidence that would convince Tan Sang we had the goods on him, and we needed to do it fast.

"So, basically, you want me to make crap up," Buzz said. "Is that what you're saying?"

"Essentially."

I proposed that Buzz engage the services of a civilian-owned surveillance satellite company, which could respond much faster than Uncle Sugar ever could. There were dozens of such companies in operation—Russian, Chinese, American, it didn't much matter—whoever could capture aerial shots of the house within hours as opposed to days would do. Civilian satellites generally can't provide the kind of high-resolution imagery that top-secret government agency birds are capable of, but that didn't matter, either. All we needed was a few passably recognizable representations of the house as taken from space. The photos could then be doctored to include infrared imagery of Tan Sang and Underwood inside the house. I knew that alone likely wouldn't be enough to convince Tan Sang we had him by the short hairs, so I told Buzz that I also wanted a time- and date-stamped shot of the colonel's black Lexus SUV parked in front of the house with the license plate visible.

"It was directly in front of the front door. There's only one spot. When you see the house, you'll see where the car would've been parked. All you gotta do is insert the car in the picture."

"You got a plate number?"

"Eight zero dash November Gulf dash six three one three two."

Buzz read it back to me to make sure he got it right, then asked me for the address. I gave that to him, too—22 Cao Bac Son. He told me that his agency had recently partnered with a Korean company on another classified project, using satellites equipped with synthetic aperture radar that could take three-dimensional pictures through clouds.

"They work fast and they don't charge much, either," Buzz said.

"How soon can you get me the pictures?"

"How soon do you need 'em?"

I checked the time on my phone—it was twenty minutes to midnight.

"In about eight hours," I said.

"You gotta be shittin' me. Eight hours? There's no freakin' way."

"Buzz, these are old men. They're taking them to prison in the morning. I don't know if either one of them will be able to survive the emotional ordeal of being locked up again that way."

"The 'emotional ordeal?' Jesus, Logan, you really are starting to sound like a shrink, you know that?"

"Just get me the photos."

He promised to upload the massaged reconnaissance shots to my phone as soon as he got them.

Back in my room, I didn't bother checking for bugs. I didn't even take my clothes off. I slipped into bed, exhausted, and tried with little success not to think about those two old men being held one floor above me, and how their fate all but rested in my hands. I thought about Phu Dung, my interpreter, and whether he was still alive. I hoped he knew somehow that I hadn't abandoned him, and that my strategy to free Cohen and Stoneburner would also prompt his release, too. Whether that strategy would prove successful was anyone's guess.

I stared at the ceiling and remembered how it felt to kiss Savannah, the tingle down my spine, the taste of her lips, the way she smiled when we made love. I missed her. I always would. I got up, too tired to sleep, drank some water, and turned on the television to some Vietnamese language movie set during the war with America. It was a love story between a man and woman, both pith-helmet-wearing Viet Cong soldiers. The guy conveyed a George Clooney-like suave. The gal could've passed for Miss Universe. The subplot seemed to involve them deceiving B-52 crews into dropping their bombs harmlessly on a patch of unoccupied jungle, rather than on their comrades. I couldn't understand the dialogue, but I followed the story line easily. The same could not be said for myriad English language Hollywood movies I've had to sit through.

Somewhere around 0115, I fell asleep. At 0427, I was awakened by frantic screaming. I walked out on the balcony in my boxers and observed people on the street running; the action appeared to be taking place around the corner on the east side of the hotel below where the two former POWs were bedded down. Something told me the commotion had something to do with them.

I threw on my jeans, shoes, and shirt, and quickly made my way out of the hotel. What I found on the pavement when I turned the corner made my mouth go dry and my rage boil over. Desperate to avoid going back to a Vietnamese prison, Captain Virgil Stoneburner, USAF Retired, had tied sheets and towels together, knotted one end to his balcony railing, then attempted to rappel six stories down to freedom. That was before a knot slipped and he fell.

TWENTY

Spectators stood around him three deep, the ones in back craning and clamoring for a better view of the gore, all seemingly jabbering at once.

I pushed through the crowd and knelt beside Stoneburner. He was on his stomach, still breathing but barely. His right leg was bent up and under his chest at an impossible angle. Blood pooled on the sidewalk around his head. Pressing two fingers against the side of his neck, I found a pulse, but it was weak. A couple of Vietnamese men, one with a cigarette dangling from his mouth, tried to roll him over on his back, thinking that might help, and I nearly took their heads off.

"Don't touch him, you understand?"

They backed off. The sirens of approaching emergency vehicles pierced the night.

"Hang in there, Captain. Help's coming." I knelt down, in his face, so he could see me. "Just stay with me. You're okay, you're going to be fine."

It was a lie, of course, one of those things people tend to say to calm the fatally injured or mortally wounded. Whether my words had any effect is difficult to say. Stoneburner's eyes were focused somewhere far beyond me. Then they lost focus completely. Some people insist that when a person passes on to whatever exists beyond this life, one can feel their presence transitioning to the hereafter. Not me. I've watched more than my share of individuals, the good and the evil, surrender the ghost up close and personal. Not once did I ever register that sort of holy, body-leaving-the-soul moment. Virgil Stoneburner was alive one minute, then he wasn't. That's just how it goes.

I picked up the top sheet that he'd fallen with and covered him with it just as two of the soldiers who'd been guarding him on the sixth floor came running. They yelled at everybody to move back, jabbing the barrels of their weapons at those who didn't respond fast enough. One of the soldiers tried to shove me out of the way, thrusting the butt of his AK at me. Without really thinking, I side-stepped the jab the way a bull-fighter might, reached back, and twisted the assault rifle from his hands, then flung it into the street as spectators scattered, many screaming in fright. As he stood there, stunned, his partner came rushing toward me, yelling and raising his own rifle to a firing position. I pivoted right as if to run, then abruptly turned into him, catching him in the throat with my left hand. He staggered back, gagging. I snatched the weapon away from him before he dropped it and pointed angrily to Stoneburner's body.

"You're responsible for this. If you morons hadn't fallen asleep or whatever the hell it was you were doing up there, he'd still be alive."

That was only half true. The other half was that Stoneburner's death was on my hands as well. Had I been more resourceful, smarter, I might've gotten him out and he'd still be alive, back in Florida by now with his wife. Guilt washed over me like a cold rain.

Two Hanoi police cars, subcompact Toyotas with sirens blaring and bubblegum lights flashing blue and red, showed up. Four cops jumped out with their pistols drawn, all yelling at me to drop the assault rifle. I did, and raised my hands. One of them wore a snarl on his face that reminded me of one of the Angry Birds on my phone. He walked up and slugged me in the gut. The blow stung but not badly. I'd been hit harder in football practice.

He shoved me at gunpoint into the backseat of one of the Toyotas without bothering to frisk or cuff me, then slid in beside me while one of the other cops got in behind the wheel. I looked back as we were driving away: the crowd of gawkers had grown exponentially despite warnings to disperse. They had pulled the sheet off Stoneburner and were snapping pictures of each other posing with the body.

∿

For the second time in less than twelve hours, I found myself in custody. Angry Bird and his partner smoked cigarettes with the windows rolled up and said nothing as we navigated the streets of Hanoi, bustling even at 0500 hours.

"So, this guy's doctor tells him, 'Sir, I'm afraid I've got bad news. You've got lung cancer from smoking. Plus, you also have Alzheimer's disease.' To which the guy says, 'Well, it could be worse. At least I don't have lung cancer.'"

Angry Bird said something tersely to me in Vietnamese. I gathered it was, "Be quiet."

Near a Georgian mansion that flew the red, white, and blue flag of the Russian Federation—Moscow's embassy, by the looks of it—we made a right turn down a side street, past a guard shack manned by soldiers armed with AKs, and into a gated, modern office complex. The sign out front was in both Vietnamese and English: Ministry of Public Safety.

I was hustled inside, strip-searched, and thrown into a windowless, one-man, five-by-seven-foot cell with fluorescent overhead lighting, a stainless steel sink and toilet, and a concrete slab for a bed. My belt, watch, wallet, and iPhone were taken from me, and I was made to trade my clothes and shoes for coarse, zebra-striped pajamas and a pair of rubber flip-flops. I was concerned that the Vietnamese would find the counterintelligence apps Buzz's people had installed on my phone, but there wasn't much I could do about that. Breakfast was soon served through a hinged slot in the cell door: a cup of tepid green tea that left a bitter aftertaste and a Styrofoam bowl of meatless ramen.

For aspiring Buddhists, incarceration offers an ideal opportunity for meditation, but I'm not much good at pondering my

~ 209 ~

own navel. The detriments, I suppose, of an unquiet mind. So I jogged in place instead, did push-ups and crunches, and sang appropriately themed Merle Haggard tunes as time slowed to an interminable crawl.

At around 0930, the cell door opened. I was shackled and placed in leg irons by three guards who smelled of beer, then escorted down a long hallway to an elevator. Two floors up, I was led along another lengthy hallway to a spacious corner office, the door of which was flanked on either side by a Vietnamese flag. Colonel Tan Sang was sitting behind a desk befitting a head of state.

"A tragedy about Stoneburner, but you will be happy to know that justice goes on. Your Colonel Cohen is being transferred within the hour to our most secure prison facility. He will be safer there."

"Safer from what?"

"The wrath of the people."

"You're the only one who's wrathful, Colonel."

He dismissed my comment with a wave of his hand and ordered the guards to free my wrists but not my ankles, then gestured to a folding chair opposite his desk. I shuffled over and sat as the guards took up station on either side of me.

"You struck a police officer," Tan Sang said. "This is a very, very serious crime in my country."

"But eating dog apparently isn't."

His dark eyes grew hard and flat. "A man facing criminal charges in a foreign land would be best served by embracing a more, shall we say, *contrite* attitude."

I noticed my phone and wallet lying on his desk. "I'm not the one in trouble, Colonel," I said, "you are. Forced labor. Sexual bondage. Peasant women kidnapped and shipped abroad. Ring any bells?"

He folded his hands in front of him a little too calmly and cocked his head, a gesture meant to convey amused nonchalance. "Making slanderous, unfounded allegations against a ranking member of the Vietnamese Community Party is also a criminal offense."

"They're hardly unfounded, Colonel."

"You have proof of these allegations?"

"Abundant proof."

Tan Sang shifted his weight slightly—some would say squirmed—and leaned forward in his chair with his hands still folded in front of him.

"As they say in your country, Doctor, I'm all ears."

I got to my feet and started to reach across the desk for my phone. Alarmed by my sudden movement, Tan Sang sat back in his chair and the guards quickly shoved me back down on mine.

"The phone," I said. "There's something on it I think you'll want to see."

Tan Sang hesitated. Then, trying not to look worried, he reached over and casually slid it across the desk to me.

"By all means," he said.

I knew then that he hadn't uncovered the classified applications imbedded in the phone's software. I was tempted to smile, but I was all too aware that my well-being was still very much in jeopardy, and hinged on the plan I'd arranged with Buzz. It was either going to work, or I wouldn't be going home for a very long time.

"Twenty-two Cao Bac Son Street," I said. "You were there last night, with Carl Underwood."

I powered up the phone, found the grainy picture I'd taken of the women held captive in the house, and handed it to Tan Sang. He peered closely at the screen and offered his own smile.

"I do not know where this was taken. I do not know who the women are in this picture. This proves nothing."

I asked for the phone back.

"You are not in command," Tan Sang said. "I am in command."

"Duly noted. Look, we both know, Colonel, I wouldn't be making these kinds of allegations if I didn't have definitive proof. There may be a way out of this, for both of us. Now, please, give me the phone."

Again, with reluctance, Tan Sang handed it over.

I checked my e-mail. There were no new messages. Nothing from the NRO with doctored satellite surveillance photographs attached. *Thanks a ton, Buzz. Where are you when I need you?* My only hope was that the photos were coming. I had to stall. I had to lie.

"Carl Underwood's already confessed, Colonel," I said, still looking at the phone like I was trying to find the definitive proof I'd alleged. "He's implicated you fully."

"Underwood? I have no idea who you are talking about."

"Well, he certainly knows you. He knows all about the women, and he knows all about your partner, Jimmy Luc, whose ear you cut off and whose body you dumped in the Red River to keep him quiet."

The blood rose in Tan Sang's face. In Vietnamese, he ordered the guards to leave his office and to shut the door behind them. They came to attention, then did as ordered. The colonel unholstered his pistol and laid it on the desk.

"If you think for one minute you will leave this building alive," he said, "you are mistaken."

I tapped the button on the phone to update the list of e-mails. There were none.

"Okay," I said, "I'm gonna lay it out for you nice and plain. Billy Hallady's back safe and sound in the states, along with his grandson. There's no extradition treaty and there's not a chance in hell of them ever returning to Vietnam. Stoneburner's dead and all you've got is Steve Cohen, who spent years being tortured by Mr. Wonderful and his ilk. The war's ancient history, Colonel. You've had your pound of flesh, so here's my proposal: you cut Cohen loose and I'll destroy any evidence tying you to Jimmy Luc's murder and to all those women you're holding captive."

Tan Sang was seething, his rage barely contained. "If you had any *real* evidence against me," he said, "you would have revealed it by now."

He raised his pistol.

I hit the refresh button on my phone.

Still no new e-mails.

Definitely not good.

Even with irons around my ankles, I was confident I could leap over the desk and hopefully avoid a bullet before turning the gun on him, but there would've been little sense in that. The building was crawling with other armed personnel. I knew I wouldn't make it very far. I needed more time. I had to keep him talking.

"So now you're just going to, what, shoot me? What excuse are you going to use, because I don't think cold-blooded murder's going to go over too big with my people, Colonel."

"You were attempting to escape."

"Escape. Right. With my ankles chained. That makes a lot of sense. Nobody's gonna buy that, Colonel. Better come up with something better."

"Very well," he said after thinking it through. "You attacked me. I was forced to defend myself."

"Attacked you with what?"

Again, he had to think about it. "My pistol. You tried to take it from me. We fought."

"Like that's gonna fly, after all the ballistics tests the FBI'll do on my carcass, all the forensics. They'll know exactly what went on here, and you can kiss your political future adios. Adios— that's Spanish for don't be an idiot. Accept the fact that I'm trying to help you before it's too late."

He launched into an angry diatribe about America's imperialistic ambitions and how if anyone had suffered, it wasn't former POWs like Cohen. The Vietnamese people, Tan Sang declared, were the true victims of a misguided and illegal war, himself included. He went on and on, but I was no longer listening because, finally, there it was, on my phone. An e-mail from Acme-Ltd.com, with an attachment. I had no clue what the attachment would show, but it didn't matter; I was about to get shot. I hit download and hoped like hell Buzz had gotten it right.

"You wanted evidence, Colonel? Enjoy."

I tossed Tan Sang the phone. As he looked closely at the screen, I watched his expression turn from contempt to what one could only interpret as resignation. His shoulders slumped and his Adam's apple bobbed. Slowly, he put the phone down on the desk, got up out of his burgundy leather executive chair with the pistol still in his hand and gazed out his office window like a man who'd just been confronted by his own mortality.

I picked up the phone and looked for the first time to see what had prompted such a reaction. In all, there were four satellite surveillance-style photos, all infrared, each taken from a high angle. The first image, a computerized extrapolation of the picture I'd shot and sent Buzz, showed the women sitting on the floor in one of the bedrooms. The second photo revealed a man standing in the hallway outside the bedroom. He was looking up slightly and over his shoulder, exposing his face to the camera. The pixilation was left purposely grainy, but left little doubt that the image was Colonel Tan Sang. Photoshop wizards at the NRO had found a photograph of him in intelligence files or perhaps other open sources and manipulated it for my purposes. They'd typed in his name and date of birth next to his face, along with his height and weight. The third picture purportedly showed Tan Sang's Lexus SUV parked in front of the house. The fourth shot was a close-up of the vehicle's rear license plate. All in all, a masterful job of visual manipulation, but for one glaring mistake: the two shots of the Lexus showed it parked with the front end facing the house.

The SUV had been backed in.

Tan Sang was still staring out the window, mulling his options. Tree branches thick with broad leaves swayed gracefully on the morning breeze like a hula dancer's arms. I worried that he would demand to take a second, closer look at the pictures. I wasn't about to give him the opportunity.

"You've got five seconds to make up your mind, Colonel. What'll it be?"

He turned away from the window and glared at me. "Who *are* you?"

"I'm the guy who can make all this go away, who can give you back your political future. All you have to do is let Steve Cohen go free."

"And what do I tell my party? What do I tell the press?"

Some might condemn me for what I said next, but under the circumstances, it seemed the only choice. One former prisoner of war was gone. I didn't want to make it two. "Pin it on Stoneburner if you want to. Tell the press he did it for all I care. He's dead. He won't mind. Case closed."

Tan Sang sat back down at his desk, pinching his lips with his thumb and index finger, looking away, thinking. Long seconds ticked by before he finally relented with a nod.

"You'll make the necessary travel arrangements for Colonel Cohen and myself," I said. "Your people will drive us from the hotel to the airport. I want two seats on the first flight out of Hanoi tonight, back to the United States. And I want it all in writing that your government will not press any charges against him."

"On one condition," Tan Sang said. "That you destroy those photographs and that you tell no one."

"Whatever you say, Colonel."

It was a lie, of course. The man was morally corrupt, an unrepentant criminal. I had every intention of ratting him out just as soon as Cohen and I were clear of Vietnamese airspace.

I stood. "Oh, I do have one more favor to ask. You'll release my interpreter, Phu Dung, and won't lay another hand on him."

Tan Sang refused, branding Phu Dung a spy. I insisted as a civilian psychologist licensed by the State of California and definitely not as a covert member of the American intelligence community that he was wrong, that Phu Dung had served as my interpreter, nothing more.

"There's no negotiating, Colonel," I said, reminding him of the surveillance photos. "He gets a free pass or the deal's off and you're done."

The colonel smoldered, then unlocked my shackles. "You have my word," he said. "Now go. Before I change my mind."

At his office door, I stopped and turned. "I'm curious. Somebody told me you're a big knife collector, Colonel. Is that true?"

He looked up from his desk, glaring vengefully at me.

~~~

After changing back into my street clothes, I walked out past the guard gate, unchallenged, and into oppressively humid sunshine. When I'd put two blocks between me and the Ministry of Public Safety, in a park where a giant bronze statue pays tribute to the Viet Cong soldiers who fought against the American military, I telephoned Buzz. He answered on the first ring.

"Virgil Stoneburner didn't make it. He fell off the balcony of his hotel room, apparently trying to escape."

"I heard. The embassy just got word."

Neither of us said anything for a few seconds.

"I'm assuming it was an accident?" Buzz asked.

"Definitively? I couldn't tell you. That's what it looked like to me."

"The poor bastard gets shot down, survives the Hanoi Hilton, goes back to the 'Nam and buys it falling off a balcony. Hard to get your head around that one."

"No kidding," I said.

"Anything you want me to tell the White House?" Buzz asked.

"Yeah. Tell 'em the scam with the surveillance photos worked. Hanoi's cutting Steve Cohen loose."

"Run that by me again?"

"They're letting Cohen go. We fly out tonight."

"Holy shit." Buzz was ecstatic. "Logan, you son of a bitch, you did it. You're a goddamned hero."

I felt nothing close to heroic. The mission had been to gather intelligence, but everyone hoped, including me, that my efforts would lead to freedom for Stoneburner and Cohen. Only one of them would be coming home alive. In that regard, I'd failed.

I wondered how Stoneburner's wife would take the news. I felt pity for her, a woman I'd never met.

My stomach roiled at the notion of having scapegoated Virgil Stoneburner and encouraged Tan Sang to brand him a killer, but there was a certain obvious pragmatism in my having done so. The dead are dead. You can't harm them any more than they've already been harmed—unless you assault their memory. The fact that I'd done exactly that, to save my former professor, was not lost on me. I vowed that if given the opportunity down the road, I would set the record straight, clear Stoneburner's name—presuming it deserved clearing.

The question of who murdered Mr. Wonderful remained very much unanswered. Was it one of the former POWs or Carl Underwood Jr.? Was it Tan Sang or untold other possible culprits? The truth was, at that moment, I couldn't have cared less about who stuck Mr. Wonderful and left his body floating in a lake in the middle of downtown Hanoi.

My disinterest would prove short-lived.

Twenty-One

Carl Underwood Jr. was hunched over an impossibly low table outside an outdoor restaurant across from the Temple of Literature, precisely where the woman who'd picked up his office phone said he'd be when I called and identified myself as an old friend from Oberlin who happened to be in town for the afternoon. He was working on a plate of what looked like stir-fried chicken and didn't see me at first as I stepped out of the cab. The man he was lunching with, Leonard Rostenkowski, noticed me right off and pointed me out to him as I came walking up to them.

"Looks tasty."

"How'd you find me?" Underwood asked.

"You're not exactly Jason Bourne." I pulled out a plastic stool and sat. "How goes it, Leonard? Taking a breather from the wife, are we?"

"You got that right." He was eating plain white rice with a fork and a face that said he was no fan of Asian fare.

Underwood looked at us both incredulously. "You two know each other?"

"We met at the hotel," Leonard said.

I asked if Leonard and Underwood worked together.

"Len's my cousin," Underwood said. "He drives a skip loader. He and his wife are visiting from Arizona."

"Cousin Len needs to take a walk," I said.

Underwood lowered his chopsticks and tried to stare me down. "I'm sorry, what?"

"I'm about to ask you some questions, Carl, which may not be suitable for family viewing, if you get my drift."

"No worries," Leonard said, pushing back from the table, "I gotta hit the can, anyway."

"Down the alley, on your right," Underwood said. He waited until his cousin was gone and gave me a hard look. "What questions?"

I held up my phone so he could see the shot I'd taken of the peasant women held in the house. "If you want a better look, I can enlarge the picture. Amazing, all the features on these phones, don't you think? You have to go back to school, just to understand 'em all."

He swallowed hard. "Where'd you get this?"

"I took it. What were you doing there with Tan Sang?"

For a second, I thought he was going to start crying. He wiped his mouth with a paper napkin, wadded it, and tossed it onto his plate. "I was, uh, conducting my own investigation," he said, his eyes never meeting mine, like he really couldn't believe so flagrant a lie, either.

"You want to try it again, Carl?"

I waited. Underwood swigged his beer and signaled for another before he finally looked at me.

"I'm a GS-12. Do you know how much I make annually? Sixty-two grand. Do you know how far that goes when you have three kids back in Virginia and a wife who doesn't understand what it is to live within your means? Her credit card got stolen the other day. I haven't even canceled it. Whoever stole it is spending less money than she does."

He forced a smile, hoping I'd lighten up.

"So you decide to pedal flesh on the side with your friend, Tan Sang, because you can't make ends meet. Is that how it works, Carl?"

"He's not my friend. We've met a couple times socially, that's all. Embassy receptions, political ceremonies, that sort of thing. I swear I didn't know what he was into. That was the first time I was there. As soon as I realized what was going on, I made him take me back to the office."

The waitress brought over a fresh bottle of beer. Underwood chugged half of it with one long swallow.

"What did Tan Sang hope to gain by you getting involved in his little enterprise? Protection? Access to intelligence files?"

"I wouldn't know. I never let it get that far." Underwood was nervously peeling the label off his beer bottle. "The guy asked if I was interested in getting dinner, getting to know each other better. It's not unusual in this business, those kinds of interactions. They're trying to find out what you know and you're trying to find out what they know. The goal is to flip him, get him to come work for you. You know how it works, I'm assuming."

I said nothing. If Underwood knew of Stoneburner's death and Tan Sang's decision to release Cohen, he didn't mention it, and I didn't say.

"My family . . ." The words caught in Underwood's throat. "I know you have a job to do, but if you destroy me, you destroy them." He polished off what was left of his beer, gazing at the bottle.

"Look at me, Carl."

He did, with obvious discomfort. I leaned closer to him, my hands folded on the table, a gesture meant to convey confidence and to let him know in a primal way that I knew everything, and that there was no point in lying.

"Tell me you had nothing to do with the murder of that prison guard."

"Nothing. I swear."

He was fidgety and sweating—typical signs of someone who's lying—but people also fidget and sweat when they're anxious, and Underwood was definitely that. His unblinking eyes held steady on mine when he proclaimed his innocence, but that meant nothing, either. Someone trained in counterinterrogation techniques, as I am sure he had been, would know that looking away when confronted is often interpreted as an indication of lying.

I waited purposely for him to fill in the gaps. He didn't try—a good sign that he was being truthful. Honest people typically volunteer necessary details and little more, while liars tend to pile on the specifics, as if to convince you of their veracity. I watched his hands. More often than not, truthful individuals refrain from touching their faces. A liar will often scratch his nose, or run his hands across his mouth if he has something to hide. Underwood kept his hands on the table or in his lap. I checked his shoes. Liars often subconsciously position their feet in a direction facing away from the person questioning them, as if they're preparing to run away. Underwood's feet were facing mine.

"Until I learn otherwise," I said, "this'll be our secret."

"Thanks." He exhaled, visibly relieved.

I was getting up to leave when he said, "I'm assuming you're aware that Colonel Tan Sang's car was spotted near the lake just before the guard was killed."

"Who spotted it?"

"I'm not at liberty to say. I can tell you, though, that the information comes from a credible source."

"You're telling me Tan Sang killed the guard?"

"I don't know who killed him. All I know is what I just told you."

Was he telling the truth, or hoping to deflect me? I couldn't be sure either way. Walking out, I crossed paths with Leonard returning from the restroom.

"I'm starving," he said. "It's rice everything around here. I'd kill for some real American food."

"You mean like tacos or pizza?"

"Exactly."

∿

The soldiers standing guard duty on the sixth floor of the Yellow Flower looked to have gotten the word that Cohen was being released because they'd all vanished by the time I returned to the hotel. Cohen said he'd received word, too—a terse phone call from a woman at the Ministry of Public Safety informing him he was booked on a flight that evening to San Francisco by way of Seoul and Hong Kong. It was suddenly as if Tan Sang couldn't get rid of him fast enough.

Cohen was subdued. One might've expected the opposite— his nightmare was almost over; he was going home—but given Virgil Stoneburner's death, I more than understood his mood.

"How do you know for certain it was an accident?"

"I don't," I said, watching him fold a dress shirt and lay it carefully in his suitcase, "but right now, we have other imperatives, the first of which is getting you home."

He paused, staring down at the floor. "Virgil was a good man. So are you. I owe you a great debt of gratitude."

"I'm just happy you're getting out of here, sir."

He rolled up a pair of trousers. "I have a little boat, out in Monterey Bay. I try to spend as much time on her as I can. I'd love for you to come up for a few days when we get back. I can pick you up at the airport. We can do some sailing, grill some steaks, decompress. You can stay as long as you'd like. What do you say?"

"I didn't know you sailed, Colonel."

"Oh, yes. Got into it a few years back. The *real* psychologist I was seeing at the time was an old navy man. He said it might be good therapy. Much less stressful than hauling around sixteen thousand pounds of bombs and jet fuel. He was right. Started out in a thirteen-foot Sunfish up at Lake Granby, in Colorado, then decided I needed a little bit more sail and a whole lot more water. Found a sweet little thirty-foot Catalina out in California and that, as they say, was that."

The notion of soaking up the sun for a few days with my old professor would've frankly been more intriguing had it not involved sailing. Not that I have anything against boats. It's just that, when you want to go somewhere, compared to airplanes, they're about as fast as a week in jail. I assured him regardless that I'd try to find time in my schedule. He seemed pleased.

"Well, I suppose I should go do some packing myself," I said and headed for the door.

"I'm reminded of what Aristotle wrote," Cohen said, watching me go. "He said courage is the greatest quality of the mind next to honor. What Virgil Stoneburner did was very courageous."

"I just wish he was going home, too, Colonel."

"I'm not talking about his alleged escape attempt, Mr. Logan." Cohen's chin began to tremble. Tears flowed. He looked away, covering his eyes.

"What is it, Colonel?"

He gestured for me to follow him out onto the balcony. Such precautions were likely no longer necessary, but paranoia in a communist state is hardly an unhealthy practice.

"Stoneburner didn't go upstairs that night to bed," Cohen said. "He was with the rest of us in the hotel bar for a while. Then he went out. Left the hotel. To where, I don't know."

"Why didn't you tell me this before?"

"I didn't want to implicate him in a murder."

As Cohen recounted events that night, Stoneburner had done some serious drinking before and throughout the big dinner with Mr. Wonderful. By the time the Americans retired to the Yellow Flower's rooftop cocktail lounge, he was thoroughly hammered.

"He started going on and on about this whole big plan of his," Cohen said. "How he found out how Mr. Wonderful liked to take walks late at night around this one lake to clear his head, how it would be easy to find him and pay back the son of a bitch for all he'd done. Then he takes out a folding knife and starts playing with it. I thought he was joking around—we all did—but he wasn't. I told him I wanted nothing to do with it. The conversation got a little heated. He essentially called me a coward, said I'd gone soft, and stormed out. Billy Hallady and his grandson left a few minutes later. I finished my drink and went to bed. What happened after that, I couldn't tell you."

"When we first spoke, you made it sound like you had your doubts about the Halladys, that they might've had something to do with it. Now you're saying you have your doubts about Stoneburner."

Cohen leaned against the railing, turning his face to the sun with his eyes closed. "When we first spoke, Mr. Logan, Virgil Stoneburner was alive and the Halladys were safe stateside, where the Vietnamese could never touch them. My goal as senior officer was to get us both home in one piece. Virg's guilt or innocence was beside the point. Now Virg is dead. He's no longer at risk."

Whether Stoneburner or Billy Hallady or both of them murdered Mr. Wonderful, Cohen was unwilling to speculate— in the same manner he would not condemn any of them for their possible involvement in the crime.

"War can wreak havoc on a man's mind long after the last bomb has been dropped," Cohen said. "Being captured by the enemy and tortured only compounds that havoc. Virgil Stoneburner suffered, Mr. Logan. We all did. He deserves better than to have his honorable service to his country impugned in any way, but under the circumstances, I'm not sure what the better course of action would be."

"One thing I don't understand: how did Stoneburner find out that the guard liked to take late-night walks around the lake?"

Cohen pondered the question with a frown. "You know, come to think of it, he never said."

~~~

The front desk clerks all stood and bowed as Cohen and I departed the Yellow Flower for the last time. "Y'all take care," Dan, the manager, said in that slightly unsettling Texas twang of his, shaking our hands and walking us outside, where our taxi was waiting. He then asked that I post a positive review on Trip Advisor when I got home. I told him that I'd only recently figured out how to send and receive e-mails; the chances of me posting a review online, I said, were only slightly better than Kim Kardashian winning an Academy Award anytime soon.

Dan laughed like it was the funniest thing he'd ever heard.

Three police cars escorted us to the airport, lights flashing and sirens yowling. I thought Colonel Tan Sang might meet us there, but he was a no-show. A phalanx of stern-faced Vietnamese government officials in green uniforms (I wasn't certain whether they were immigration or military authorities) carried our luggage and whisked us through the terminal, past several security checkpoints to what passed for an executive lounge. The room was about as luxurious as a bus station waiting area, but it was quiet and that counted for something. We sat on molded orange plastic chairs, alone, and waited.

Cohen gazed wistfully out at the runway. "The last time I flew out of this airport was in 1973," he said. "They drove us out in buses. There was a C-141 waiting for us on the tarmac. That red, white and blue star on the aft fuselage . . . something I'll never forget."

"Must've been quite a moment."

Cohen closed his eyes, remembering. "Even after we took off, we didn't dare think we were free until the pilot came on the intercom and said we were outside Vietnamese airspace. The whole plane went nuts, everybody cheering and crying. That's when I felt relief. Only then. They gave us cigarettes and coffee. After we landed in the Philippines, we had steak, corn on the cob, ice cream, strawberry shortcake. As much as we wanted. Best meal I ever had."

Our magic carpet ride came in the form of a Korean Air Boeing 777 and departed at 2250 hours. We flew business class. Don't ask me who paid for the tickets. To this day, I don't know. I slept most of the way, that first leg, anyway, awakening only to eat. The food was outstanding. Smoked New Zealand salmon, chicken Aventino, and cheesecake. Cohen drank one glass of champagne after another. The flight took six hours and change, followed by a fourteen-hour layover in Seoul, followed by a four-hour flight to Hong Kong, followed by another, nearly sixteen-hour layover.

On the last leg of the journey, fifteen hours in an overbooked Cathay Pacific Airbus A350, our seat assignments were separate. Cohen sat somewhere forward of the wing while I was relegated to a middle seat in the very last row of the plane. The Airbus's audiovisual system had malfunctioned, along with my overhead light, meaning that reading was out of the question and there were no movies to watch. I tried to sleep but couldn't. Same with meditating. Mostly I tried not to think about Savannah and focused on connecting the dots that might lead me to who killed Mr. Wonderful. Or killers. By the time we landed in San Francisco, bleary-eyed and exhausted, I was no closer to figuring it all out than when I'd left Hanoi. My brain was fried. And I still had another one-hour flight to Rancho Bonita.

Cohen was flying on to Monterey, anxious for the solitude of his boat. He'd spent the majority of his post-Hanoi Hilton years studying the great philosophers, seeking some silver bullet I suppose that he'd hoped would help him forget the war. The closest he'd come was chancing upon some obscure Irish author whose name he couldn't remember, but whose words resonated. "To forgive is wisdom," the author wrote, "to forget is genius."

"I had hoped this trip to Vietnam would bring me some peace," he said as we stood in the US Customs enforcement line, waiting to be let back into the country. "I'm afraid it did the opposite."

"I'm just glad you're back. I'm glad we both are."

A US Immigration and Customs Enforcement officer sitting in a little glass booth motioned him forward, ran his passport through a scanning computer, asked him a few perfunctory questions, and welcomed him home. I got the same treatment. Standing a few feet beyond the Customs checkpoint was a lanky blonde in flat heels with kind eyes and an off-the-rack navy skirt suit. A San Francisco Department of Airports ID badge hung from a yellow lanyard around her neck.

"Colonel Cohen?" she said, smiling, her hand outstretched. "Hi, Barb Gollner, airport administration. Just to give you a heads up, there are a few news media folks waiting to chat with you out in the main terminal. We can certainly make arrangements to have you exit the airport without having to deal with them, if that's your preference."

"I'd be happy to talk to the press."

"Very good, sir. Right this way, please."

"Looks like the cat's out of the bag," I said as we followed her.

Cohen stopped and turned to face me. "There are elements to all this, what went on behind the scenes, that I'll probably never know, but it's important for me that you understand, I'm so grateful for all you did. Thank you."

"I was doing my job."

"The invitation stands," Cohen said. "Come up and spend some time on the boat. It'll do you good. It always does me."

My clothes were sticking to my skin. I could barely keep my eyes open. I needed a hot shower and a night in my own bed before I could begin to even think about more traveling.

"I'll be there," I said.

When I went to shake his hand, he hugged me the way a father might've. He didn't let go for a long time.

The "few" news media types to which Ms. Gollner referred in fact constituted a sizable, unruly gaggle of reporters and camera operators who engulfed Cohen like a rock star the moment he emerged from the Customs area. He took the onslaught in stride, answering their questions with fighter-pilot cool, one at a time. No one paid the slightest bit of attention to me as I rolled my suitcase down the concourse, toward my connecting gate. That was fine by me. My part of the saga was over. That's what I assumed, anyway.

Turns out I couldn't have been more wrong if I had wanted to be.

Twenty-Two

Kiddiot rubbed against my legs, purring and chirping, thrilled that I was home. When I picked him up to hug him, he licked my cheek with that cute little pink sandpaper tongue of his, as loving a pet partner as there's ever been.

And if you believe all that, there's a bridge for sale in Brooklyn I'd like to show you.

He treated me with his usual indifference, jumping off the bed and sauntering toward me, bushy orange tail flicking side-to-side, as I unlocked the door and entered our garage apartment. Then, picking up speed, ears back, he hustled past me and ran out into Mrs. Schmulowitz's backyard.

"I was thinking about taking you to one of those fancy kitty day spas on your birthday," I hollered after him, "but you can forget about that now, you ungrateful pelt."

I booted the door shut.

My shoes felt like cement blocks. I sat down on the bed and pulled them off. My socks and shirt, too. All I wanted was sleep, but that wasn't in the cards.

"If you're a burglar," Mrs. Schmulowitz shouted from outside, "I have a shotgun in the house and I know how to use it."

"It's me, Mrs. Schmulowitz." I got up and opened the door.

She was standing there empty-handed, wearing her favorite New York Giants baseball cap, her frizzy hair (this week's color: midnight black) sticking out underneath, black stretch pants and an oversized, white T-shirt emblazoned with a picture of Magic Johnson driving the lane on Larry Bird.

"You don't really have a shotgun, do you, Mrs. Schmulowitz?"

"Who needs a shotgun when your whole body's a weapon, am I right? The point is you're home, bubby. Mazel tov." She gave me a heartfelt hug, then walked in like she owned the place which, in fact, she did. "Big news while you were gone. That meshuga kitty of yours got himself a girlfriend."

"You're kidding. Kiddiot actually *likes* something?"

"Not just likes, Bubeleh, *loves*. A mangier cat you have never seen. When this cat goes to the beach, other cats try to bury her. But your cat appears to have overlooked her looks, and isn't that what love is all about? There truly is somebody for everyone in this world."

I yawned.

"You look pooped," Mrs. Schmulowitz said. "Why don't you take a little nap? When you wake up, I'll cook you dinner. My famous chicken soup."

I'd had more than my fill of chicken soup in Hanoi, but I couldn't very well say no. I thanked her for her kindness and told her I'd see her in a few hours.

~~~

Sleep eluded me. Images of Virgil Stoneburner's body, sprawled on the pavement outside the hotel where he'd fallen, played on an endless loop inside my head. I'd been lying there nearly an hour when Buzz called me from Cleveland.

"Are you watching this?" he asked.

"Watching what?"

"This. On TV. Your former professor, Steve Cohen. He's leading the news on CNN. Why didn't you tell me he was having a press conference?"

"There were reporters waiting at the airport when we got in. I don't know how they knew he was there but they did. I probably should've called and let you know what was going on. I was just too wiped out."

"Didn't you tell Cohen to keep his mouth shut?"

"Was I supposed to?"

"For Chrissake, Logan, standard operating procedure dictates that a classified op remains classified until it's been deemed not classified, does it not?"

"It does. I'm sorry, Buzz. I guess I wasn't thinking." A long silence on the other end followed. "You there?"

"Yeah, I'm still here. I'm just trying to figure out how we stuff the genie back in the bottle. This thing is rapidly spiraling out of control. I just got my balls handed to me over the secure terminal by the president's chief of staff. His boss needs the whole truth and nothing but before he has to stand up in front of the cameras and tell the American people what the hell happened over there. So what I want to know from you is this: what the hell *did* happen over there? Did one of our guys murder this guard or not?"

"Hard to say. I'm not done digging."

"I understand that, Logan. But if you had to guess . . ."

"If I had to guess, my money would be on Billy Hallady or, more likely his grandson, Sean."

"Why the grandson?"

"Because younger men kill far more often than older ones, who know better. And because this one has a history of violence. Because he idolizes his grandfather who was abused by the North Vietnamese. Because he got the hell out of Dodge hours before the body of his grandfather's chief tormenter was found stabbed to death."

"Kid sounds guilty as hell to me," Buzz said. "I want you on a plane first thing tomorrow morning to Salt Lake City. Find him and you get me the truth. Beat it out of him if you have to."

"I'm sure he'd be a lot more cooperative if he knew there was the chance of immunity from the Justice Department."

"I'll run it past the appropriate personnel. Meanwhile, you get yourself to Utah A-SAP. I'll have my people make the flight arrangements and e-mail you your itinerary. And one more thing, Logan. You damn well better keep me in the loop this time. Remember, I know where you live."

I went to bed early that night after a bowl of Mrs. Schmu-lowitz's chicken soup which, I have to admit, was every bit as good as the *pho ga* I'd had in Hanoi.

Kiddiot showed up shortly after midnight, squeezing through his rubber cat door and slurping water loud enough from his dish that it woke me up. I tried to coax him onto the bed with me, but he jumped onto the kitchen counter instead, then atop the refrigerator, where he usually slept. He was still snoozing there, a fluffy orange ball with his tail curled around his face, when I left for the airport four hours later.

~~~

In theory, I could've flown myself to Salt Lake City in the *Ruptured Duck*, but with the wind at his back, the *Duck's* top speed is only about 120 knots. At that rate, factoring in at least one fuel stop, plus deviations for mountainous terrain and, pos-sibly, weather, it would've likely taken me all day to get to Utah. Much faster to hop a commercial airliner. Probably smarter, too, as jet-lagged as I was.

I stopped off along the way at Larry's hangar, across the field from the main terminal, to pick up any messages that had been left on my office answering machine while I was overseas. The red digital light on the machine was blinking the number seven. One call was from that cat rescue agency in San Jose, asking if I'd reconsider serving as the agency's spokesman. Delete. Two calls were hang-ups with no messages. Delete, delete. Two were from prospective students. I jotted down their contact informa-tion. Message number six was an automated robocall offering me an "exciting new way" to reduce my monthly mortgage pay-ment, which would've been cool if I could've afforded a house and had a mortgage to begin with. Delete. The seventh call was a 619 area code and one that definitely got my attention:

"Hey, Logan. Hope you're doing well. This is Alicia Rosario in San Diego. Remember me? Anyway, I'm planning to be up in your neck of the woods on vacation in a couple of weeks and I was thinking about maybe, possibly, taking a few flying lessons. Lemme know if that works for you. Maybe we can get together, okay? Ciao for now."

Did I remember her? Was she kidding? Alicia Rosario was a savvy and seductively earthy homicide detective who worked for the San Diego County Sheriff's Department. I'd met her a couple of years earlier on a gig that had taken me down the California coast from Rancho Bonita to America's self-proclaimed "Finest City." Our mutual attraction was undeniable, but I'd pulled back before we could become intimate. Back then, I was still in love with Savannah, who was now gone. I jotted down Alicia's call-back number that had been captured on the phone's caller ID and left it in a rarely disturbed spot where I knew I'd never lose it—my unpaid bills file—and promised myself to call her when I got back from Utah.

~~~

"That's the only car you have available, a Fiat 500? It's not even a car. It's a riding lawnmower. It's what clowns drive in parades."

The Jamaican-born clerk ignored me, squinting at her computer monitor from behind the car rental counter at the Salt Lake City International Airport. "So it says here you are employed by General Motors Employee Relations, Midwestern Operations. Is this correct, sir?"

"That is correct."

"Yes, well, it says here the rental has been prepaid, and the subcompact is all your employer is willing to pay for."

"But a 'subcompact' implies that it's a *car*," I said. "What you're renting me is not a car. It's a skateboard with cruise control."

It was pointless, I realized, to argue, but it still felt good. She handed over the keys along with my rental agreement and told me where in the lot my tiny clown mobile was parked. It was easy to find, given that it was less than half the size of every other car on the lot. That it was also painted lime green didn't help matters.

Always trying to save the taxpayer a buck. Thanks, Buzz.

People stared as I drove through Salt Lake City. Several pointed. Some laughed. One young guy in a black Ford Mustang wearing his Utah Jazz baseball cap backwards pulled up beside me at a traffic light, rolled down his passenger window, grinning, and yelled, "Hey, bro, does that thing mow the lawn, too?"

An aspiring Buddhist tries to avoid confrontation and seeks never to take the bait. I forced a pleasant smile, my hands on the steering wheel, and stared straight ahead.

~~~

The address on Scan Hallady's driver's license corresponded to a two-story, graffiti-marred apartment building across from a cement-mixing plant, a couple of miles north of downtown Salt Lake City. Square and utilitarian in form, the building looked like it had been modeled after a military barrack. Hallady's unit, number six, was on the top floor. I knocked.

An older Latina opened the door. I could hear young children laughing and playing inside.

"*Hola.*"

"*Hola.* I'm looking for Sean Hallady. Is he here?"

"*Yo no hablo Inglés.*"

"Sean Hallady." I showed her a copy of his driver's license. "*Aqui?* Is he here?"

She shook her head. "No. He no live here."

"Did he move? Do you know where I could find him?"

She shrugged and smiled apologetically, her palms facing up.

"OK, *señora, gracias.*"

I rapped on a few other doors. People either weren't home or they'd never heard of Sean Hallady. One older Arabic man with skin like cellophane who lived on the first floor gave me the number of the real estate company that he said owned the building. I called and left a message, saying I was from the California State Lottery Commission and that I was trying to contact the lucky winner, to pass along the hundred grand he'd won. They never called back.

The file Buzz's crew e-mailed me indicated that Sean Hallady had been working as a food server for the past year and a half at Bindings Grog and Good Eats, a popular beer and burger joint at the Snowbird ski resort. It took forty minutes to drive there, up from the smog bowl that is Salt Lake City. This being near the end of April, the daily crowds of skiers and snowboarders had thinned. So, too, had the ranks of the restaurant's workers.

"Sean's working part-time these days," said the manager, a clean-cut young man who looked like he belonged in the Eisenhower era. "He won't be in until the day after tomorrow."

"Any idea where I can find him on his off days?"

"We're not really allowed to give out that kind of information." He said it like he was afraid I might slug him. "I'm really sorry."

"No worries. I'll find him."

"Could I at least tell him who was looking for him?"

"Let's keep it a surprise."

As I walked toward the door, a waitress in her early twenties with about ten piercings in each ear and a blue streak in her platinum-dyed hair said, "You're looking for Sean?"

"I am."

"You a cop or something?"

"No. I just need to talk to him. It's kind of important."

She pursed her lips, eyeing me, debating whether I was trustworthy, before turning and shouting over her shoulder, to where her manager was standing, "Taking a smoke break, Jason."

"Around back, Angie," came the response. "I don't want to have to keep telling you."

"Okay, okay. Thank you."

I followed her outside and around the corner of the restaurant, near the trash cans and a bunch of propane canisters.

Plowed snow was piled along the edges of the driveway. She dug out a pack of Spirit cigarettes from the back pocket of her jeans.

"They don't like us smoking out front. Not good for public relations."

"Or your health."

"Can't live forever." Angie lit up with a red Bic lighter. "Is Sean in trouble or something?"

"Why would you think that?"

"I dunno." She turned her head, and blew smoke out the side of her mouth. "He's just been acting funny lately, that's all. Not himself."

"Funny how?"

"Just . . . funny. A little freaked out, I guess. He took this big trip with grandpa to Vietnam. It affected him, you know?" She flicked ashes and looked down at the ground.

"Is Sean your boyfriend?"

"Sean? God, no, nothing like that." She sort of laughed. "I mean, he's sorta cute, but he's way older than me, like thirty. Besides, I think he's into drugs pretty hard core."

"What kind of drugs?"

"You name it. Anything he can pretty much get his hands on. So what is this about, anyway?"

I lied and told her I was a friend of Sean's family, and that they were deeply concerned about his welfare. I also told her we were both veterans. There was truth at least in that part.

"Do you know where he lives, Angie?"

"All I know is somewhere down in town." Another drag on her cigarette, then she said, "I do know he likes to go shooting. Real big into guns. Always trying to get me to go with him. I was gonna go, once, but . . . I dunno. He's just weird, you know?"

"Where were you going to go shooting?"

"At one of those . . . what'd you call 'em?"

"A range?"

"Range. That's it."

"Do you remember the name of the place?"

"I'm really not into guns. I'm, like, the only person in Utah who's not, you know?"

≈

Angie wasn't far off the mark in her assessment of the popularity of firearms in Utah, judging by the number of shooting ranges in and around Salt Lake City. The Survival Club, the Rifleman, Snapshots. I visited three of them before I scored a bull's-eye at Blaster Bill's, an indoor pistol range on the town's south end.

"Yeah, he comes in here every couple weeks and runs through a box or two of .45 reloads. Why? What'd he do? Rob a bank?" the clerk asked as he scrutinized Sean Hallady's photo from behind a glass display case filled with handguns for sale and rent. "Bill" was the name tag pinned to his National Rifle Association T-shirt. He had a sandy crew cut, reading glasses, and a handlebar mustache that curled upward at the ends. Holstered to his right hip was a long-barreled, Smith & Wesson .44 Magnum, the model of revolver Clint Eastwood made famous in *Dirty Harry*.

"No, nothing like that," I said. "I just want to talk to him."

Bill gave me a knowing look over his half-glasses. "Mister, nobody comes in here just wanting to *talk* to somebody. Either you're a cop, he owes you money, or he's sleeping with your lady. Which one is it?"

"Mr. Hallady recently visited a foreign country. An incident happened while he was there. I work for the government. It's urgent that we locate him."

"When you say 'the government,' you mean the feds?"

I nodded.

"Let's see some ID."

"It's not the kind of agency, Bill, if you get my drift."

He eyed me skeptically. "Well, if you're one of *those* agencies, why can't you just go find him yourself?"

"I'm confident we will eventually. I was hoping you might help us shortcut the process."

"What makes you think I know where he is?"

"Target ranges usually keep the names and home addresses of their shooters on file for liability purposes."

"Right. So what you're wanting me to do is just turn over his address. What is this, a police state? Brave New World? Typical government. You guys think you're all-powerful. Well, guess what? You're not. Maybe 'We the people' doesn't mean anything to you, but it sure as hell does to me."

"Actually, Bill, Huxley's *Brave New World* was a satirical look at the future, not an NRA manifesto condemning the evils of authoritarianism. You're thinking more of Orwell's *1984*."

Bill didn't like being talked down to, especially by a man who was smaller than he was. He folded his arms across his chest defensively and told me he didn't have to cooperate with me, federal government or no federal government, and there wasn't a damn thing I could do about it.

"Tell you what," I said, trying to keep things cordial, "how 'bout the two of us have a good ol'-fashioned shootin' match? Best out of five rounds. If I win, you give me Hallady's home address. If you win, I'll give you my official Special Forces chronometer." I held up my left wrist so he could see my watch.

"Special Forces my ass," Bill said. "That's nothing but a thirty-dollar Casio."

"Exactly. Do you really think operators wear Rolexes and Tags in the field? You want a watch that's reliable and expendable, that's waterproof down to a decent depth and keeps good time. All the rest is marketing and Hollywood."

"I'm not interested in your watch." He pointed to the door. "Don't let it hit you on the ass on your way out."

"Okay," I said, looking at the boxes of bullets stacked on the wall behind him, "let's try it another way. How about I promise I won't come back here in an hour with a search warrant and a team of agents who have nothing better to do today than turn this dump inside out looking for armor-piercing, cop-killing handgun ammo which, as we both know, is illegal."

He stroked his chin, thinking it over. "Okay, fifty-foot range," he said, "but I get to pick the guns."

"Game on."

Predictably, Bill chose to fire the .44 Magnum he carried on his hip. He picked a snub-nose, .357 Colt Python for me. He knew that his Magnum's long barrel afforded greater accuracy than a revolver with a two-inch barrel. What he didn't know was that I owned a Colt Python; I'd put thousands of rounds through it in training. I'd even terminated a few miscreants with it when I was with Alpha. I couldn't help but smile when he pulled the little snubby out of the display case.

"This is gonna be like taking candy from a baby," Bill said, smirking.

"Never were truer words spoken."

He was correct. It *was* like taking candy from a baby—a big pouty baby with a handlebar mustache. Two of Bill's rounds fell just outside the ten-ring. None of mine did. True to his word, he dug up Sean Hallady's address.

Like they say: it ain't bragging if you can do it.

Hallady lived on Emerson Street south of downtown Salt Lake City, not far from Blaster Bill's, in a tidy brick duplex with a flat roof and a raised, weed-strewn planter box separating the two entrances. His apartment was on the right. Affixed to the front door was a faded American flag decal. Below it was a yellow bumper sticker with red letters that said, "Marine, your best friend, your worst enemy."

I knocked. There was no answer. I knocked again, harder.

"Sean? You in there?"

The door opened wide and there he was. Only it wasn't so much Sean Hallady I noticed. It was the gaping muzzle of the .45 semiautomatic aimed at my face.

TWENTY-THREE

Hallady's bare chest was a tribute to bad tattoo art. Inked above his left nipple was a likeness of Jesus with the words, "I ain't afraid of no ghosts." On his right chest were renderings of a scorpion, an M-16 rifle, and a marijuana leaf. He was clutching a bottle of Budweiser in his left hand. There were traces of white powder below both nostrils.

"Who the hell are you?" he said, his eyes asymmetrical and unfocused.

"I'm just a simple country doctor who doesn't appreciate guns being pointed in his face. Do me a favor, Sean, and put the pistol down."

"Well," he said, slurring his words, pointing the .45 sideways, the way bad guys do in the movies, "maybe I don't feel like it."

"Looks like you could use another beer."

Woozily, he held the bottle up for a closer inspection. That's when I backhanded his right wrist and twisted the .45 from his grip.

"Hey, man, you can't do that."

"Apparently I just did."

"That's my gun, dude! Give it back."

"Later." I slid the .45 into the back of my jeans and pushed him inside. "First we need to have a little chat."

"What the hell. This ain't your house. This is my house!"

"Take a seat, Sean."

I shoved him down hard on a brown corduroy couch that had definitely enjoyed better days. On his battered coffee table were copies of *Soldier of Fortune* magazine and the ossified scraps of a pizza, still in their cardboard box. A Marine Corps eagle, globe and anchor flag was tacked to one wall, NASCAR posters elsewhere. Dirty clothes were strewn about the carpeted floor. The TV was tuned to an episode of the *The A-Team*. I turned down the volume.

"My name's Logan. I'm working with the government. I need you to answer a few questions about your trip to Vietnam."

"Fuck that noise. Come barging in here all big and bad. I ain't talking to you." He folded his arms across his chest. "I ain't saying shit to nobody about nothing."

"I'm trying to help your grandfather, Sean."

"My grandfather?" His eyes got wet. "My grandfather's a great man. He was a hero. In Vietnam."

"So I understand. Lemme get you that other beer."

"Fuckin-A," Sean said.

The refrigerator stank of curdled milk. By the time I returned to the living room with a fresh Budweiser, he'd dozed off with his neck craned back and mouth open. I patted his cheek.

"Wake up, Sean." He wouldn't. I stomped on his bare left foot and he came to with a start. "Here's your beer."

"Cool, thanks, man." He took a long draw and belched.

"Sean, I need you to walk me through what happened that last night in Hanoi."

"Whadda ya mean? Nothing happened."

On TV, Mr. T fired a rocket launcher, sending a truckload of miscreants pirouetting in slow motion across the sky. Hallady was mesmerized by the pyrotechnics. I turned off the tube.

"Sean, I need you to try and focus."

He tried, blinking.

"Personally," I said, "it doesn't matter to me what you did over there. What's done is done. What's important is that we close out the books on this whole thing, put it all behind us, so people can get on with their lives, right?"

Sean Hallady was looking up at me as if I had two heads. "I have no clue what you're talking about. What night?"

"The night you and your grandfather killed the guard, Mr. Wonderful."

"Whoa. Whoa. Whoa. Wait, what the—are you shittin' me? That guy got *murdered*?" He grinned and pumped his left fist. "Dude, that is out-fucking-standing."

I said nothing, waiting for him to elaborate. A look came over his face: realization, followed by fear.

"Wait a minute—you think *I* killed the dude?"

I waited.

"Okay, look." He rubbed his left temple. "I don't know where you came up with that, okay, but that's a complete total raft of bullshit, okay? I didn't murder nobody. Not in Vietnam, not nowhere. You don't believe me, gimme a lie detector. I'll take one right now."

"What about your grandfather?"

"No way."

"Revenge can be a powerful motivator, Sean."

"My pop-pop, he don't have it in him to murder a fly. Anybody who says he does is a goddamned idiot." Sean was starting to get agitated again. "Listen, you know what? This is my house, okay? I live here. And I don't have to sit here, in *my* house, listening to some guy I never even ever met come in here, in *my* house, and talk smack about me and my pop-pop. Now the way I see it, you got two choices: you either leave right now on your own, okay, or they're gonna be calling an ambulance on your ass." He started to get up.

"Sit down, Sean." I shoved him back down on the couch. "We're not done."

"I didn't do nothing! And neither did my grandfather. He's a war hero, and you got no right coming in saying stuff like that. This is bullshit, man!"

"How do you know? Mr. Wonderful gets stabbed to death and the two of you fly out of Vietnam not long after. You've got to admit, it sounds pretty suspicious."

"Look, I'm telling you, there's no way he killed anybody. If you saw him, you'd understand. We got back to the room and went to bed. My cousin's in medical school down in New Orleans, okay? She was getting an award for being number one in her class. Half my family went. It wasn't like he ran out or something. We took off the next morning when we were supposed to. The tickets were bought a long time ago, okay? You can check. I mean it ain't like I'm making this up or some shit."

"How much did you drink that night?"

"Enough."

"Meaning you got drunk."

He shrugged.

"Did you pass out?"

"I don't remember."

"So you did, in other words."

Another shrug. Hallady sipped his beer. "Maybe."

"So, maybe, your pop-pop got up when you were sleeping and left the room without you knowing."

"Look, I'm telling you, he would've never done nothing like that. It ain't like him. My pop-pop, he don't have a mean bone in his body."

"He swore an oath to 'get' Mr. Wonderful if it was the last thing he ever did."

"Where'd you hear that?"

"I read it in the newspaper."

"Yeah? Well, that's bullshit. Newspapers lie all the time."

"So do guys who get kicked out of the corps and use their girlfriends as punching bags."

"I ain't lying."

"If I find out otherwise, I'm coming back and you're going to prison for a long time."

"What about my gun? I got rights, you know."

I ejected the pistol's magazine and thumbed all seven bullets onto the floor. I pulled the slide back, ejecting the live round seated in the firing chamber, and tossed the empty .45 on the couch cushions beside him.

"Hey, man," he said, "you want a beer?"

"No, thanks." A thought hit me as I headed for the door. "You don't speak Vietnamese, do you Sean?"

"Are you serious? Dude, I have a hard enough time with English."

~~~

I called Buzz from the Salt Lake City International Airport as my plane to Los Angeles was about to board. Mindful of the butt-chewing he'd given me for not keeping him apprised of my movements, I recounted how Sean Hallady had denied even knowing of Mr. Wonderful's death, but that he'd possibly further implicated his grandfather by revealing how Billy Hallady may very well have wandered out of the hotel as Sean snoozed in the hours preceding the murder. My game plan, I told Buzz, was to catch a connecting flight from LAX to Rancho Bonita, grab a few hours' sleep, then get up early the next morning and fly myself in the *Ruptured Duck* to Redlands, California, where I'd track down and confront the elder Hallady, hoping to exclude him as a suspect or extract a confession.

Buzz reminded me that the White House, anxious for answers, was still on the warpath. Losing the trade agreement could cost untold American jobs, and losing jobs could prove a liability to the president's political party in the upcoming elections.

"The White House wants to get ahead of the story before it breaks," Buzz said. "That gives us no more than a day. Any chance you can get to Billy Hallady tonight?"

"If you sent that private jet of yours, I could."

"The bird's tied up on another op."

"That's your only jet? What kind of two-bit operation are you running out there, Buzz?"

"We're working for Uncle Sam, Logan, not Warren Buffett."

To satisfy Buzz's demands, I agreed to rent a car after arriving at LAX at 1800. I would then drive to Redlands, about ninety minutes away. With any luck, I told Buzz, I'd make contact with Hallady that night.

"Get on it," Buzz said. "Do the best you can."

I did the best I could. Unfortunately, United Airlines didn't. The inbound jet on which I was scheduled to fly to Los Angeles had encountered an unspecified mechanical issue, requiring a replacement aircraft be flown in from Chicago—a minimum six-hour delay. There were no available seats on any other United flights departing that afternoon from Salt Lake City to anywhere in the Southern California area. Nor were there on any other airlines. And pulling rank proved pointless.

"It's imperative I get to Los Angeles," I told the blue-blazered, June Cleaver look-alike ticketing agent holding down the fort at United's customer service counter.

"Imperative. Great word. Haven't heard that one this afternoon." She pecked away on her computer keyboard, pausing every few seconds to tap her teeth with her pen and frown at her monitor. "Unfortunately, every flight's showing full. The best I can do is rebook you on the replacement aircraft coming in. That'll get you into Los Angeles around eleven."

"OK, look, here's the deal," I said, keeping my voice down so the thirty people behind me couldn't hear. "I'm traveling on official federal business, on a matter of national security. I can give you the telephone number to call of the people I'm working for if you don't believe me. Please, there must be *one* seat available on a flight leaving sooner."

"Honey, do you know how many times a day I hear that 'I'm-on-official-government-business' routine?" She handed me back my boarding pass with a sympathetic smile and gestured over my shoulder to those waiting in line. "Next, please?"

I called Buzz, got his machine, and left a message explaining my predicament, then brooded. By the time I got into Los Angeles, rented wheels, and hit the road, it was more than an hour past midnight. Fortunately this car wasn't a Fiat, but a silver, four-door Toyota Camry.

Satirist Dorothy Parker once famously described the greater Los Angeles area as "seventy-two suburbs in search of a city." Nowhere is that truism more in evidence than east of LA in the grandiosely named "Inland Empire," a jumble of hardscrabble municipalities that meld together along Interstate 10 into one vast, polluted, contiguous, graffiti-splashed pastiche of commercial warehouses and junkyards, of billboards advertising strip joints and ambulance-chasing attorneys. It is, by any definition, an inordinately unattractive stretch of the modern Americana best driven through in the dark. Then there is Redlands. With its lush, Midwestern-style college campus and grand Victorian homes, the town sticks out among its lesser neighbors like a French poodle at a pit bull convention. Traffic that morning was light. I arrived shortly before 0300 hours—too late, I realized, to go knocking on an old man's front door, but not too late to reconnoiter where he lived.

Based on the specifics Buzz's crew had forwarded, Hallady resided on Cyprus Circle in a tidy, pea-green bungalow with an arched roofline and a front porch flanked by Grecian columns that looked like an architectural afterthought intended to class up the place. Parked in the driveway, under security lights that lit up the entire property, was a tapioca-colored Oldsmobile Delta 88 station wagon, circa 1977, with wood-grain siding and a bumper sticker that said, "Republicans, working like crazy to support the lazy."

I parked three doors down where I could keep an eye on the house, tilted the seat back, closed my eyes, and slept nearly four hours straight—the first time I'd done that in as long as I could recall. I found a Denny's about a mile away near the freeway, availed myself of the men's room, and ordered coffee, black, along with a short stack of blueberry pancakes, if only to convince myself that my body was a temple and that I was eating healthily. When I was finished eating I walked outside, sat on the hood of my rental Toyota, and returned Alicia Rosario's call from the previous day.

"Hope I'm not calling too early."

"Not at all. I'm just getting off work."

"Off work when most people are going to work. Such is a cop's life."

"You got that right."

She asked me how I'd been and said she'd been thinking about me. I made a joke, something about probably owing her money, and she laughed, assuring me that wasn't at all the case. Neither of us spoke for a few seconds. Then she said, "So the last time we saw each other, you were thinking about getting back together with your ex. How'd that work out for you?"

Alicia Rosario was a homicide detective. My guess was that she already knew all about Savannah's murder—the story had been widely reported—and that she was testing me, gauging whether enough time had passed such that if we did become romantically entangled, the relationship wouldn't involve her trying to nurse an emotional basket case back to some semblance of mental health.

"She was killed, Alicia. You may have read about it."

"Actually I did. I'm so very sorry, Logan."

I thanked her.

"How're you doing with all of it, emotionally, I mean?"

"Good days and bad. Sort of like life, you know?"

"Yeah. I do. There's a lot of evil in this world."

"Sadly true."

Another pause. Her tone brightened. "So, anyway, you got my message about flying lessons? Sounds like it would be a lot of fun."

"Famous last words. When were you thinking of coming up to Rancho Bonita?"

"Whatever works best for you. I've got a bunch of leave just sitting on the books. If I don't use it pretty soon, I lose it. So, you know, whenever. The sooner the better definitely works for me."

We made arrangements to get together the following week. I would've offered to let her stay at my place, but there's only the one bed, and I didn't want her getting the wrong idea. Besides, if she bunked with me, she'd also have Kiddiot to deal with. I wasn't about to subject anyone to that kind of abuse, especially a woman to whom I found myself attracted. He'd probably find her attractive, too, but one really never knows what a cat thinks of anyone. Especially mine.

My watched showed 0820. I drove back to Billy Hallady's house, hoping to finally uncover the truth behind a brutal murder that had occurred 8,000 miles away, involving a man who'd probably had it coming for a long time. And that's what I found. The truth. Only it wasn't exactly the kind I had anticipated.

Twenty-Four

The bell chimed "America the Beautiful" and the dog inside started barking like crazy. After about twenty seconds, a corpulent old lady, in pink curlers and a pink terry cloth robe, cracked open the front door. The skin of her face was baby pink.

"Ferdinand, hush!" she said to the miniature schnauzer at her feet, yapping and snarling at me from behind the screen door. Ferdinand ignored her.

"Good morning, ma'am. I apologize if I woke you up. My name's Logan. I—"

"Whatever you're selling, we don't want any."

"I'm not selling anything, Mrs. Hallady. I'm here to speak to your husband."

"My name's not Hallady, and my husband's been dead for eight years."

She started to close the door. I opened the screen door and blocked her effort.

"Ma'am, I'm sorry, please, but this is very important."

She took a step back, her eyes wide with fear. "If you don't go away, right now, I'm calling the police."

I knelt and let Ferdinand sniff my hand. He stopped yapping and wagged his stubby tail as soon as I petted him. My new best friend.

"I'm looking for Billy Hallady. I've come a long way to talk to him. I was told he lives here."

"Billy Hallady is my brother; this is his house," she said. "What is it you want to talk to him about?"

"It's about Vietnam."

"You don't look old enough to have been in Vietnam."

Her name, she said when I asked, was Dot. I told her that, like her brother, I'd flown combat aircraft, but not in Vietnam. I told her how much she reminded me of my own mother, whose face I can no longer remember, and how much I loved dogs, which was no lie. I told her that her brother and I had mutual friends, and that I was interested in discussing his recent "vacation" in Hanoi because I was thinking about going there myself. Anything to build rapport and get me inside without having to force my way in.

"Billy's still sleeping," Dot said. "He usually gets up around nine."

"I'm happy to wait. Promise I won't be any trouble."

She thought about it, watching the way her dog was reacting to me. "Well, if Ferdie thinks you're not some psycho, then I suppose you're not. You want some coffee?"

"Please."

I followed her through the living room. The furnishings were a shrine to Naugahyde. In the kitchen was a Formica dining table and harvest gold appliances, circa the Nixon era.

"You want a doughnut?"

"More than life itself."

"I'll take that as a yes."

She poured coffee into a chipped green mug from one of those old, stove-top percolators, then strained to grab a box of Hostess mini powdered doughnuts off the top of the refrigerator. I helped her.

"I gotta keep those things up there or my brother would eat himself half to death," Dot said. "Have a seat."

The significance of her words was lost on me in the moment. As I sat down at the table, my mind was on nothing more than those doughnuts. Some people have a weakness for strect drugs, others for trashy baked goods. You pick your poison in life.

Dot was one of those individuals you meet who have no qualms about sharing their life stories without prodding or, in her case, pausing for breath. In the span of five minutes, I learned all about her two divorces, her failed gastric bypass surgery, her unfulfilling career as grocery store checker, her bouts with cancer, her hysterectomy, the daughter—who took up with a drug dealer—she never talks to anymore, and the son who "decided" to "go gay" and was living a bacchanal life somewhere in the San Francisco area. Not once did she mention her brother, the former prisoner of war, with whom she lived. After a second cup of coffee and having consumed more doughnuts than I'm prepared to admit, I was getting antsy.

"Any chance Billy's up yet?"

"I'll see." She got up from the table, walked to where the kitchen intersected a hallway, and yelled, "Billy, wake up and get your butt in here! There's somebody here to see you."

From down the hall I heard a man hack up some morning phlegm with considerable effort, then respond, "Who is it?"

"What did you say your name was again?" Dot asked me.

"Logan."

"Says his name's Logan!" Dot shouted. "He wants to talk to you about Vietnam!"

"Get in here and help me with my leg" came the response.

"Oh, for heaven's sake." Dot disappeared down the hall. "It's always something with you," I heard her say.

Checking my phone, I found one new text message from Buzz. It said, simply, "And?" I typed, *Meeting with Hallady now.* I debated having one more doughnut and opted otherwise. A man has got to know his limits. Mine in this case was six.

Dot returned, coughing phlegmatically herself. "He's coming." She grabbed an asthma inhaler out of a drawer, held it to her lips, and took a hit. "You know, the head checker at the Safeway I worked at, his name was Logan. Real fresh one, that guy. Couldn't keep his hands off me in the break room. Any relation by chance?"

"It's a common name, Dot."

"Well, you never know."

Rheumy-eyed Billy Hallady hobbled into the kitchen on crutches, coughing. Uncombed and unshaven. Faded long-sleeved pajamas. His left leg, which he had to mechanically kick forward to walk, appeared to be prosthetic from the knee down.

"Mr. Logan." He shook my outstretched hand with his left one, which he could barely raise above his waist. With Dot's assistance, he lowered himself into the chair across the table from mine. "What would I do without you, kid?" he said to her, smiling yellowed teeth.

"You'd probably be dead in a week." She parked a single doughnut in front of him and returned the box to the top of the refrigerator. "Don't ask for any more because you aren't getting any."

Hallady gave me a wink. "Isn't she something? After my wife died, I had nobody else to take care of me so my little sis here volunteered for the duty."

Dot let Ferdinand out in the backyard, brought Hallady a cup of coffee, and pecked him on the top of his bald scalp. She said she had a doctor's appointment at ten thirty, reminded him of his own appointment at noon, promised to be back in time to drive him, and left to go get dressed.

"So, my sister says you're planning a trip to Vietnam and you wanna know what's it like? I was just back over there, you know." He took a bite of doughnut and strained to raise the coffee cup to his lips.

"That's what I came to talk to you about, Commander."

A light came on in his eyes. "You're the gentleman who went to see my grandson yesterday. He called last night. Told me what you said, how you think I killed that guard. I got a call from somebody in Washington after I got back, asked me the same thing. I told her I didn't know what the hell she was talking about."

"Did you kill the guard?"

He set his cup down. "In high school, I was a three-sport letterman. There wasn't a ball that didn't have my name on it. When I took my commission, I weighed one hundred and sixty-five pounds. I could bench over three hundred pounds. All muscle. Not an ounce of fat." Slowly, painfully, he hiked up the sleeve covering his withered right arm. His bicep looked like something a wild animal had chewed on. "This is what that bastard did to me. Strung me up and left me to hang for days, the tips of my toes barely touching the ground, until my shoulders came out of their sockets. Stomped me. Beat me with that tire iron until the interrogation room floor ran red. And you want to know if I killed him? Hell, yes, I killed him. A thousand times. Ten thousand times. Every night in my dreams."

Hallady, I realized, was physically incapable of assaulting anyone.

He turned and watched Ferdinand chasing a squirrel in the backyard. "The VA says I'm 100 percent disabled. I don't have the strength to brush my own teeth anymore. How the hell do you think I'd have the strength to pick up a knife and stab a man with it?"

"What about your grandson?"

"What about him?"

"He was a marine."

Hallady looked back at me, shaking his head. "Sean's a pussycat. He doesn't have it in him."

"How can you be so sure, Commander? He knows how much you suffered. He worships you. He'd do anything for you."

"You're barking up the wrong tree, Mr. Logan. My grandson didn't put that gook out of his misery, and neither did I."

The way he broke eye contact, though, and nervously licked his lips, staring down at his hands, told me he knew things he wasn't saying.

"You know who killed him, don't you?"

"I'd like you to leave, Mr. Logan."

"Not until you tell me the truth."

"I got nothing to say to you."

"The people I work for answer directly to the president, which means whatever you tell me goes straight to the White House."

He looked up at me, glowering. "You think I give a good goddamn? I didn't vote for that son of a bitch."

"Commander, you're a retired naval officer with a distinguished combat record. A national hero, a patriot. This is a matter of national security. You have an obligation to tell me what you know."

I stood as Hallady abruptly grabbed his crutches and willed himself out of his chair, grimacing in pain. I tried to assist him, but he pushed me away. "The only obligation I have," he said, seething, "is to the eternal memory of those boys I went over there with who never came back. You can find your own way out."

He teetered angrily toward the back door.

I wanted to ask him how he'd been able to sit through dinner at some fancy hotel with a sociopath who'd left him a cripple. How do you break bread with a man, exchange pleasantries with him, when he's robbed you of your dignity and health, when he took such apparent delight in your agony? Had I been among the captured pilots tossed into the Hanoi Hilton and survived Mr. Wonderful's brutality, I'm sure I, too, would've dreamed of killing him a thousand times over. Part of me wanted to thank Billy Hallady for his sacrifice. Part of me knew no expression or gesture of appreciation could ever do that sacrifice justice.

"Just one question before I go, Commander. Do you speak Vietnamese?"

"Hell, no."

He pushed open the back door and maneuvered himself outside, no easy feat on crutches. Ferdinand came running up with a little rubber ball and tried to get him to throw it, but Hallady paid no attention to him. He walked to the far corner of the yard, his back turned to me, his gaze to the west. He might've been weeping. I couldn't tell from where I was standing.

Could I have threatened him, forced him to divulge all he knew? Maybe. But there are some things you just don't do, no matter how pragmatically or legally justified. Ethical behavior, the Buddha believed, is based on whether an action is harmful to oneself or others. One's own personal "code of conduct" is how I remember Steve Cohen once defining that otherwise invisible boundary that deters people from doing bad things. I wasn't about to get tough with an infirm old warrior in the name of some international trade agreement about which I couldn't have cared less.

Besides, without even knowing it, Hallady already had given me the answer I was looking for.

TWENTY-FIVE

With the Los Angeles freeway system its usual overburdened quagmire, the drive back to Rancho Bonita took nearly three hours, twice as long as it should've. No accidents, just too many, many people. How they all endure putting up with being stuck in vehicular purgatory hour after hour, day upon day, without shooting each other more frequently than they do, I'll never know. Gridlocked on the westbound 101 somewhere between the Lankershim and Cahuenga exits, I began to fantasize about the A-10s I used to fly, and how its Gatling gun would've easily blown a path through all those other cars and trucks impeding my progress. But then I remembered the Buddha's teachings. *Patience in all things. You'll live longer.*

I turned on the radio and surfed through innumerable stations—Spanish speakers, rap "artists," an evangelical conman imploring his listeners to send him money, and some over-orchestrated country-western yahoo waxing poetic about his big red tractor—before I hit upon Linda Ronstadt singing "Desperado," the Eagles's maudlin salute to lonely guys everywhere. I thought about Savannah and allowed myself to wallow in the luxurious misery that song always brings out in me, but only for a minute. I turned off the radio, trapped on the 101, going nowhere fast, and focused on who killed Mr. Wonderful.

Reconstructing that night in my mind, the question all came down to one salient consideration: if any of the three former American prisoners of war had, in fact, murdered Mr. Wonderful, or if Billy Hallady's grandson, Sean, had done the deed, how could any of them have learned that the former prison guard enjoyed late-night walks around the lake in downtown Hanoi where his body was discovered? The Halladys didn't speak Vietnamese. Neither did the late Virgil Stoneburner.

Steve Cohen spoke Vietnamese fluently.

Hard as it was for me to conceive, there was no denying the possibility that my reasoned, insightful former professor, whose love of philosophy and alternative thinking had ultimately helped reshape my taste for violence, had himself committed the most violent of acts.

I called Buzz and told him that I was driving home to Rancho Bonita, where I intended to turn in my rental car, then fly the *Ruptured Duck* up to Monterey that evening to confront Cohen.

"And how sure are you that it is Cohen?"

"I'm not, Buzz, but that's as good as I've got right now."

"The president doesn't want to know if it is as 'good as you got,' Logan. He wants to know if Cohen's the guy, yes or no. If Cohen *is* the guy, they're gonna need time with the legal beagles over at Justice to figure out what to do with him."

"Understood. I'll get there as fast as I can."

"You're gonna need a backup team," Buzz said. "We've got assets in San Francisco. I can have a quick reaction force on station by midmorning. DOD's got that language institute in Monterey. It's a secure facility. You can stage there before engaging."

"The only thing a quick reaction force'll do is scare the guy into having a coronary. We're talking about an old man here, Buzz, not al-Qaeda."

"A cornered dog is still a cornered dog. Young or old, Logan, they're both capable of biting your face. You've been around. You should know that."

"Look, I go back a long way with this guy. I just find it hard to believe he's capable of going postal on me, guilty or otherwise."

"You didn't believe he was capable of murder, either, before you called just now to tell me you think he may be dirty."

"Touché."

I made arrangements to rendezvous with Buzz's QRF force at 0900 the next day in Monterey, a scenic seaside community south of San Francisco that I was more than passingly familiar with. When I was with Alpha, I'd spent three months there at the Defense Department's language institute, learning enough Arabic to order a decent falafel, and to make myself understood when ordering HVTs to drop their weapons, before shooting them anyway. Dead, I found, was always a much easier way to go when hunting high value targets who were wanted dead or alive. Less risk that way of being misunderstood linguistically.

From Washington's perspective, Buzz said, the situation involving the Vietnamese was beginning to unravel. A newspaper in Boca Raton, where Virgil Stoneburner lived, had somehow gotten wind of his death in Hanoi and run a short piece, which had been picked up by other papers in south Florida. The White House was beginning to field inquiries from other media outlets.

"One way or the other," Buzz said, "this thing is gonna break wide open, probably by no later than tomorrow. The newshounds are gonna want to know whether your guy did it or not. Sounds to me like he did."

"We'll find out."

"Just so we're clear on the stakes, Logan, the most powerful man on the planet is personally counting on you—and, no, I'm not talking about me. Plus, international free trade and socioeconomic stability in Southeast Asia hang in the balance. Not to put pressure on you or anything."

"What pressure?"

Buzz wished me good hunting and hung up.

Miraculously traffic on the 101 started moving again—then quickly stopped. Again. I'd advanced approximately fifty meters over the past two minutes. At this rate, I'd make it back to Rancho Bonita sometime next year.

My intention was to fly that night to Monterey, but those aspirations were put on hold the moment I reached the crest of the Conejo Grade west of Thousand Oaks. Across the farm fields of the Oxnard Plain, as far north as I could see, the coast of California was blanketed in fog. I could tell the ceiling was unusually low, probably less than 200 feet. Taking off at night in that kind of soup wouldn't necessarily pose a problem. However, if the *Duck*'s engine suddenly quit and I had to attempt a landing, alone, without an autopilot, well, that was potentially a big problem. I decided I'd wait until morning and reassess the weather before launching or not. Worst case: I could always catch a few hours' sleep, roll out of the rack at zero dark, and drive in my truck to Monterey. From Rancho Bonita, I'd be looking at about five long hours on the road, versus two in the air. When you're a pilot, driving is an anathema, a mode of transportation intended for mere mortals. I preferred to fly.

~~~

Mrs. Schmulowitz was clad in a pair of farmer's bib overall shorts. She'd been gardening all day.

"I'm making liver and onions for dinner," she said, washing her hands at the kitchen sink. "I'll make you some, too."

I'll eat just about anything—and have—but *liver*? No can do.

"That's very nice of you, Mrs. Schmulowitz, but, really, I'm not hungry."

"Not hungry? You must not be feeling well. C'mere, let's have a look at you." She quickly dried her hands on a New York Giants dish towel, reached up, and pressed her left palm to my forehead. "Not feverish." She probed my neck. "No swollen glands. Stick out your tongue."

"I feel fine, Mrs. Schmulowitz. I'm just not in the mood for liver, that's all."

"Liver's good for you. It's loaded with iron."

"How about we go out to eat instead? My treat."

"You have no money, bubby."

"Actually, Mrs. Schmulowitz, I'm doing pretty well right now. C'mon, for once, let me spring for dinner."

She tapped her chin, debating my offer. "You know, come to think of it, I am in the mood for a little schnitzel."

"Schnitzel it is."

"*Wunderbar*! I'll go change my clothes. I won't be but a minute."

∼∼∼

Unfortunately, the only German restaurant in Rancho Bonita was run by a dictatorial woman from Munich named Gert who wore lederhosen and reeked of unfiltered Camels. Every hour or so, she'd go around handing out lyric sheets printed in German, put on German music, and demand that diners sing along without telling anyone what exactly they were singing. Mrs. Schmulowitz dubbed her "Grandma Adolph."

"How's your schnitzel?" Gert asked me between songs, more of an inquisition than a question.

"No complaints."

"*Gut. Gesunder appetit.*"

After she moved on, Mrs. Schmulowitz said, with one eyebrow raised, "Notice how she didn't ask me how *my* schnitzel was?"

"How is your schnitzel, Mrs. Schmulowitz?"

"My schnitzel is fine. That's not the point. Do you want to know *why* she didn't ask me?"

"Because she's jealous of your dazzling beauty."

Whatever my landlady was about to say in condemnation of our hostess in particular and the German people in general went right out the window amid my apparently successful effort to avoid conflict by employing gratuitous flattery. She knew what I was doing and blew me a kiss across the table anyway.

"*Oy gevalt*, the last time a man commented on my 'dazzling beauty,' Jimmy Carter was in the White House. I will admit to you right here and now, bubby, that I lusted after that man. Which is why I purposely avoided visiting our nation's capital when he was in office. That reminds me of a story."

I smiled and nodded in all the right places as Mrs. Schmulowitz droned on about the time she led a field trip to Washington. After the kids had all bedded down that night in the hotel, she said, she ended up plying the streets of Georgetown in the backseat of Henry Kissinger's stretch limo with a magnum of Dom Pérignon. When Kissinger got too frisky, as was his reputation, apparently, Mrs. Schmulowitz let him have it "right in the mansicles."

Truthfully, though, I wasn't paying much attention. My thoughts were on the morning, how I was going to get to Monterey and, once there, how I was going to extract a confession from Steve Cohen about what had happened that night in Hanoi. Whether or not he was a killer, as far as I was concerned, the psychological scars he bore from his years as a prisoner of war, the sacrifices he'd suffered for his country, afforded him a certain respect. In that context, the notion of trying to dislodge the truth from him through manipulation or other interrogation techniques seemed distasteful to me. He deserved to be dealt with in a straightforward manner, and that's what I intended to do.

Twenty-Six

Sunrise came officially at 0616 hours. I was up, showered, and on my way to the Rancho Bonita Municipal Airport a half hour before then—but not before tucking my two-inch Colt revolver into a side pocket of my flight bag. With all due respect to the Buddha and his preaching about passivity, nothing is quite as comforting as having a reliable firearm within easy reach when heading into harm's way.

Curled asleep atop the refrigerator, Kiddiot never budged as I left.

The fog from the previous evening had lifted significantly by the time I parked my truck and got to the plane. I telephoned Flight Service and filed an instrument flight plan to the Monterey Regional Airport, a distance of about 190 miles, then did a walk-around inspection of the *Duck*, making sure all was airworthy. A squadron mate I'd flown with during Desert Storm told me once that there are only two things that can happen to a pilot. The first is that you'll walk out to your aircraft one day knowing it's your last flight. The other is that, one day, you'll walk out to your airplane *not* knowing it's your last flight. I hoped that this flight, as I always hoped, would not be the latter.

Finding no major anomalies on the *Duck*, I climbed in, buckled up and, after receiving the necessary clearances from air traffic control, was soon ready to depart.

"Winds variable at three," the tower controller said in my ears. "Cessna Four Charlie Lima, cleared for takeoff, Runway two-six."

Feet off the brakes. Throttle to the firewall. One eye on the centerline, the other on the gauges. At fifty-five knots, I began smoothly pulling back on the yoke. The *Duck* raised his nose like a dog sniffing the air and, just like that, we were airborne. Almost immediately, we were enveloped in dark gray clouds.

No matter how many times you do it, it's an oddly exhilarating feeling that instant when you lose sight of the ground at the controls of a hurtling piece of machinery that can kill you faster than just about anything if you don't keep a careful eye on your flight instruments. But on that morning, climbing out of Rancho Bonita at a respectable 800 feet per minute, I wasn't in the coastal overcast very long. The layer quickly gave way to piercing sunshine, revealing the whole of the earth below enveloped in a soft blanket of white.

Leveling off at 8,000 feet, I could see all the way from the Pacific, east to the Sierra Nevada and beyond. It was one of those mornings that make you feel good just to be alive.

I hoped I'd still feel the same way after confronting Steve Cohen.

~~~

Del Monte Aviation, the executive air terminal at the Monterey airport on whose ramp I parked, catered to high-rolling corporate jets, but they couldn't have been any more welcoming to me and my scruffy 172. The smiling line attendant, a freckled towhead who introduced himself as "Nick," had the *Duck*'s wings tied down even before I opened my door. He offered me a ride in his golf cart to the terminal, which was less than one hundred meters away. I told him I could use the walk.

"You need your windscreen washed or anything?"

"That would be great, Nick. Thanks." I tipped him five bucks, grabbed my flight bag out of the backseat, and headed inside.

A muscular dude in black steel-toed jump boots, Levis, and a forest-green polo shirt was waiting for me with his hands on his hips. He bore more than a passing resemblance to the late actor Charles Bronson, right down to the flinty eyes.

"You Logan?"

"I am."

"Name's Hersh. Any friend of Buzz's."

"Nice to meet you, Hersh."

We shook hands. I told the friendly brunette behind the reception counter that I planned to be in Monterey most of the day and asked that my plane be refueled, then grabbed a couple of freshly baked chocolate chip cookies from a tray on the counter and followed Hersh out the automatic-opening door.

Parked at the curb was a black Lincoln Navigator. Occupying the driver's seat was a gum-chewing, light-skinned African American woman in her midthirties. She wore big round sunglasses. Her shoulder-length hair was dyed blonde and braided in beaded cornrows. A pistol protruded from underneath her untucked, blue-denim work shirt. The shirt was embroidered with butterflies.

"This is Mercy," Hersh said as I climbed into the front passenger seat. "She's running this op."

She made no attempt to shake my hand. She didn't even look at me. "You packing a gun, cowboy?"

"Got a two-inch revolver in my bag."

"A snubby? Hell, man, that's no gun. That's a joke."

"So size does matter. Is that what you're saying?"

She didn't smile. "I need to break out some ID."

I handed her my driver's license. She studied it over the tops of her sunglasses. Her eyes were light green. Satisfied I was who I was supposed to be, she gave me back the license, put the Lincoln in drive, and merged into traffic.

"When did you guys get in?" I asked.

"Last night," Hersh said from the backseat.

"You based in San Francisco?"

"That's on a need-to-know basis," Mercy said, cracking her gum, "and you don't need to know."

"Well," I said, "this has all the makings of a beautiful friendship."

Back in the day, operators didn't treat each other with such brusqueness—those assigned to the same unit, anyway. But times change, I suppose, and so do people.

They didn't say anything else for the rest of the ride and neither did I.

Our destination was an old motor lodge on Lighthouse Avenue in nearby Pacific Grove advertising "air-conditioning, free ice and HBO" on its marquis. The kind of motel you can rent by the hour, if that's your thing. In room number four, a pierced and heavily tattooed carrot top in his midtwenties was watching a television cooking show. Feet up on the desk, Houston Rockets cap on backwards, he swiftly turned to point a short-barrel, pump-action shotgun at us as Hersh and I followed Mercy inside.

"Blue, coming in," she announced.

The carrot top lowered the shotgun and returned his attention to the cooking show.

"Turn off the TV, Byron," Mercy told him.

"I'm learning how to get the lumps out of my hollandaise sauce."

"Turn off the TV, Byron, *now.*"

Byron sighed. "I was afraid you were gonna say that." He reached over and hit the off button. "This the dude?"

"This is him," Hersh said.

"Byron," he said, leaning over and shaking my hand.

"Logan."

"Pleasure."

"Let's get this done, people," Mercy said, taking off her shades. "We're burning the taxpayers' dough."

Hersh pulled the bedspread off one of the beds. Underneath it was an elaborate series of enlarged, eight by ten color photographs showing Monterey's harbor and marina from various angles and elevations.

"The subject's boat is berthed here," Mercy said, pointing it out on one of the photos. She pointed to another picture. "We've set up a two-man observation post on this unoccupied boat across from his slip, here. They've maintained eyes-on since zero seven thirty. The subject spends most of his time inside the boat's cabin, comes out on deck every so often."

"Is he alone?" I asked.

"Affirmative."

Mercy then proceeded to lay out an assault plan that nearly rivaled Normandy in its detail: one guy advancing from this position laying down a base of fire; another guy advancing from that position; a third guy to distract Cohen using flash-bangs; the others to rush and overpower him with their weapons locked and cocked.

"This is what we old school types refer to as 'overkill,'" I said. "You can employ security and overwatch tactics all you want, and that's fine. You can talk all you want about establishing a base of fire, and that's fine, too. What I'm going to do is walk in there, alone, and have a heart-to-heart with him. Steve Cohen's a war hero, not a terrorist."

"Look," Mercy said, "no one's saying the guy didn't bleed for his country. But according to our records, that 'hero' has more handguns and rifles registered to his name than half the rural police departments in America. He's also been arrested repeatedly for making violent threats, mostly to his neighbors. The only reason why he's never been prosecuted is because of his distinguished service record. Were you aware of that?"

"No."

"Are you aware that his wife committed suicide in 1985, and that he blamed the Vietnamese for it?"

"He told me his wife left him."

"That's one way to put it," Byron said, trying not to chuckle.

Mercy dug into a file folder and handed me a Veterans Affairs report that outlined Cohen's domestic history. It described my former professor's chronic depression, and how his wife, Margaret, bore the brunt of his emotional abuse until, one night, leaving the apartment she rented after they'd split, she drove to a park in downtown Colorado Springs and blew off the top of her head with one of the many handguns he kept in their house.

I had no idea.

Clearly Mercy and her team weren't there to make nice. They'd convened in Monterey ostensibly to take Cohen into custody, the operative word being "ostensibly." More realistically, their purpose was to take him out. What more elegant solution could there be? The late Capt. Virgil J. Stoneburner had already taken the fall for the death of Mr. Wonderful. What good could be gained by forcing another former prisoner of war to stand trial? This way, with Cohen dead, the trade agreement could go through without a hitch, and big business would make big money on both sides of the Pacific. The whole thing reeked.

"Guilty or not, Cohen still deserves a fair trial," I said. "I'm not going to stand by while some sniper puts a round in him if he happens to sneeze funny. Your team will stand down until I say otherwise."

"You have no say here, Logan," she said, giving her gum a workout. "You're here strictly as an observer. We do it my way, and if you don't like my way, you can sit this one out. Find yourself a comfortable seat. Byron here will show you how to make hollandaise sauce."

"I would if you'd have let me finish watching my show," Byron said.

I walked outside and called Buzz.

"Technically, she's correct," Buzz said. "She is in charge of the op."

"Look, I don't know where you found this woman, but I'm telling you, she's bad news."

"Mercy's ex-FBI, eight years with the bureau's Critical Incident Response Group. She's good people."

"Maybe so, but this is the absolute wrong play, Buzz. You cap a seventy-five-year-old former POW for allegedly trying to resist arrest instead of talking him out, I guarantee you, by tomorrow morning, the president's approval ratings'll be in the toilet."

"Who said anything about capping him? All we're doing is taking proper precautions before we take him into custody."

"Like hell. You forget, I've been on a few of these ops. I know how the game is played."

"That was then, Logan. Alpha's long gone. We play by a different set of rules now."

"Look, you hired me to do a job. Let me do it. Give me ten minutes with Cohen. If I can't get him to come out peacefully, then feel free to bring in the artillery. Buzz, you and I go way back. Let me do it my way. Just this once."

Silence on the other end. I could hear him exhale. Then he said, "Put Mercy on the goddamned line."

I walked back inside and held my phone out to her. She stopped her chewing, giving me one of those cold, if-looks-could-kill-you'd-be-a-corpse kind of stares, then took it.

"Yeah?" She listened, trying to get a word in, but Buzz wouldn't let her. After several futile attempts to defend her game plan, she caved. "Fine," she said. "You're the boss."

I was to be given ten minutes. One chance to make Cohen come quietly. If something bad happened in the process, like me getting shot, there would be no calling in local law enforcement, no cordoning off the marina and negotiating, waiting him out. Mercy and her people would move in with swift and deadly precision, neutralizing the threat to public safety.

"Fair enough," I said.

"You might need these," Byron said, handing me a silver pair of handcuffs.

I shoved them into the front pocket of my jeans, extracted the revolver from my flight bag, and stuffed that into the back of my waistband, under my shirt. I hoped I wouldn't have to use the weapon. I knew there was a distinct possibility that I might.

TWENTY-SEVEN

The sun was out but the wind that spring morning was off the bay and had a bite to it that made me wish I'd brought along a jacket. In the kelp beds offshore, I watched two sea otters swimming and chasing each other, or whatever it is sea otters do. The air reeked of dead fish.

Snuggled between John Steinbeck's famous Fisherman's Wharf and Monterey's longer but lesser known Municipal Wharf, the marina where Steve Cohen berthed his sloop was a small, vibrant community unto itself. Here and there, weekend sailors in sweaters and Top-Siders were busy hosing off decks, repairing sails, coiling ropes, or just hanging out and chatting with each other. There appeared not to be a single ethnic minority among the sailors, nor anyone under retirement age.

"What has twelve arms, twelve legs, and twelve eyes?" one old guy asked me as I strode past his boat on the way to Cohen's slip, which was on the seaward end of the dock. He was sitting in a cheap, low-rise lawn chair and hoisting what I guessed was not his first margarita of the morning. His blue baseball cap said "Dubai Yacht Club." The scar tissue and precancerous blotches on his ruddy face said he was no stranger to the dermatologist's office.

I played along with him. "I don't know. What has twelve arms, twelve legs and twelve eyes?"

"Twelve pirates!" he said, cracking himself up and sloshing his drink on the dock.

I managed to smile and kept walking.

What I don't know about sailing vessels would fill volumes, but I knew enough to recognize that Steve Cohen's boat was a beauty. Sleek and immaculately maintained, with elegant lines, she was neither big nor small, pretentious nor modest. Painted in cursive letters on the stern was her name: *Great Escape*. I noticed as I drew closer that the lower part of the hull was painted a glossy bluish green. There appeared to be no one on deck.

"Colonel Cohen?"

No response.

Across the marina, I spotted Mercy's Lincoln Navigator. She was aiming a camera out the driver's window, pretending to take pictures of the ocean, but the lens was aimed at me. Nearby a pair of bearded, middle-aged men in Hawaiian shirts were doing the tourist thing, leaning against a railing, ostensibly admiring the view. One of them had a pair of binoculars. They, too, were focused in my direction.

"Colonel? Hello? Ship ahoy?"

Cohen suddenly emerged from below deck. He appeared startled to see me, if not alarmed.

"Cadet Logan," he said with a plastic smile, "what're you doing here?" His hair was mussed and his clothes—a gray, Air Force Academy sweatshirt and a pair of baggy old khakis—were rumpled. He seemed to have aged considerably since I'd seen him last.

"I was in the neighborhood and thought I'd take you up on your offer, come hang out. Gorgeous boat, Colonel. What do you call that paint color, anyway?" I said, pointing to the hull.

"Aquamarine."

"That's what I thought. Mind if I come aboard?"

He shot a quick glance down the companionway ladder he'd just climbed, leading to the cabin below. "Actually, now's not a good time. I'm square in the middle of something. Can you come back a bit later? We'll go have lunch."

"I'm afraid I can't do that, Colonel. I think you know why I'm here."

His plastic smile melted. "No, as a matter of fact, I'm afraid I don't."

"It's about Mr. Wonderful."

"The guard?"

I nodded.

Cohen forced another smile intended to mask his rising anxiety. "If you or whoever it is you're working for are implying that I was involved in any way with what happened that night, I'm going to have to ask you to contact my attorney. Beyond that, I really have nothing to say. Now if you'll excuse me."

I stepped off the dock and onto the boat, walking toward him. "What happened to Socrates, Colonel? Didn't you tell me it's not right to return an injury, no matter how much you've suffered from it?"

"You're trespassing, Mr. Logan," he said, backing up and bracing himself on the tubular metal handrail leading below deck. "I can have you arrested."

"Colonel, listen to me, I'm trying to do you a solid here. The people I'm working with have a tactical team in place. They're prepared to assault your boat, and they would love nothing more than to put a round in your head because that's what they get paid to do. We need to talk, earnestly, and you need to do exactly what I tell you, or this day is going to end very badly for you."

He glanced about, looking for the snipers. "What makes you think I killed him?"

"You're the only one who speaks Vietnamese. Stoneburner and Halladay and Halladay's grandson? None of them would've had any way of knowing where to find Mr. Wonderful that night."

"That's all you've got? My foreign language skills? If your efforts at persuasion had been as thin as that during our philosophical debates in class, I can assure you, Mr. Logan, I'd have failed you."

"Not just your language skills, Colonel." I watched his hands. "You have a long history of violent behavior. Your actions precede you."

"You mean that little dust-up with my neighbors, the property line dispute? They were the ones who came after me. I was merely defending myself. The case never even went to trial."

"The knife you killed the guard with had paint on it. The paint was oil-based, waterproof, the same color as your hull—aquamarine. If I had to put money on it, I'd bet that further analysis will prove them to be an identical chemical match."

Cohen's trousers were baggy enough to hide a full-frame handgun. Had he reached into his pockets, I would've drawn my revolver and might've been forced to shoot him, but he didn't do that. He did something I never expected: he began to sob.

I closed the distance between us and reached out to comfort my old professor, to tell him that, regardless of what he'd done, everything would be okay, one way or the other. That was my first mistake, letting down my guard. The second was in not realizing that there might've been someone else on the boat, in the cabin below.

Carl Underwood Jr. was standing at the base of the ladder, arms extended in a two-handed combat crouch, aiming a 9-millimeter Glock up at me.

"Try anything funny," he said, "and I'll blow your shit away."

I knew that Mercy and her team were watching us at that moment through their field glasses. Assuming standard tactical procedures were in effect, I also was aware that at least two high-powered sniper rifles were likely trained on Cohen from covering fields of fire. Unfortunately none of that surveillance or weaponry did me much good considering that Mercy's team couldn't see Underwood and were therefore unaware of his presence. I was tempted to alert them via some sort of subtle distress signal—mouthing the word "gun," perhaps—but the rising panic in Underwood's eyes told me he wouldn't hesitate to shoot if spooked.

I turned around and, facing the ladder, climbed down into the boat. Cohen followed me.

The cabin was trimmed in varnished teak and smelled faintly of diesel fuel. Underwood backed up, careful to maintain a safe margin between us, giving him time to fire should I lunge at him, his eyes never leaving mine.

"Check him for weapons."

"Please," Cohen said, "this isn't necessary. Mr. Logan's a former student of mine. He's not going to—"

"Shut up and do what I tell you," Underwood said, cutting him off.

Cohen frisked me. The revolver wedged in my belt wasn't hard to find.

I repeated to Underwood what I'd told Cohen, that a heavily armed tactical team had the boat surrounded, and that there was no way out for either of them.

"The absolute best thing you can do," I said, "is to lay your piece down on that table, then we walk out of here together, the three of us, nice and easy. I'll buy you both a cup of coffee and we can talk this all out. C'mon, Carl, what d'you say?"

Underwood snatched my revolver from Cohen. He now had a gun in each hand trained on me. "I had it all worked out, every detail," he said. "Then you came along and had to screw everything up."

"What did I screw up, Carl? Tell me?"

"What did you screw up? Everything. Try my father's honor, for starters."

"Your father? I don't understand."

"Carl senior was one of the most courageous men I have ever known," Cohen said, looking at Underwood. "You've done his name proud your entire life, son, but he never would've wanted all this. Now, please, Carl, put the gun down."

And then it dawned on me: Carl Underwood, *Junior*.

"Your father, Carl Senior, died at the Hanoi Hilton," I said. "He was tortured to death."

"He passed in my arms," Cohen said. "Made me promise to look after his son if I ever got out alive. I've tried all these years.

To the best of my ability, God knows, I've tried to be the father he never knew."

Underwood's eyes were wet. "You have, Colonel. I'll always be grateful."

"We wrote letters back and forth, talked on the phone almost every weekend," Cohen said. "Christmas vacations with my wife and his mother. We tried to spend as much time together as we could, didn't we, Carl? I owed your dad that much."

"Including helping Carl Jr. murder Mr. Wonderful?" I asked.

"Colonel Cohen had nothing to do with it," Underwood said angrily.

"What about the knife, Carl?"

"You won't find my prints on it. I wore gloves."

"Why did you tell me about the paint? You knew I'd find out it matched the colonel's boat."

"You said you were working for the White House. I threw you a bone, to get you off my back."

"You knew that the whole trade agreement, the big State Department dinner, would make good cover. It allowed you to ask questions about Mr. Wonderful—his schedule, his habits, where he'd be that night—without raising suspicions. Nobody'd ever suspect a thing. You wanted me to think the Vietnamese killed Mr. Wonderful. That's why you told me Tan Sang collected knives. It's why you told me his car was seen that night near the lake. You hoped Washington would blame him for the murder, create a stalemate, force the Vietnamese to release Stoneburner and Colonel Cohen."

"You've got it all figured out, don't you?" Underwood said.

"Not all. The paint on the knife. I still don't get how it got there."

"I was at Langley for meetings about a month ago. I stopped on my way back to Vietnam, to see Colonel Cohen. We talked about his big upcoming trip to Hanoi, how nervous and excited he was about going back after all these years. He was working on his boat. I was happy to pitch in. A speck of paint got on the blade. I should've noticed it. I didn't."

"You knew Colonel Cohen would be arrested along with Stoneburner. They'd be the likely suspects, and you killed the guard anyway."

"I thought they'd all be home by the time they found the son of a bitch. I thought they were all going back with Billy Hallady." He turned to Cohen. "Isn't that what you told me, Colonel. You were all going back at the same time?"

"I never said that, Carl."

"Makes sense, though," I said. "Once everybody was back stateside, Hanoi could scream bloody murder all it wanted, but there's no extradition treaty with the US. Everybody would be safe, your father's death would be avenged, and Mr. Wonderful would be sitting in an urn on his widow's shelf. Is that how you saw it all going down, Carl?"

"If you think I'm going to prison for doing what had to be done, you're flat wrong," Underwood said. "All you're doing is opening up old wounds. I can't let you do that."

He leveled my revolver at me.

"Carl, please," Cohen said, pleading, "don't do this. I'm begging you."

"Don't you see, Colonel? This is the only way. Doctor Barker here, or whatever the hell his real name is, shows up unannounced and says he has evidence implicating you in a murder. He wants money to keep quiet. Then, when he realizes you can't be broken, just like my father, he's overcome by guilt and shoots himself with his own weapon."

"For god's sake, Carl, you're delusional," Cohen said. "Give me the weapon."

Underwood thumbed the hammer back. With a frightening calmness, he whispered, "No."

I went for his legs at the very instant Cohen lunged for the gun. Grunting and straining, the two men grappled for no more than a second or two before it went off.

At first, I wasn't sure who'd been shot. Then, slowly, Cohen slipped from Underwood's grasp and collapsed. I could see a bullet hole in the center of his sweatshirt, the edges of it blackened by gunpowder. There wasn't much blood, really.

In that moment, Underwood, his face filled with the horrific realization of what he'd done, seemed to forget I was there and knelt beside Cohen, cradling him. The sorrowful cry that escaped his lips is something I'll never forget. Then before I could react, he raised the revolver to his right temple and squeezed the trigger for a second time. This time, there was plenty of blood.

I hoped the gunshots would draw a response from Mercy's tactical team, but hope never saved lives. I thumbed 9-1-1 into my phone and applied direct pressure to Cohen's chest wound with my other hand. He was still breathing but barely.

"The way is not in the sky," he whispered. "The way is in the heart."

"The Buddha."

Cohen nodded, pleased that I recognized the quote. Then he closed his eyes.

"Don't do this, Colonel. C'mon, hang in there. Stay with me."

Outside, people were yelling my name.

"Down here!"

I could feel wetness on my cheeks. For a moment, I thought I'd been grazed by a bullet fragment. But it wasn't blood that had dampened my skin.

Twenty-Eight

Each morning, we are born again. What we do today matters most. The Buddha said those words more than 2,500 years ago. They are, however, as fresh to me as every new sunrise. It was in that context of essentially being reborn that I was better able to compartmentalize the death of Carl Underwood Jr. and my inability to have prevented him from taking his own life. A man can steep forever in guilt, dwell forever on the capricious nature of fate, its inexplicable cruelties. At some point, he has to let it all go and move on, to savor the new day, or slowly perish emotionally. I chose the former course.

Journalists didn't make the process easier. For two weeks, unconfirmed, often half-baked reports of what had occurred in Hanoi and in the Monterey marina dominated front pages and the nightly news. Thanks to the White House's masterful job of spin control, though, much of what passed for factual reporting was reduced to little more than conjecture as administration officials maneuvered to bury the truth and salvage the big trade agreement with Vietnam.

The glossed-over version fed to the public was that Carl Underwood Jr. was a troubled man with a history of mental illness that had gone mostly undetected during his tenure with the State Department. His rumored ties to the CIA were categorically denied. Cohen, meanwhile, was described as a "family friend" with whom Underwood had a "close but conflicted personal relationship." Underwood died in what was officially described as an attempted "murder-suicide" after Cohen threatened to tell authorities what he knew of Underwood's role in the death of Mr. Wonderful. The White House version made no mention of my presence in the case. It was as if I never existed, which was fine by me.

Airlifted to the Level One Trauma Center at San Francisco General Hospital, Cohen would undergo emergency surgery and spend nearly a month in the intensive care unit, recovering from his wound. I stayed with him for the first couple of weeks until he insisted I go home.

"Beautiful things happen when you distance yourself from the negative," he told me.

Turns out my former philosophy professor was right.

About a week after I returned to Rancho Bonita, I got an e-mail from my interpreter, Nguyen Phu Dung. Colonel Tan Sang had made good on his word to release him unharmed. Phu Dung said he'd made his way to Laos, where he had relatives, and that he'd begun the long application process, seeking political asylum in the United States. I wrote back and offered to help any way I could. I told him we'd go flying when he made it to California. I also told him I would show an old MiG-21 driver how a *real* fighter pilot handles an airplane. As of this writing, I've yet to hear back from him. I hope he knows I was only yanking his chain.

Mrs. Schmulowitz was thrilled to have me back—not only because she once again had someone to cook for, but because, she said, she was exhausted, having to play with Kiddiot all the time in my absence.

"You can't believe the tricks I've taught him," Mrs. Schmulowitz said, pouring me a cup of coffee in her kitchen. "This cat, he's a genius!"

With that, she opened a drawer near the sink and got out a wad of aluminum foil as Kiddiot sat looking up at her intently, swishing his tail side to side and making little chirping noises.

"Okay," Mrs. Schmulowitz said, "watch this."

She tossed the foil ball across the kitchen floor.

Kiddiot went skittering after it like he was being chased by coyotes. I never realized he was capable of that kind of speed. He batted the ball maniacally as he slid across the floor on his belly, before gently picking it up in his mouth and returning it like a well-trained Labrador retriever to Mrs. Schmulowitz's outstretched hand.

"Here. You try it."

She handed me the foil ball. I tossed it just as she had done. Kiddiot sat impassively and watched it roll across the floor until it stopped. He scratched his right ear with his right rear paw and yawned. Then he got up and walked out of the room.

"Don't feel bad, bubby. You know he loves you."

"Actually, Mrs. Schmulowitz, I don't know that, but that's okay." I gulped the last of my coffee and set the cup in the sink. "Anyway, I'll see you later. I'm late for a date."

"A date? A date with who? I have to be the last person on the planet to hear of these things? Who is she? What does she look like?"

"I really do have to go."

"Go!" she said, pecking me on the cheek. "Have a ball. I hope you score. You know, if everybody in this world scored more often, there'd be no wars."

"From your lips, Mrs. Schmulowitz, to the Buddha's ears."

∿

I drove up to the airport. Larry wasn't there. Alicia Rosario was, though, waiting outside his hangar in a banana yellow VW bug convertible with the top down.

"Hey, sorry," I said, parking next to her and jumping out of my old Tacoma pickup. "I promise I'll be on time for our next lesson—assuming you still want to go flying with me after this one."

She smiled, her eyes cloaked behind aviator sunglasses. "I suppose we'll just have to see, won't we?"

Maybe it was the exquisite proportions of her face, her brown skin against the white tank top, or the way her ebony hair, which had grown longer since I'd last seen her, caught the breeze and the light. Maybe it was the low-riding jeans that highlighted the curve of her hips, or her open-toed sandals and burgundy toenails, or the fact that she's a cop. Hell, there's something inherently alluring in that alone—the whole beautiful-woman-with-a-gun and-handcuffs fantasy. Whatever it was, all I knew was at that moment, as Alicia Rosario stepped out of her car, I found myself undeniably attracted to her. When she put her arms around my waist and hugged me, it only confirmed the sentiment.

"How're you doing, Logan? It's been what, a couple years? You look great."

"You look more than great. How've you been, Alicia?"

"Oh, you know. Same old, same old. I figured I needed a little change of pace, so here I am, right?"

"I'm really glad you came. I didn't think you would. San Diego to Rancho Bonita, that's no easy drive."

"Hey, the sun's up, got my top down. California dreamin', you know? Besides, anybody who got in my way, I just waved my badge at 'em."

"Personally? I might've shot them."

She laughed. Neither of us mentioned the night in San Diego when we'd come exquisitely close to making love but hadn't. Savannah and I were working hard back then to reconcile. Savannah was now gone. Times change. People change. And now, fast-forward, here we were.

"My plane's right over here." I punched my computer code into the reader on the chain-link fence outside Larry's hangar, then held the security gate open for her. We walked out onto the flight line. Winds were light and out of the southeast. The sky was cloudless. A perfect day to introduce anyone to the joys of flying.

"You remember the *Duck*," I said.

"Do I remember?" Alicia laughed. "Pretty difficult to forget an airplane I once nearly got killed in."

"Yeah, I could see how the experience might reinforce certain memories."

"I'm just glad you got it all fixed up. Looks good as new."

"The *Duck* says thanks."

Distracted as I was by memories of what she looked like naked, I was determined to maintain my certified flight instructor professionalism. She'd called to say she was interested in taking flying lessons, not to explore the possibility of rekindling a fledgling romantic relationship. I intended to keep it that way. Aboveboard. Honorable.

"The first things we need to talk about," I said, "are safety procedures. Safety is paramount in aviation. As my first instructor told me, 'Unless you know what you're doing, an airplane can kill you faster than just about anything.' Now, before we actually get in the airplane, I'd like to demonstrate the—"

Alicia held up her palm to silence me. "Before we get into all that there's something I've been meaning to demonstrate, too. And I've been waiting nearly two years to do it."

She kissed me.

In that instant, I was transported back to my days studying literature at the Air Force Academy, to that line from the English poet, Percy Bysshe Shelley: "Soul meets soul on lovers' lips."

Did I give Alicia a flying lesson that day, or did we retire instead to my apartment where we spent the afternoon teaching each other how to soar in different ways? I could tell you, but then I'd have to . . . well, you know . . .